the
TATTOOED
HEART

MICHAEL GRANT

the TATTOOED HEART

A MESSENGER OF FEAR NOVEL

 KATHERINE TEGEN BOOKS
An Imprint of HarperCollins Publishers

Katherine Tegen Books is an imprint of HarperCollins Publishers.

The Tattooed Heart: A Messenger of Fear Novel

Library of Congress Cataloging-in-Publication Data
Grant, Michael, date.
    The tattooed heart : a Messenger of Fear novel / Michael Grant. — First edition.
        pages   cm
    Summary: "The Messenger of Fear and his apprentice, Mara, ask those who have
acted out of prejudice, intolerance, greed, and narcissism to play a game to win their
redemption"— Provided by publisher.
    ISBN 978-0-06-220743-2 (hardcover) — ISBN 978-0-06-241517-2 (int.)
    [1. Justice—Fiction. 2. Good and evil—Fiction. 3. Apprentices—Fiction.
4. Games—Fiction. 5. Fear—Fiction. 6. Supernatural—Fiction.] I. Title.
PZ7.G7671Tat 2015   2014041259
[Fic]—dc23   CIP
                                                                           AC

Typography by Carla Weise
15 16 17 18 19 CG/RRDH 10 9 8 7 6 5 4 3 2 1
❖
First Edition

Parts of this book are inspired by Aitazaz Hassan Bangash,
who died saving his school from a suicide bomber. I've changed
names, locations, and details to serve my story.

For Katherine, Jake, and Julia

1

FROM CHILDHOOD I SUFFERED FROM OCCA-
sional nightmares featuring the most vivid monsters
and the most intense of emotions. A constant theme
was helplessness. I was often paralyzed in my dreams.
Or, if I could move, it was in slow motion while everything and everyone around me moved at normal speed.
I would often wake myself by screaming. Deliberately,
you see. In the throes of the horror I would tell myself to
scream, to scream until I was awake.

When my father died, my dreams changed and
became bittersweet. I had one terrible dream in which

I saw him dead. After that he was never dead, just far away. I never saw him in his casket, nor did my unconscious mind conjure the moment when an enemy's bullet took his life. He was always alive and his eyes shone not with fear but with regret and love. I would savor those dreams and seek to prolong them. And when at last, reluctant, I woke, I would find my pillow wet.

I think maybe dreams provide a type of balance. When life is good, dreams remind you that fear still lives out there in the world. When life is bad, dreams offer hope.

I am Mara. I am sixteen years old. And my dreams now are most often of my home, my school, my friends, past pets, objects I hold dear, and my mother and my ever-absent, ever-present father. They are dreams of loss and alienation, but not nightmares.

Life is my nightmare now, and paradoxically, my dreams have become escapes.

So, in the seconds before my eyes fluttered open, I was at my friend Suzee's pool party for her thirteenth birthday. The sun was shining, but not hot—it seldom gets really hot in Marin County, California. The pool in the dream was overflowing, lapping around the legs of my chaise longue. My flip-flops were floating away. But in compensation the water was carrying a bag of blue corn tortilla chips toward me and in the dream I thought, *Well, that's a fair trade.* I waited patiently for the flip-flops and the snacks to pass each other, indifferent to the fact that a current cannot flow in opposite directions at once.

In reality, after that pool party, after that lovely, languorous day, I had a terrible nightmare in which the water kept rising until, immobilized, I began to drown.

Now my subconscious mind goes back to that pool party as a pleasant antidote to the traumas I endure daily. The mind strives for balance, doesn't it?

Balance has become a very important thing to me. Balance is the explanation for the indignities and cruelties I must inflict on the Messenger's targets. I justify myself with that concept, hoping it is not an illusion or a lie, hoping that I am doing good and not evil.

I no longer live in the land of suburban pool parties, I live in . . . well, it's hard to summarize the nature of my existence for the simple reason that I do not yet fully understand it myself.

What I do understand is that there are things

at work in this dull world that are more vivid, more bizarre, and more awful than rational people can easily accept. Everything about this life I now lead spells dream, and yet it is terribly real.

I have moved through solid objects.

Understand this: I do not mean that I have imagined doing so, or that we're still in dreamland, or that some spectral projection of me has done this. I mean that I have moved *through* solid objects.

I have been transported effortlessly through time and space. I've been to a past I never experienced and to a future that is not mine.

I have caused the world to rewind, to advance at half speed, to accelerate as though reality itself was just Netflix on my laptop.

I have dived deep into the tortured unconscious minds of people I did not previously know.

These are not my powers, but power granted to me by gods older than any known to mortal man. It is the gods who labor to keep the world balanced on the edge of nonexistence so that it should not fall into oblivion.

Balance, you see, always balance.

Yes, it is the gods who right the wobbly balance of

justice, and their instruments are Messengers of Fear. And I, as punishment for my own terrible sins, have been made the apprentice of one such messenger.

I know him only by that name: Messenger. And I know the day is coming when my name, too, shall be only Messenger.

He was in the kitchen when I woke and stumbled in in search of coffee and breakfast. Please note that I do not say "my" kitchen. There is nothing about this place I inhabit that is truly mine. It is a place, or perhaps just a cunning and convincing illusion of a place, where I sleep and eat and recuperate in between following Messenger on his duties.

But were I to open the front door I would not see the suburban neighborhood that should be this abode's native habitat. Rather I would see the mist, the soul-crushing yellow mist that surrounds this place. And yet through the kitchen window I could see the sun-blanched leaves of a tree. A real tree? I very much doubt it, but whoever or whatever created this space had some concern for my well-being and must have known I'd go slowly mad if I never saw sunlight.

"Did you rest well?" Messenger asked.

"I did," I said, smiling at the memory of trading flip-flops for corn chips.

"I took the liberty of making coffee."

I could smell it. I poured myself a cup and took a sip. I'd always taken coffee sweetened and with milk before. I took it black now. The bitterness no longer seemed significant to me. Indeed there was something reassuring about it.

"Are we traveling?" I asked him.

"Yes. We have a complex situation."

I don't think he'd ever referred to one of our missions in quite that way before. I might have asked him what he meant but the Messenger of Fear is not easily questioned. He speaks or does not, as he chooses.

He is a boy, not yet a man, though as with everything now I'm never sure if what I'm seeing is really him. He is tall, thin, and has long very dark hair and eyes the blue of a sunlit tropical ocean.

He is beautiful, Messenger is. I am perhaps pretty, or maybe just cute, but Messenger is beautiful.

He wears the same thing each time I see him: a long black coat that goes down to midcalf, a steel-gray shirt, black pants, and tall black boots. Yes, that almost completes the outfit. I say almost, because there are details, like the buttons of his coat, which are small silver skulls. And the two rings he wears.

The ring on his right hand is Isthil, goddess of wickedness and justice. She is stern, magisterial, and shown on the ring carrying a sword.

The other ring is a face. It's a young face, contorted by unendurable terror.

"Let me get dressed," I said. I popped a strudel in the toaster and went to shower and dress. There's a closet with several rather dull outfits, all perfectly sized, none really mine.

When I got back Messenger was sitting on a stool and doing nothing at all. He's good at that. In a world where no one who owns a phone can ever be without some diversion, he is diversion free. He is patient, and that patience is slowly beginning to be mine as well, simply because there is no point in impatience.

By the time I was ready, the toaster strudel was cooked and cooling in the toaster. I wrapped it in a paper towel and began to take careful bites even as we were out of the house and—without a flash, a sound, or even a sense of movement—instantly somewhere else.

We stood on gravel and loose stone beside a road that had once been paved but had since fallen into disrepair, so that the gray of pavement was like a series of scabs over the richer soil beneath. Grass poked up here and there but seemed to lack sufficient moisture to thrive.

Across the road were cultivated, irrigated fields, and there the crop grew. It was a rich green, neat rows of what looked like tall grass that bent over at the top. Beyond that, in the distance, a vast field of pink flowers. This field was being worked by men bent low with bags slung from their shoulders. Other men with automatic rifles patrolled the edges of the field and appeared to be supervising or protecting or controlling, or some combination of the three.

Beyond the lovely but sinister flowers the land rose into terraced hills and, still farther, far off in the distance, the gray and white suggestion of snowcapped mountains.

Between the road and the fields was a small, off-white building. It was not an impressive sight. It was roughly square, a single ill-proportioned story in height, whitewashed brick on the sides, stuccoed brick in the front. There were three doors, all in a line, too many obviously for such a small structure, with the two flanking doors smaller than the central one, which was itself only tall enough to allow a six-footer to scrape beneath the top of the casing. The doors were painted green, a darker green than the Dr. Seuss–like tree that provided a comically small patch of shade.

The only feature of note was a small tower, just twice the height of the building itself and narrow, like a blunt, brick rocket. It leaned just a little to one side.

But my eye was drawn away from the building by the sight of a group of people walking slowly up the road toward us. A dozen people, perhaps, it was hard to be sure, but certainly no more than that number. The men were dressed in what looked like long shirts over loose-fitting pants, all of unadorned cotton. The women wore voluminous black with only their faces and hands showing.

Four of the men carried something, and I could already guess, from the muted crying, from the down-cast eyes, from the slumped shoulders, from the way some supported others, that this was a funeral procession.

The body came into view as the mourners neared. It

was wrapped in white cotton. A red rope tied the top of the shroud just above the head, a second rope gathered the shroud just beneath the soles of the feet. Two more such ropes were wrapped around the body's midsection, keeping the shroud in place. It had the unmistakable gravity of sacred ritual.

The body was large and at first I thought it was too large to be that of a child, but then I noticed that some of the men were of large size as well, so perhaps it was a family trait.

As the procession reached us more men came from the small brick building and joined silently in.

"Their mosque," Messenger said, nodding slightly toward the building.

"It isn't very impressive," I said. I suppose I had images from news stories of the huge mosque that protects the Kaaba Stone in Mecca, or even of the overwhelming Hagia Sophia.

We were, of course, invisible and inaudible to the mourners. Had we wished to we could have walked right through them. But death and grief impose limits, even on those with great power. We kept our distance. I finished my pastry, feeling foolish and disrespectful but needing food and having no better plan.

"This is a poor, rural area," Messenger said. "Farmers and shepherds. Their mosque is humble."

"Why are we here?" I asked. "This is a very long way from home. Does your duty extend this far?"

"This is the victim, or one of them," Messenger said. "Our business is with the ones responsible."

"But how did . . ." I let it drop for two reasons. First, Messenger showed what he wanted to show, when he wanted, and in whatever order he thought necessary for me to understand.

Secondly, there was a new person with the mourners, a person who clearly did not belong since her eyes tracked us as she approached.

She was dressed all in black: loose trousers beneath a flowing robe, with her head covered in a black hijab. Black but not dull or even quite monochrome, because as she drew close I saw that the fabric swirled with woven patterns which, unless my eyes deceived me, moved and changed in subtle and fascinating ways.

Her clothing was unadorned, but she wore rings, and I knew instinctively that they were of Isthil and the Shrieking Face.

"She's a messenger," I said.

Messenger's silence was confirmation.

The procession passed by, and the young woman in black joined us. She was quite beautiful, with dark skin, unusually large eyes, and a quirk in her mouth that spoke of humor.

"Messenger," she said.

"Messenger," he acknowledged with a nod. "This is my apprentice."

No names. I was disappointed. I was certain that Messenger had a name, at least had had a name once upon a time, but evidently I would not learn it here and now. Even my name was dropped from the introduction.

I stuck out a hand, an instinctive offer of a handshake, a gesture this new Messenger declined with a wry smile.

"You must be new not to know that a messenger is not to be touched," she said in accented but easily understood English.

"Sorry," I apologized.

"Thank you for allowing this intrusion," Messenger—my messenger—said.

"We serve the balance," the woman said. Then, "It makes no difference, but he was a good boy. Fifteen years old. Brave. Kind. He burned fiercely for justice."

Without a word being spoken by either my mentor or his counterpart, we three were half a mile down the road, past a village that was really little more than a cluster of a dozen brick and plaster buildings, none even so grand as the humble mosque. We stood in a dusty field marked with twenty or thirty stones, some cut to rectangles, others obviously just hauled here in their natural rough state.

It was the placement of these stones that told the tale, for they were evenly spaced, six feet from left to right, in approximated rows. It lacked the carefully manicured grass, or the cut flowers, or the chiseled limestone markers and grandiose marble obelisks I recalled from my own sad travels to cemeteries, but cemetery it was.

A hole had been dug, long enough and wide enough for a body, deep enough to discourage whatever wild creatures roamed this strange and unfamiliar landscape.

Now the mourners stood praying in three rows.

Men stood in front, closest to the grave. Women behind them. Children in the row farthest away.

A woman's knees buckled and she released a small, despairing cry. She was held standing by women on either side. It was beyond doubt that here was the mother.

The shrouded body was placed on its side in the hole.

"Facing Mecca," our new companion explained.

"How did he die?" I asked.

The female messenger nodded and the three of us began to walk away. But as we did the world scrolled backward around us. We walked at what seemed a normal speed, but the dead body leaped from the grave and was once again on a stretcher being carried backward down the road.

Faster and faster the scene moved past us, though there was no sense that we were moving at anything but a leisurely pace.

The funeral procession passed backward by the tiny mosque, down the road, to a village somewhat larger than the one we'd earlier passed through. This village was clustered around a trickle of a stream that barely moistened the rocks and seemed at any moment it might be drunk up entirely by the parched earth.

We watched silently as the body was placed on a wooden table in one simple home with low ceilings and a scattering of thin mattresses. The walls had once been painted a cheerful turquoise but earlier colors of paint and bare brick showed through.

Now only men were in the room and in reverse motion they untied the ropes, and unwound the shroud, and revealed a body. The boy was heavy and dark-skinned. And he had a bullet hole in his chest, another in his neck, a third in his arm that had very nearly severed it so that just above the elbow was nothing but strings of gristle still attached to the lower part.

A fourth bullet in his face had removed half of his head.

I had never seen anything like that wound. It was . . . what word would suffice? How can I describe the damage? How am I to explain without resorting to horror movie clichés?

His face, from the hairline, down to the bridge of his nose, down to the place on his mouth where the lips dimple a little in the middle, and from there down to the bare white bone of his jaw, was no longer there.

It was all too easy to see what he must have looked like if I simply duplicated and reversed the remainder of his face. But no sane person can see such a thing and calmly reconstitute what is no longer there. The outrage is too great. The anger that wells up inside you is too powerful. There is no looking at such a thing and reasoning, there is only the most profound sense of wrongness, of an unspeakable sin.

Tears filled my eyes. Not because I knew the boy, I didn't, not even because I could see the pain and sadness on the faces of those who had undertaken the heartrending job of wrapping him for burial, though I could. I cried because it was wrong. I cried because it should not be, should never be.

Messenger did not cry, neither did his female counterpart. They both looked on with the clenched, stony resolve of those who are past crying but not yet past feeling.

"What was his name?"

"Aimal," the female answered. "His name was Aimal."

The reality around me had slowed to a stop. Now all the men were as frozen as the boy on the table. His shroud was gone and the men were held motionless in the act of cleaning the body with damp rags.

Motionless tears hung on the cheeks of a man I took to be Aimal's father. But as if he had read my mind—and he may well have—Messenger said, "That is not the father, that is Aimal's uncle. The father is in America. As are those we must deal with."

"The ones who killed Aimal?"

Messenger shook his head. "The men who killed Aimal are not our concern."

"Then why are we here?" I asked. Was this soul-searing display unnecessary? Had I been burdened with yet another gruesome memory for no good reason?

"The wickedness we pursue is not murder, but murder's source," Messenger said. "It is hatred we pursue. Hatred."

2

WE DID NOT BID THE FEMALE MESSENGER GOOD-bye. One second she was there and the next she was gone. And a second after that, we, too, were gone.

There was a brick marker that read *Theodore Roosevelt* on a limestone banner and beneath it the words *High School*. I somehow knew we were in Iowa.

The same combination of red brick and limestone comprised the school itself. The central portion was three stories tall, three generous stories, so that the structure was taller and more impressive than the simple number of floors might indicate. The wings extended to left and right and were of just two floors each. There were architectural details rendered in stone—window framing, a stone railing across the roofline—that gave the school a slightly ornate look, an almost Old World look. It very nearly evoked *Downton Abbey.*

Just before the front door was a tall flagpole. The Stars and Stripes snapped in a breeze stiff enough to ruffle the mature hardwood and fir trees that flanked the entrance and which were dotted haphazardly across the lawn.

It looked like the very model of a high school—what a traditional high school ought to be.

As usual, I had questions. As usual, I didn't ask. It's not that Messenger will *never* answer a question, but he prefers not to, and for whatever reason, I don't want to nag at him. He's the master, I'm the apprentice. I've accepted that. More or less. And as the teacher he gets to choose how and when to tell me things.

Frustrating? Extremely.

We walked at a normal pace across the lawn. Kids were pouring from buses that had pulled up in the parking lot. At the same time freshmen and sophomores and juniors were piling from their parents' cars, and the luckier seniors were pulling up in cars of their own.

The familiar morning rush. And we joined it, invisible to the crowd as it filled the main hallway. How did we squeeze through dense-packed bodies without touching anyone around us? I don't know. It's something I've now seen happen many times, and even when I pay the closest attention it's hard to explain. It's as if reality bends to get out of our way. Like we're a force field that no one feels. Limbs and heads and torsos all seem to warp, like some kind photo booth effect.

Testing it, I deliberately passed my arm through a girl. Her body appeared to split in two at the waist, upper half and lower half seemingly completely disconnected, yet she chatted glumly to a friend all the while and her legs kept moving her forward.

Messenger noticed my experiment, raised one eyebrow slightly and said nothing.

We walked in this way until we arrived at a narrower hallway leading into one of the wings. There Messenger's focus seemed to settle on one particular group of three boys walking together in that bouncy, playfully shoving way that boys sometimes have. There was nothing particularly noteworthy, just three boys, probably sophomores or juniors, all three of them white, all three dressed in jeans and T-shirts with logos of bands or defiant slogans.

Here the crowd had thinned a bit and I took notice of a particular girl moving in the opposite direction from the boys. She was wearing a hijab of sky blue over her head and neck. Other than that she was dressed in jeans and a long-sleeved white blouse. I liked her shoes.

It was the hijab that one of the boys grabbed as she went by. Grabbed it from behind and yanked it back off her head.

"Hey!" the girl yelled, and tried to put the scarf back in place.

"See, she does have hair under there!" This from the smallest of the three boys, a short, cute kid with longish brown hair.

"Drop dead," the girl snapped.

"Just playin' with your towel, towel-head." This was not said in a playful tone, and it came from the boy in the middle. He was tall, powerfully built, with short blond hair. He was wearing sunglasses so I could not see the color of his eyes.

A second girl, just arriving on the scene, saw what was going on and said, "It's called an abaya, moron. And leave her alone, Trent."

This second girl was not in Muslim dress. She was in the navy blue and white uniform of a cheerleader.

"Wasn't me," Trent said, faux innocent. "It was Pete. Wasn't it, Pete? See, Pete thought maybe she had horns under there and that's why she's always wearing that towel."

"Idiot," the cheerleader said, and rolled her eyes.

The bell rang and everyone went hurrying away.

The Muslim girl looked shaken and angry, but she said nothing more and the incident appeared to be over.

Messenger and I now stood in an empty hallway, ringing with the muted sounds of lessons filtering through a long row of closed doors.

"This is connected to the dead boy, Aimal," I said, careful not to give it a questioning inflection. But Messenger was not enticed into answering my non-question question.

I did not know where we were, exactly, nor where Aimal had been, but I was pretty sure there were thousands of miles separating the two locations. However, in Messenger's world, space and time are a bit . . . different.

I did not believe we were there because one jerk kid had harassed one girl in one school. The penalties Messenger imposes can be . . . Well, they are the fuel of my nightmares.

"Where should we follow the story next?" Messenger asked.

"What?" The question was so out of the blue I wasn't sure how to answer. Since when did Messenger consult me? And, anyway, didn't he already know all the answers? Didn't he know exactly how this story—whatever it was really about—would end up?

But he was still waiting for an answer so I had no real choice but to attempt one. "We either follow Trent—he's the ringleader—or the girl."

"As you wish."

"Well . . . which one?"

"Both."

And then something extraordinary happened. Extraordinary even by the standards of the extraordinary reality into which I have entered. The world around me split in two.

We stood, Messenger and I, in a void, blackness ahead and behind and above, and far more disturbing, black emptiness below as well. I saw no floor or ground beneath my feet, but I was not weightless, either.

But this void was as narrow as a footpath, and to either side of this void was the world. Two worlds. Or two iterations of the same world. The effect was as if we had been standing in a darkened room and two enormous movie screens had been set up, one to our left, the other to our right, each infinitely tall and long and wide.

Two real worlds. I had only to turn my head or even just move my eyes to see one then the other. Both at once if I stared straight ahead.

But, as hard as it is to imagine, and despite my suggestion, you must not think these were movie screens. They each were real, each happening, each completely three-dimensional. I knew that I could step into either, so that they were less like screens than like living dioramas.

To our left, the girl. To our right, Trent. We could hear both. I could smell the lamb stew the girl was heating in the microwave of her kitchen.

The girl's phone dinged an incoming text. Without thinking I stepped into her world, hoping to read it over her shoulder. Instantly a wall closed between me and Messenger. I saw neither him, nor Trent.

Frightened, I stepped back into the newly appeared wall, passed through it, and was with Messenger again.

This made me feel foolish. Obviously Messenger understood all this better than I, but that didn't mean I wanted to seem like some kind of newbie.

That in itself struck me as absurd and I laughed.

Messenger shot me an inquiring look.

"Just . . . takes getting used to," I explained lamely and stepped back into the girl's world. Her name was Samira. I saw it on her text. The person she was texting was named Zarqa.

Zarqa: Heard u were hassled. RU OK?
Samira: It was nothing. Just jerks.
Zarqa: What happened?
Samira: They pulled off my abaya. NBD.
Zarqa: It is a big deal. U shd tell sum1. Bullying.
Samira: No.
Zarqa: Grl we have to stand together.

The microwave rang and Samira cut the conversation off with a quick GTG and a heart emoticon.

Samira set her phone aside and removed her meal.

I stepped back to Messenger. "Her name is Samira. I think that was another Muslim girl texting her."

"All right, I admit it: I'm mystified."

The words were what I was feeling, but they did not come from me.

Oriax had appeared.

Oriax is a female. She's a female in much the same way that a billion is a number, or a Porsche is a car, or a twenty megaton nuclear bomb going off is fireworks.

Age? Whatever age she wants you to see. She may be eighteen. She may be older than human civilization.

I knew enough of her to know that she is sadistic, cruel, evil, not really human, and incredibly beautiful. Dark hair, dark eyes, an outfit of scraps of leather melded seamlessly to form a dominatrix look that fit her like it was painted on—and might well be. Her boots were extreme high heels but minus the heel, a look only possible when you have hooves.

"Well, hello there, mini-Messenger. What was

your name again? Pawn? Puppet?"

She had a throaty purr that sounded like an intimate whisper. The illusion is so real that when she punctuates the *p* sound in *puppet* I swear I can feel her breath on my ear, and it makes the hairs on the back of my neck stand up.

"Mara," I said. "My name is Mara."

She moved like a tiger—sinuous, precise, dangerous. She was beside me and though I'm straight I felt my throat tighten and my breathing become labored, such is her animal appeal.

"You know, Mara, you don't have to dress like a schoolgirl. I could arrange for something a bit more . . . well, let's just say something that would make it harder for Messenger." She laughed wickedly at that, then with a wink, added, "I mean harder for Messenger to ignore you so completely. As a young woman."

"I'm not . . . ," I began, and then realized there was no safe way for me to conclude that sentence. Instead I blushed and fell silent.

"I don't think he's even really noticed the way you look at him sometimes, or the way your heart speeds up when he comes close or—"

"What is it you want, Oriax?" Messenger asked wearily.

"Oh, you, Messenger. Always. You're just so very delicious. I could eat you up." She licked her lips, which today were glowing mauve, and leered, but for a chilling moment it occurred to me to wonder if she might not mean that literally.

I had stood by helplessly while she had tricked a boy into accepting a punishment that left him shattered as a human being. She had laughed and sung a grim little song as he was made to experience being burned alive. Was there anything too foul for her? Was there any sort of limit? I doubted it.

"I'm fine," I said, responding way too late to her offer to improve my appearance.

"Why this girl?" Oriax gestured at Samira, who had gone on eating, disregarding the three of us. "Because someone pulled her silly scarf?"

"Don't pretend to be blind to the connection, Oriax," Messenger said. "Hatred grows like a cancer, spreading ever outward from its source. It's a poison in the human bloodstream that spreads far beyond its origin. *'If you prick a finger with a poisoned thorn say not that you are innocent when the heart dies.'* Isthil teaches that no one who does evil can ever be blameless for the consequences."

"Oh, well then," Oriax said, dripping sarcasm, "if Isthil said it—"

And just like that, without a word from Messenger, without any sort of warning, we were back in that void between two realities.

On our left, still within Samira's reality, an irritated Oriax realized we'd given her the slip. She seemed not quite able to find us, though we could still see her.

On the other side of the void, Trent was with Pete. The third boy was no longer with them and in fact I never saw him again. I hoped he'd seen the malice in his friends and chosen a better path for himself.

Trent and Pete were sitting on swings at a park playground. Trent glared and frightened off the younger children who approached.

"Have you heard from your dad?" Pete asked.

Trent shook his head angrily. "He's gone. Up in North Dakota, looking for work."

"Yeah, but—"

"Hey. Douche nozzle. You think I want to talk about

my dad? He's gone. Maybe he'll come back, maybe not. Okay? We done?"

Pete swung a little, a short arc, with his feet dragging the ground. "Okay, man."

"Probably just drinking," Trent muttered. "Up there drinking and not giving a damn about anything."

"He used to be kind of cool before he lost his job," Pete observed.

"Yeah, well, he did lose it. So that's that, right? They gave it to some Mexican." At that point his talk turned scatological and racist and I won't attempt to repeat it.

There was a depth of barely contained anger in Trent. His friend, Pete, seemed like a more balanced person but one who was under the sway of his larger companion.

"My dad's okay," Pete said. "He still—"

"Do I give a damn?" Trent asked with weary mockery.

Pete was taken aback but forced a sickly smile and said, "No, man, even I'm not really interested in my dad."

"He's got a job anyway."

"Yeah, but he kind of hates it because—"

"But he's got a job. Right? So he's not off somewhere

all messed up from being out of work. Right? So shut up."

Pete shut up.

I've often wondered about people like Pete. I have never understood why angry thugs like Trent seem able to attract more normal followers.

But then I winced, remembering. I had been a bad person. I had done a terrible thing. And yes, I'd had friends and acolytes the whole time.

Self-righteousness rises in me sometimes, and then I remind myself that I do not have the right to look down my nose at others. I am the apprentice to the Messenger of Fear, and as such I deliver a measure of justice. But it had begun when I accepted the truth of my own weakness. My position as apprentice was not an entitlement, it was a punishment.

"Oriax can't see us?" I asked, mostly just to distract myself from painful memories.

"Eventually, but not immediately. Her powers are different. Very great, but different. But she will find us in time."

"Then let's use the time to figure this out," I said.

"The time?" He cocked his head, waiting.

It took me a few seconds to grasp the hint. "Yes, the

time. But I don't think I want to see more of Trent. I want to understand the connections. I want to see what led to the death of that poor boy with his face blown away."

Just like that, one-half of this split-screen reality replaced Trent and Pete with the solemn scene of the far-distant funeral.

Messenger seemed accepting of my initiative, even approving. "Proceed."

"What?"

"Don't be timid, Mara," he chided. "You've seen that we can travel through time. So do it."

I glanced back along the void. Would going backward take us backward in time? This was not how we'd previously done it. Messenger had always just made it happen.

But of course this was the simple version. This was Time Travel 101, an introduction before greater secrets and techniques could be learned.

I turned and walked with far more confidence than I felt, back along the narrow black bridge between facing realities. And yes, to my satisfaction, time went into reverse.

On her side Samira spit her food into her bowl,

placed the stew in the microwave, took it out and put it in the freezer, walked backward from the kitchen.

Far more disturbing, the shrouded body of Aimal once again leaped from its grave and landed on the stretcher, which was then borne away.

I walked faster, faster, and time reeled backward at a geometrically quicker rate. Now Samira was back at school being harassed, and Aimal's body was being ritually washed by his male relatives, and Samira was in class, and Aimal was quite suddenly alive. I noticed that the time lines were not synchronized, not matched up. I sensed that Aimal's was the more recent event.

Distracted by that realization, I saw that I had moved too quickly. I reversed my direction and slowed my pace.

Aimal now was in the dirt yard of a bare, one-room cinderblock schoolhouse. There was a single tree providing scant shade from a blistering sun. There were other kids, younger, older, many kicking a soccer ball. Others read. Others just sat in small groups, chatting.

If you ignored the opium poppy fields and the distant but intimidatingly sharp-edged mountains, and the poverty of the school, it could be any school.

A pickup truck came barreling down the semi-paved road, kicking up a plume of dust. There were two men in the cabin, one more in the back.

The kids in the yard didn't notice. But Aimal did. He rose slowly to his feet, the biggest of the boys. He shaded his eyes and watched the truck and peered closely at something particular.

Without even realizing what I was doing I stepped into his frame and peered as though through his eyes. I saw the thing he focused on.

It was the upraised barrel of an assault rifle.

3

AIMAL BEGAN YELLING. IT WAS NOT ENGLISH, OF course, but I understood it nevertheless.

"Hide! Hide!" he yelled. "All the girls must hide!"

But by the time his shouts were noticed and conversation had fallen silent and all heads had turned toward the truck, two men were already leaping from the back and both were armed with assault rifles.

"Run! Run!" Aimal shouted.

Some of the girls responded now. There were only six of them, ranging in age from ten to perhaps fifteen. But now they saw what Aimal saw and understood what

Aimal understood, so they ran.

POP! POP POP POP!

That's what it sounded like, the gunfire.

One of the girls fell facedown in the dirt. A cloud of dust rose from the impact.

A second girl ran to the fallen one and a piece of her shoulder blew away, a twirling chunk of bone and meat, trailing blood.

Now everyone, boy and girl, was screaming, screaming, but only Aimal was running the wrong way. Not away from the guns. Toward them.

He waved his arms and shouted, "No, stop, stop, this is against Islam, this is against God, you must stop."

He ran until he was between the gunmen and the girls, some of whom kept running. But two of them seemed to have collapsed in sheer terror.

"Get out of the way!" a gunman yelled, and waved his rifle at Aimal. "It's not you we want."

Aimal shook his head, almost a spasm it was so quick and violent, like he could not control his bodily movement. He was terrified. He was terrified and barely able to keep his knees from buckling.

He saw what would happen.

He saw and knew and *understood* what would happen and still he did not back away.

"Go away! Leave us be!" he shouted at the gunmen.

"We are only here for the girls, get out of the way!"

He shook his head again, slower this time, slower, knowing . . . knowing that—

POP! POP POP! POP POP POP POP!

The two men standing, and one still in the truck, opened fire.

The high-powered rounds did not simply strike Aimal's body, they dismantled it. Before he could fall his right arm was hanging by a spurting artery and his spine had exploded through his back like a bony red alien, and the side of his face was obliterated, turned to red mist and flying chunks of meat and bone.

He fell and now the two girls who had been unable to move cowered and screamed and died, their bodies jerking and jerking and jerking as the gunmen emptied their magazines into them.

One of the gunmen ran into the tiny schoolhouse and came out with a man so undone by fear that he had stained his clothing. The teacher was forced to his knees.

"School is not for girls," a gunman said, and fired two rounds into the teacher's groin. The teacher howled in pain and writhed on the ground.

"And since you are a girl now, it is no place for you, either."

They executed the teacher with bullets in his head and neck.

Someone, Messenger or maybe even me, froze the scene then.

Shocked boys stood staring. One surviving girl lay slumped over her dead classmate. In the distance another girl was frozen in midstep, running. Aimal lay in dirt turned to mud by his blood.

I felt as frozen as the scene around me. I knew I was panting and yet did not feel I was getting air. The very skin on my body seemed to reverberate with the concussion of those gunshots.

We've all seen movies and games with shooting. Sometimes it's in slow motion, sometimes it's played for laughs, sometimes it's shown as tragic and awful, but nothing in media prepared me for the real thing. For murder.

It's always been an ugly word, *murder*, but still we

manage to sanitize it. We jokingly say we'll murder someone. I've said it. But I don't think I'll ever be able to speak that word lightly again. When you see it, in reality, right there in front of you, actual *murder*, you want to cry and tear your hair and claw at your own face and fall down on the ground and demand to know why such a filthy thing could happen.

Why would you shoot a fleeing child in the back?

What could possibly justify that?

What kind of god could ever sanction such a thing?

The murderers were two older men and one younger, so young he might be no older than me. What poison had been poured into that young man's soul that he could do such a thing?

"Are we here for him?" I asked.

"No," Messenger said. "A different justice awaits them. No, we have business elsewhere."

He was looking at me with something very like concern.

"If you're going to tell me it gets easier, please don't," I said.

"I don't know if it gets easier over time," he said.

"But whatever time has passed for me, it has not been enough to make it less terrible."

He let time flow again, and now I watched as the killers drove away. And I watched as the stunned and shattered survivors lifted themselves up off the ground and rushed to the dead. They cried. They wailed. They sobbed that God is great, and maybe he is, but he wasn't there on that day.

Something happened to me then, a spinning feeling, a feeling of being sucked down into the earth. But I suppose it was nothing that supernatural. In fact, I just fainted.

I woke with a start.

My first feeling was confusion. Just where was I?

I was no longer at the blood-soaked school yard.

I was lying on cold stone. Beside me on my left was a large rectangular pool with greenish water. On my right was an outdoor café with umbrellas shielding round wooden tables and canvas director's chairs. Many of those chairs were occupied by people dressed for tropical weather drinking cups of espresso or mineral water or tiny bottles of unfamiliar sodas.

I sat up, self-conscious at being passed out in a

strange place with people chatting not five feet away. The language being spoken was not one I recognized. The people were a mix of white and black and a few who were Asian, like me.

Of course they could not see me. At least I hoped they couldn't as I wiped away a trickle of sleep drool. Then I raised my eyes above the tables that had preoccupied me and was stunned to find myself in the courtyard of what looked like a white limestone palace. There were pillars and arches all around me. And at one end of the courtyard a sort of open tower rose. Beyond that moldering tower, great trees pressed close all around, almost menacing in their insistence. And farther still, above the immediate foliage, rose vivid green mountains that soared up into mist.

Not the sinister yellow mist that so often appeared in the demimonde I now occupied, but a genuine mist, the steam of low-flying clouds.

"I've been here before," I said, searching for Messenger. But no, that wasn't quite true, was it? There was familiarity to the location, but it was not a memory of my own experience, rather it was a memory of . . . of a video.

It took me a few minutes to clear my confused thoughts and put my finger on it. A music video. An old one. Something I'd come across on YouTube. Snoop! That was it, Snoop and Pharrell.

And the song was . . . "Beautiful."

I was probably more proud of myself than I should have been for a simple feat of memory, but this world I now inhabited is strange at the best of times, and it is very easy to lose your way when not only space but time can be rearranged according to Messenger's whim.

I did not know what the place was called. But I knew it was in Brazil.

I closed my eyes and saw the school yard. I saw, as if it was on a loop, the bullets tear into helpless children. I wanted to be sick but fought the urge. My feelings were unimportant, my emotions secondary: I had witnessed terrible evil. It had made me sick. But how small were my emotions when weighed against what I had seen?

I stood up and had the passing thought that I was a very long way from home with no airline ticket, no passport . . . It takes a while to adjust to this new reality—I'd lived sixteen years in a world where airplanes carried you across vast distances and time could not be traversed except in one direction and at one speed.

At least I was not there in that school yard. I was in a green, humid place where people sat at ease drinking soda and laughing. Of course no scene is so innocent that it reassures me entirely. The world I now occupied seemed to demand a permanent state of readiness, a constant flinch.

I walked to the nearest table and waved my hand in front of a woman's face. No reaction. I was still invisible to her. I breathed a sigh of relief at that. If I were visible I'd be questioned, and all my answers would be likely to suggest that I was insane.

Messenger had to be nearby, so I went in search of him, passing through an arched passage and out onto stone steps. From that elevation I looked out over what must be a park. There was a lawn and beyond it tall trees.

I closed my eyes, swallowed hard, pushed my hands down to press the palms against my thighs, holding myself there, feeling my own physical reality.

It is a cliché—one I've seen in many books—to say that you feel the earth spinning beneath you. But that is how I felt, as if the planet had wobbled a bit on its axis and its spin through space could be felt.

The world I had known was fraying, coming apart. My world now encompassed ancient gods, messengers who could move through time as easily as flip through a calendar app. My world now contained Oriax, Daniel, and the Master of the Game, and far more evil than I wanted to acknowledge.

What else existed unseen? What other disruptions and horrors would Messenger show me? What would be left of what I used to know?

I caught a glimpse of a dark figure moving through the trees and ran down the steps and across the lawn and paused, realizing that I did not need to run. I could simply decide to be there, beside that dark figure. I could do what Messenger could do, couldn't I? At least I could when he told me to. Did I need his proximity to use my new powers?

The idea made me queasy. What if I did it wrong? What if I ended up in some entirely different place?

So I ran across a lawn so it was like running on a mattress. I found a wide and leafy trail through the trees and followed it, slowing my pace a little so as not to look like an anxious puppy in search of its master, or like a lost child looking for a parent.

Coming around a bend I spotted an old stone tower, something that might have been lifted from a medieval castle. And there below it stood Messenger.

He was not alone. He was in heated conversation with Daniel.

I don't know what Daniel is. To all appearances he's a casually dressed youngish man, not imposing in the least. But from Messenger's hints, and more from Messenger's obvious deference, I judged Daniel to be a powerful being, someone with a sort of supervisory role over Messenger and by extension, me.

I stopped, stepped off the path into deeper shadow to be less visible, and shamelessly eavesdropped.

"I was not aware that I was never to stray, even for a few minutes, from the path of duty." This was Messenger, and he did not sound deferential, he sounded defiant.

"It is not a rule," Daniel said calmly. "You perform your duties well, Messenger, I have no complaints."

"Then why are you here?"

"I am concerned for you," Daniel said. Where Messenger was defiant, Daniel was understanding.

"I would have thought I'd earned some trust," Messenger said, still huffy in a low-key sort of way.

Daniel put his hand on Messenger's shoulder. "You have. And beyond that, you have earned some affection."

Messenger slumped and the defiance was gone from his body language and his tone. "I know you think I'm obsessed."

"Yes," Daniel said, and smiled sadly. "I wish I could help you."

"I know that you may not," Messenger admitted. "And I know that my searches are in vain. I know, Daniel. I know the chances of seeing her, it's just that . . ."

"The search has become an expression of faith," Daniel said.

"My only faith is in Isthil. And, of course, in her servants."

"Yes, Messenger, I know the *correct* answer. But the truth is otherwise. Isthil is only your second love. Ariadne is your first. You search for a glimpse of her, knowing how improbable it is, but the act of searching is, for you, an expression of love."

Messenger had nothing to say to that. He hung his head and the two of them stood in silence until Messenger said, "She once told me there were a dozen places she wanted to see before she died. She loved old places, places that were unique, places that seemed to hold a mystique."

"She sensed even then the presence of our world," Daniel said. He emphasized the word *our* so that there was no doubt he was referring to whatever impossible dimension we occupied. Daniel looked around, saw me, let me know that he had seen me, and said, "She was not mistaken. This place has meaning to the gods."

"But she is not here."

"You know I cannot answer that."

Silence again as Messenger absorbed that answer, and after a moment nodded his acquiescence.

"I do not forbid you, Messenger. Even you are allowed a life, pleasures, as you carry out your destiny. But as a friend, I wonder if you do yourself harm. I wonder if your already burdened heart only becomes heavier."

"I can't give up," Messenger said with a note of help-lessness. "That would be despair. That would do more than burden my heart, it would destroy me."

Daniel nodded and smiled wistfully. "Love is a power to equal that of the gods. Your apprentice is with us."

Messenger turned his gaze on me, not searching, knowing where I was. "She needed rest. She has seen terrible things."

Without willing it, I was with them.

Daniel said, "You have begun to see the nature of your duty, and the pain it will cause you. But you have not broken."

"I . . . I didn't mean to . . ." I was about to say I had not meant to eavesdrop, but of course I had, and there is little point in lying to people who know instantly whether you are speaking truth. "I don't understand why—"

"You are not *my* apprentice," Daniel said, cutting me off. "I am not *your* master."

With a nod to Messenger he was gone.

An uncomfortable silence stretched between me and Messenger. Then he took an audible breath and said, "This place is called Parque Lago Azul. It is in Brazil."

"I recognized it."

"Did you? Ah."

I wanted to ask him about Ariadne. The shadow of Ariadne had been on him since our first encounter and at times his obvious devotion to this girl annoyed me. Oriax would no doubt have some snarky remark to offer on the subject, along with the rude suggestion that I was attracted to Messenger in a most un-apprentice-like way, and thus jealous.

Was I jealous of Ariadne for being the object of such love? How could I not be? Who does not want to be loved beyond all reason? Who does not want to be needed as Messenger needed his Ariadne?

For Messenger I felt sadness. He did not speak of his pain, but knowing some small part of what his life had been during his service as Messenger, having touched him for a fleeting second and thus felt viscerally some fraction of what he had felt, I could only be sad.

But another part of me was jealous in a different way, not of him as a boy in love with someone else, but of the fact that he had something to hold on to.

Did I?

Had I ever loved anyone in that way? Could I ever love someone that way?

Yes, I thought, in time. But the one I might someday come to love was not to be touched.

4

WE WERE BACK AT THE IOWA SCHOOL. IT WAS TIME
to see what was happening with Trent.

Trent was in the office of the school's vice principal, along with Pete. The vice principal's name—on her
desktop nameplate—was Constance Conamarra.

"I've got a report of an incident between the two of
you and a Muslim student yesterday," she was saying.

Messenger and I stood in the corner of the cramped
room, invisible, of course, inaudible. But I felt conspic-
uous just the same.

"That's bull . . . um, not true at all," Trent said. "Is it, Pete?"

"Totally not true. Whatever that chick said—"

"I never mentioned it was a girl," Conamarra said.

That stopped Pete, but not Trent, who said, "Whatever. Okay, look, I was just playing around, no big deal."

"Actually it is quite a big deal. It's a three-day suspension big deal. And I'd be within my rights to make it much worse, believe me."

Pete groaned but Trent's face turned sullen with rising fury.

"No way," he said. "You can't suspend me just for grabbing some towel-head's scarf, that's b.s."

"I can and I have," Conamarra said.

"This is crap! Special treatment just because she's some terrorist."

"Samira Kharoti is a terrorist?" The vice principal's voice dripped scorn.

"They're all terrorists. Bunch of foreigners come over here and start getting treated like celebrities. She's not special. She's not some big thing." He did a hand-waving gesture around that "big thing" that started off sarcastic and ended with a violent thrust. He practically spit when he did it.

"All you had to do was leave her alone, Trent. *And* this is not your first incident. Last month you—"

"Yeah, whatever," Trent said, shoved his chair back, and stood up. Conamarra was a small woman, and between Trent and Pete they made an intimidating pair. "Everyone's special, because they're girls or black or Mexican or a towel-head or—"

"That. Is. Enough. You can come back to school on Monday. Until then, you are not to come on to school grounds."

They left on a wave of muttered curse words and slammed the door behind them.

In the hallway Trent said, "I'm going to find that bitch and give her something to complain about!"

"What are you talking about?" Pete asked.

"That Samira bitch. I'm going to have a little talk with her."

"Dude . . ."

"What?" Trent snapped.

Pete put up his hands defensively. "Hey, I'm already suspended, I don't want—"

"Are you pussing out on me?"

"I'm not—"

"Are you seriously pussing out on me? A little bit of trouble with Conamarra and you turn into her puppy dog? Oh, oh, pet me on my little head, please pet me, waaaah."

"Aw, man, it's not like that."

"That's just what it's like. Don't you know what this is? All of them against *us*. Ni—ers, Jews, Mexicans, now we have to put up with camel-jockeys, too? They're taking over, man, taking over. Taking. Over."

"Dude, I just don't want to get all into some big thing over this," Pete pleaded. Then his eyes lit up with a crafty light. "Hey, how come it's just the two of us? Why isn't Marlon down here with us?"

"Conamarra probably got to him first, and he wimped out, just like you're doing. That's the game, man, they play us against each other. Make us weak."

They had made it most of the way down the hallway when a security guard stepped in front of them and spoke into a walkie-talkie. "I got them both, right here. Yes, ma'am."

To the boys the guard said, "You two need to get your stuff from your lockers—which are not down this hallway—and get off the school grounds."

An argument followed, but in the end Trent and Pete, with their backpacks full, walked off the grounds to Pete's car.

The car had no backseat in which Messenger and I might conveniently wedge ourselves, so we simply walked alongside the car. The fact that I accepted this rewriting of the laws of physics without much shock is, I suppose, a sign that I was adjusting to Messenger's world. Then, too, I had seen this trick before.

We walked alongside the car as it accelerated to thirty and then forty miles an hour. Somehow we were ambling along at forty miles an hour, stopping at stop signs, then effortlessly accelerating despite the fact that when I looked down at my feet they were doing no more than walking. There was no stiff wind in our faces, we were not huffing and puffing, we were simply effortlessly keeping pace with a car moving several times faster than the fastest runner. The car still sounded like a car, and all the other sounds of the road roared in our ears, but I could hear the conversation in the car as clearly and as intimately as

I always heard Messenger's voice.

It was not a conversation I enjoyed hearing. Much of it was a string of angry expletives and racial slurs covering every ethnic group, but mostly focused on Muslims.

And the theme that grew from that obscene anger was one of revenge. Revenge for the suspension from school. But not revenge against the vice principal, no. No, the talk was of getting *them*.

Them.

"Is there anything more exciting than a pair of angry fools with a *them* to pursue?"

Oriax.

She was beside us, walking along on her absurdly tall and impossibly pointed boots. As always she had a new outfit, not more revealing than the earlier one but every bit as likely to cause a sudden cessation of conversation among those who appreciate female sensuality.

I did not resist the feeling. At that moment my brain was still reeling from the shooting of Aimal and the girls and the teacher. I would have preferred any thought to that memory.

Probably it was shameful that I was so desperate to push that horror aside. But I had already seen far too many things I'd give anything to purge from my memory. If this was to be my fate I would see many, many more. They would be tattooed on my flesh until all of me was covered. I knew my sanity would be at risk, *was* at risk.

And I had no Ariadne to hold on to.

"What do you think they'll do?" Oriax asked, and clapped her hands in gleeful anticipation.

The answer was not long in coming. Trent pulled a bottle of peppermint schnapps from under his seat.

"Of course!" Oriax said. "I should have guessed. They'll need that."

Messenger ignored her as he usually did, as though his refusal to engage would discourage her. It was clear he had no power to make her go away. He could lose her sometimes in the swift movement through whatever impossible geography comprised our universe, but he could not forbid her to be present.

I decided on a different approach. If I was truly to become the messenger myself someday, then Oriax would become my problem to deal with.

And curiosity has always been my strength as well as my weakness.

"What do you get out of this, Oriax?" I demanded.

She smiled at me, parting her mauve lips to reveal white teeth that looked a bit sharper than teeth should be. "Excellent question, mini-Messenger. I will answer it if you'll agree to answer one of mine."

Messenger's eyes flicked a warning, but I took Oriax's challenge. "Okay. I agree."

"Excellent," she purred. "What I get out of this is the pleasure of seeing and helping to inflict pain. I savor human despair. I revel in human weakness. But equally, I take enjoyment from offering its opposite: pleasure." She made a sort of philosophical sound, a worldly sigh, a commentary on life's interesting vagaries. "It's fortunate, really, because in a way it's also my . . . job." She spoke that word with evident distaste. "I am what I am, and I am what I do, and I enjoy what I do."

She leaned toward me, very close, and I felt my heart race. It was not a rational thing, nor even strictly a sexual thing, it was something almost like gravity—invisible, inescapable, inevitable. When Oriax did that, I could no more ignore it than I could ignore the heat of the sun or the pull of the earth's core.

"And now, my question for you, mini-Messenger. It

is this: Have you fantasized about our lovely, handsome Messenger? Have you imagined yourself in his arms? In his bed?"

I started to blurt an answer, but Oriax held up a cautioning hand. "If you lie, I will know it. And so will Messenger."

My mind went instantly to a dream I'd had, one of my more unsettling, though not at all terrifying, dreams.

No one should be held responsible for their dreams.

"I never imagined Messenger *having* a bed," I managed to say as a blush rose up my neck to burn my cheeks.

"Hah!" She seemed delighted with my pathetic evasion. She knew she had landed a blow. She knew she had made things awkward between Messenger and me. Awkward to say the least.

She was, as she'd said, reveling in human weakness.

Darkness had fallen completely by the time the car pulled into a cemetery that was much more opulent than the one we'd visited so far away. The car crept along manicured paths between stark marble testimonials to lost love. There were impressive marble crypts and small granite crosses. Here and there a Star of David.

"There!" a slurring Pete said, and pointed.

Trent stopped the car and the two boys stumbled out. The sun had gone down and the shadows were growing long.

We followed them onto the springy grass to a modest granite headstone. It read *Mohammed Marwat, beloved husband, father, brother.* And a fairly recent date of death. It was decorated with an engraved crescent and star.

"Yeah. Raghead," Trent said.

Pete offered some expletives of support.

Then Trent kicked the headstone. His reward was pain that had him hopping and cursing. He limped back to Pete's car and rummaged in the trunk until he found a tire iron and a can of red spray paint.

With the tire iron he began digging at the foundation of the stone, wedging the crowbar end beneath it and, finally, toppling it onto its back while Pete kept watch.

More loud cursing.

"And now, the paint," Oriax said with a wink.

Trent shook the paint can, musing about his message. In the end he decided on his favorite word, *Raghead*, which he misspelled as *Rag-hed*. Then added an expletive. And finally the words, *Go home.*

"And there we have your basic grave desecration," Oriax said with satisfaction. "Are we really all here for a little grave desecration? This is your mission, Messenger? Trivial."

And then Trent urinated on the stone and Pete did likewise.

"Okay," Oriax said with tolerant humor, "now, it's an enhanced grave desecration. But really, Messenger, are you going to subject these two cretins to the full-on Messenger treatment? I'm surprised you'd want to show mini-Messenger the true pitiless savagery of your absurd goddess's so-called justice."

I expected Messenger to ignore her. But instead I found him looking at her very thoughtfully. And Oriax didn't like it. She seemed to blanch, although that's too strong an image for the very slight, barely noticeable pullback.

I wondered if she was frightened of Messenger. But no, in the times I'd seen them together she had never shown any fear. But she had just now winced— and again, that's too strong an image for a change of expression that was so well concealed as to be almost unnoticeable.

Almost unnoticeable.

And yet I was sure that she had done something or said something she now regretted.

"Well, I have other, friendlier folk to see," Oriax said lamely, and disappeared.

"What was that about?" I asked.

"Indeed. What *was* that about?" He repeated my question while, of course, offering no answer.

"Thanks for clearing that up," I grumbled, just relieved to have something other than my fantasies, my *alleged* fantasies, as the main focus of conversation.

He sighed and relented. "Not all of us who live in this world beyond the normal have the same abilities and gifts," Messenger said. "Oriax's kind sometimes sees further than we are able."

"Further? As in deeper into? Or as in further away?"

He shook his head very slightly. "Further ahead. Time, not space."

In my mind I heard *Pop pop pop*. I saw brain and bone and blood. I sucked in air but seemed to be suffocating, as though the air held no oxygen. I realized I was trembling.

I realized as well that the murder of Aimal, and the

girls, and their teacher, was yet to come. It was in the future, still. Right now, across the world, Aimal was alive.

Somehow this led to that, though the how of it was not yet clear to me. What was the Isthil gospel that Messenger had quoted to Oriax? *'If you prick a finger with a poisoned thorn say not that you are innocent when the heart dies.'* Was this the pricked finger?

I did not want to show Messenger any more weakness, which is how I thought of my fainting at the school yard. If I was to be Watson to his Holmes, then I had to be able to hold my own. Keep up. I clenched my fists together behind my back and squeezed until deep crescents were pushed into my palms and my forearms ached. But I hid it. I pushed the murder sickness down inside.

"Well," I said, "where are we off to next?"

He stood silent in deep thought, ignoring me. Finally he must have reached some kind of conclusion because he said, "That's enough for now. You'll be wanting food and rest."

He was quite right, but I wondered whether he had gleaned that from an unwanted intrusion into my mind—he was certainly capable of that—or whether he was just noticing the sag of my shoulders and the unconcealable agitation on my face. Either way I found myself alone in my . . . I must find something to call the place where I ate and slept and showered. It seemed absurd to call it home, but it was all the home I had for now.

As always there was food in the kitchen: fresh fruit, cereal, and milk, Flake bars—a habit I'd picked up during a childhood visit to the UK—and even a frozen pizza. All things I would ordinarily eat.

I made myself a dinner-breakfast of egg, cheese, and English muffin sandwich and wished this place had come with internet, or at least TV. But this place existed outside of normal space and time so the cable company did not exactly have its lines here.

There were books, however. Some were the sorts of books I normally read for pleasure, but there were some heavy, leather-bound tomes as well, that could not have been placed there by accident. There was a shelf of these just to the side of the fireplace.

Someone or something had arranged kindling, logs, and matches, and I took that as an invitation.

Before there was computer-plus-internet to shine a light on our faces there was fire. I built a decent little blaze that crackled impressively and threw off the odd spark. I pulled cushions off the sofa and sat there within range of the comforting heat with a small pile of obscure books.

"*Thesis and Antithesis: The Search for Balance*," I read aloud. "Wow, that sounds like the dullest book ever written." As did a book simply titled *Justice* that weighed about as much as one might expect so portentously titled a book to weigh.

In the end I opened a large but not terribly thick book with a magnificently embossed blue leather cover.

"Isthil," I read aloud.

Messenger had taken me to Shamanvold, that awe-inspiring pit where the names of all Messengers are inscribed alongside bas-reliefs of the Heptarchy, the Seven Gods, of which Isthil was one.

I opened the book and read.

In the beginning was the void.
Into the void came existence.
But existence was precarious,

Suspended above the void,
Surrounded by the void.
A guppy at the shark's mouth.
A feather floating before the waterfall.
A pebble wobbling at the lip of a bottomless pit.

Ours is not the first existence.
Existence has occurred before.
And existence has failed.
It has fallen into the shark's teeth.
It has been swept down into the rushing water.
It has tipped and fallen into the pit.
Existence blinks into being,
And in a blink is gone.

"Well, that's cheerful," I muttered to the fireplace.

Into existence came the Seven.
Summoned by the will of existence itself.
Summoned to serve existence.
Summoned to ensure that this time,
Existence should not fail.
Summoned to maintain the balance,

Of the guppy, the feather, and the pebble.
Summoned to extend the length of that blink.

And thus was Isthil born . . .

I read on, skimming past the long origin story, looking for the passage Messenger had quoted. And there, at last, amid a series of homilies and parables, I found it, though Messenger had slightly misquoted.

"The fool says, 'I never intended to kill, I meant only to wound.' But I tell you that if you prick a finger with a poisoned thorn you may not claim innocence when the heart dies. Do not plant a weed and pretend surprise when it grows to strangle your garden. For, I tell you that to hate is to kill, for from hatred grows death as surely as life grows from love. Therefore do not nurture hatred, but love, even for those who hate you in return. Hatred wins many battles, and yet will love triumph."

The message came from a strange god, not my God, but it was no different than the lesson of my own faith, and perhaps many other faiths as well. Whatever Isthil really was, divine or mortal, god or pretender, I thought her words wise.

I decided I must read further, but the warmth of the fire and the lingering horror of seeing children shot down as I watched helplessly took their toll.

I did not dream of Isthil or of the balance of the world. I dreamed of places I had known, and people: a mother. A father now lying in his honored grave. Teachers. Friends. All of them in my dream seem to be on the other side of a pane of thick glass. I could hear their voices only as unintelligible murmurs. I saw their faces, but distorted by distance and the eternal yellow mist that in some way separated me from ordinary life.

And then, yes, I dreamed of Messenger. I saw him in my mind without his long black coat. Without the symbols of his office, the ring of horror and the ring of Isthil.

To my unfettered subconscious imagination he was the boy he was before becoming the Messenger of Fear, or at least how I imagined he must have been. Tall and beautiful as he was still, but sitting on a rock at the edge of the ocean, laughing as waves sent cold, salt spray to dampen his chest and shoulders, and the rope-gathered linen pants I had dressed him in.

Yes, I looked with more than casual interest at his

chest and shoulders, at his long black hair as it blew behind him, at his compassionate eyes. Yes, Oriax, I confess.

But even in my dream I knew it was false, for I knew that Messenger's body was covered in the tattoo-vivant marks of the horrors he had seen and made to happen.

I did not, in my dream, look at the single such terrible decoration that now marked my own body. I never looked at that, not in dreams, and only reluctantly in reality.

But in my dream Messenger did not look at me as I looked at him. Instead he whispered a single word. The crashing waves tore that word from his lips, but I knew in my heart that what he had said was, "Ariadne."

Ariadne, not Mara. Nor could it ever be Mara.

I think I cried in my sleep then, though I remember no dream, for my pillow was damp upon waking.

"It's time," Messenger said, but he was no longer the laughing boy by the ocean. He was back, looming above me, the real Messenger of Fear, grim and relentless.

5

"ARE WE GOING AFTER TRENT AND PETE?" I asked.

"Yes. But not yet. Later. For now we have a very different matter to address."

I was on the point of asking him where we were about to suddenly appear next, but by the time I could form the question, we had already stood in a wrecked, abandoned room.

It took me a while to establish just where we were. Messenger, of course, did not volunteer to help, preferring I suppose, that I use my own powers of observation. I don't think I'd ever been particularly observant before, but I had changed and grown since becoming what Oriax liked to call "mini-Messenger" and I now paid a great deal more attention to my environment.

In this case the environment was an abandoned business of some sort. That it was abandoned was evident from the filth, the dust, the cobwebs and spiderwebs, the lack of any light aside from the ghostly greenish-gray of streetlights filtering in through a grimy window and grimier glass door.

There was a waist-high counter that surely once held a cash register. Behind the counter was a twisted mess of wire racks, a torn cardboard poster for Camel cigarettes. Strewn across the linoleum tile floor of the room were random bits of shelving, an upended round cooler splashed with the Pepsi logo, and a liberal scattering of trash—candy wrappers, empty chips bags, plastic cups, paper hot dog holders, empty water bottles, cigarette butts, and dried feces.

Against the back wall were empty spaces that would once have held refrigerated cases.

"It was a convenience store," I announced proudly,

as though I really was playing Watson to Messenger's Sherlock.

Messenger was not wildly impressed by my powers of deduction.

The place stank of human and animal waste, of rotting garbage and dust. The room appeared empty. I heard a slight scratching sound, assumed it was a rat and carefully scanned the floor around me while wondering if there was a weapon at hand should the rat come my way.

Messenger moved to the back of the room, to the empty rectangles where the cold cases had once dispensed beer and soda and packs of salami and cheese. The glow of streetlights did not reach this far, but to my surprise the space was not entirely dark. There seemed to be a candle within, judging from the buttery light that flickered and at times disappeared entirely.

The scratching sound came again and something about it contradicted my assumption that it was an animal. It was too slow to be a rat. Too random.

I leaned into the void and saw the candle first, and the person lying near the candle second. I saw that it was a girl, a girl hard to place age-wise, though I guessed she might be seventeen or so. She had dark hair that looked as if she had made an effort to gather it all together with a scrunchie, but wisps and entire hanks of hair had escaped. Her face might be pretty. I wasn't entirely sure, as it was both dirty and marked with too much makeup.

She was dressed like a bargain basement Oriax, but the net effect spoke not of supernatural allure but rather of vulnerability and despair.

I don't know why it took me so long to notice the syringe in the crook of her elbow. Maybe I just didn't want to see it.

It lay there, the needle still in the vein. A trickle of blood had started to dry. A leather belt lay loosened around her bicep. A tablespoon with a blackened bottom was on the floor beside the guttering candle.

"Her name is Graciella Jayne, though she has taken to calling herself Candy. She is seventeen."

"Is?" I asked sharply, for I had leaped to the sad conclusion that she was dead.

"She lives still," Messenger said. He cocked his head, as did I upon hearing a sound of footsteps and low conversation. From the direction of what must have been the store's back door came a boy and a girl, both much the same age as Graciella.

Both looked to be in the same . . . business . . . as Graciella, the boy dressed in a skintight T-shirt that bared his lean midriff, while the girl wore the shortest of shorts and a top that would have doubled for a bathing suit.

"Candy!" the boy cried. They rushed to Graciella and knelt beside her. The rush of bodies extinguished the flame and for a moment they were in near pitch-darkness. Then a lighter flared in the boy's hand and the candle was relit.

"Oh, my God, she OD'd," the girl said.

"Is that the stuff she got off Jenks?"

"Same stuff we've got, Mouse. Jesus."

The two of them looked at each other and slowly the boy named Mouse pulled a small, rectangular packet of white powder from his pocket. A logo had been stamped on it. A pink pony.

"We have to call 911," Mouse said.

"I have to boot up first," the girl said.

"Are you crazy? You want to end up like her? That stuff is cut with something bad."

"Maybe not, maybe it's just real high-test, you know? Too pure will kill you. So I could just shoot half a spoon. Three-quarters, you know?"

Mouse stood up. "I'm calling 911." He pulled out a cell phone and, shaking his head at the girl's plaintive look, called in an overdose.

The girl began slapping Graciella's face, saying, "Wake up, Candy, come on. Wake up."

Graciella managed a low moan, but only one, and then she slid back into coma.

"Okay, come on Sue Lynn, we gotta get out of here before the EMTs show up," Mouse said.

"This neighborhood, it'll take them twenty minutes," the girl said. "And don't call me Sue Lynn. I'm Jessica now. And I have got to fix. It's nighttime, Mouse, I'm getting sick."

All the while I watched Graciella. Her breathing was shallow. Her skin was gray and covered in sweat. Gray even by the gentle amber light of the candle. It was all I could do to stop myself asking Messenger the question: Can't we help her?

I knew the answer to that. The answer is always the same. We may not interfere. We are not there for the victims. We are there for the people who create victims.

Yet first we must understand what has been done, that is the rule, that is the way of the Messengers of Fear.

The EMTs arrived, as Jessica had predicted, after about twenty minutes. By then Mouse and Jessica were gone. Did they go to shoot up? Almost certainly. Would their lives end in tragedy? Probably.

Would I find myself someday looking down at the dead body of one or the other or both, wondering what wickedness I was there to punish? That was a grim thought that would bring feelings of hopelessness in its wake. I pushed the thought away.

The arrival of the EMTs gave me my first inkling of where we were. The patch on their shoulders indicated Nashville, Tennessee.

The EMTs, a man and a woman, moved with practiced efficiency, barely speaking because they had seen OD'd junkies before, many times. They hung a transparent bag of fluid and pushed a needle into Graciella's arm. But the veins had been weakened to near collapse and the needle did not work. The EMT pulled it out, tried again. Again nothing. It took her six tries to find a vein that could handle the flow of fluids. The other EMT took her pulse, blood pressure, checked her eyes, and said, "Pinpoint. BP is seventy over thirty-five. Breathing shallow and irregular."

"Naloxone?"

"Yep."

A shot into the muscle of her thigh this time. They radioed in to the emergency room at Vanderbilt University Hospital.

"BP's rising, ninety over forty."

"She'll live," I said, as though I were part of their conversation and not invisible and inaudible.

We watched as they brought in a gurney, kicking trash aside to allow them to roll it. A third EMT arrived and helped them lift Graciella onto it and pass a strap over her waist.

Then, without warning, Messenger and I were outside the red brick hospital. Ambulances pulled up but none were carrying Graciella; she was already inside. We walked through the doors, slid past nurses, technicians, doctors, and patients, and came upon Graciella in one of the beds. A young foreign doctor stood at the foot of her bed addressing half a dozen medical students.

"Heroin overdose. EMTs reported low BP, low pulse,

nonresponsive, breathing shallow. They administered fluids and Naloxone. The workup indicated what we already knew: OD. When results come in I expect we'll find she's positive for at least one STD, and almost certainly positive for hepatitis. Malnourished, of course."

"She looks young," one medical student offered.

"I'd say fifteen, sixteen, give or take, younger than she looks," the doctor said wearily. "She's most likely a runaway turning tricks. She is still in a coma, but brain function appears normal."

I turned away. She looked too vulnerable lying there being discussed by strangers as though she wasn't even present. Of course in a way she wasn't present.

"She's a junkie," I said to Messenger, and perhaps my distaste was too obvious for he shot me a cold and disapproving look that I took as a rebuke.

I bristled at that. "It's what happens to junkies," I said harshly.

"Yes," Messenger said.

"People shouldn't take drugs," I said, coming off more self-righteous than I intended. "I mean, come on, who doesn't know that heroin is dangerous?"

"And you want to look no further?" he asked.

"I guess I don't have a lot of sympathy for people who screw up their lives in some obviously stupid way. There's people who have terrible things just happen to them. There are people being shot in the back in a school yard. That boy . . . those girls . . . and now this stupid girl, who nearly killed herself and may do so yet."

"You spare no pity for the foolish."

"I do have pity, it's just . . . I mean, you can't compare that brave boy standing up to gunmen and this girl here."

He was silent, but it was a silence that carried the weight of disapproval.

The doctor and the medical students had moved on to another case. Graciella lay alone. All alone. A pretty but ragged girl with tubes in her arms and up her nose, scabs on her inner arms.

"Where are her parents, for God's sake?" I snapped. "That's who should be taking care of her."

I should have known what would happen next—we stood outside a very nice, upscale suburban home in a location I could not guess at. There was a suggestion of impressive, pine-covered hills in the distance, the sky was threatening, and the air was chilly but not cold.

"Her home?"

"It was," Messenger said. "And it is still, in this time."

"You mean she's in there right now?" Did my reluctance show? For I was strangely resistant to seeing her in a time before she became a disease-ridden drug addict. But I couldn't fail in my duties. Messenger was deliberately waiting, patient as always, and I knew he was testing me.

I took a deep breath and walked straight up the sidewalk and through the front door into a tall entrance hall that revealed twin, curved staircases going up, with a formal dining room to the right and an equally formal living room, both furnished in a heavy, rather old-fashioned way, all dark wood and embroidered upholstery.

I heard laughter and the sound of running feet. A girl, no more than six years old, came running past, giggling, chased by an enthusiastic terrier.

It might be Graciella, I thought, but this child was a universe away from the scabbed junkie who lay in a Nashville hospital.

We walked on, heading back toward the kitchen

where a woman with a blond ponytail stood slicing vegetables for a salad. She worked awkwardly due to a cast on her left arm.

"Her mother," I said, and at that a man entered. He was a strikingly handsome man of perhaps thirty-five but with prematurely silvered hair. He came up quietly behind his wife and made to put his arms around her waist but at his touch she flinched and cried out, "No, please!"

It was more than a startled sound, there was something brittle and high-strung in it, a panicky sound. Something was going on between the two parents. The man's face darkened in anger.

"I hate it when you do that," he snapped.

"Do what?" the woman asked, trying to conceal her emotions. "You just startled me is all."

"I haven't had a drink in two days and you still treat me like . . . like, I don't know. Like you hate me touching you."

She turned and I saw naked fear on her face. It was so surprising that I took a step back.

"John, I didn't mean . . . I mean, I was just startled."

"Have I ever laid a hand on you when I was sober?"

the man asked, his expression one of hurt and perhaps wounded pride. "I just want to give my beautiful wife a hug."

"Of course," she said, but it came out almost as a gasp.

He carefully, gently, raised her injured arm and seemed to be inspecting the cast.

She stood rigid.

"It was an accident," he said firmly.

"I know, John, you didn't mean to . . . It's just that when you. . ." She looked into his eyes and looked away quickly.

"So, it's like that, is it?" He seemed almost pleased in a spiteful way. "Make a mistake, pay forever, right? Well, you ever hear the phrase, 'might as well be hanged for a sheep as a lamb'?"

"I don't . . . I . . ."

"I'm sorry," he said with savage mockery. "Is that a little over your head? Let me explain it in words of a single syllable. It means if you're going to blame me for what I haven't done, I might as well go ahead and do it for real."

He opened the door of their expensive refrigerator,

drew out a bottle of beer, and rummaged in a drawer for a bottle opener.

"John, please."

"Please, John. Please, John." He popped the bottle top and drank half the bottle in a single long swig. "Please, John, please work like a dog to buy me this beautiful home, John. Please, John, buy me a nice new car. Please, John, pay for the country club and the private school."

"Sweetheart, you know—"

"Shut the hell up. Just shut up."

I saw Graciella, the six-year-old Graciella, standing at the edge of the room, framed in an arched doorway.

"What do you want, honey?" her mother asked.

Graciella shook her head.

"Then go up to your room and play. Or outside. But don't bother Mommy and Daddy right now, okay, sweetie?"

"You're scaring her, Alison. You don't have to leave, Graciella. You can stay. Daddy's all right." He said "all right" in a way that elongated the vowels, sardonic, sullen. "Daddy just wanted a little affection. But I guess that's too much to ask, isn't it?"

Graciella knew something was wrong. Her face was serious, her eyes huge, looking from her mother to her father. I felt extremely uncomfortable but, I told myself, a difficult childhood is not a reason to become a junkie. I was pretty sure of that. After all, who doesn't have some kind of problem with their parents?

Messenger turned away and headed up the magnificent staircase to the bedrooms upstairs. It had been day, now it was night. And I sensed that more time than that had passed.

Messenger hesitated at a door. "This may be difficult to watch."

I almost laughed. Suddenly now Messenger was concerned for me? I'd already seen things that could haunt my dreams for a dozen lifetimes.

I nodded. But secretly I smiled. What was there left that could possibly be that awful?

We passed through the door and into a darkened bedroom. Graciella was asleep, but she was an older Graciella, perhaps nine or ten now. Her curls lay spread across her pillow. She breathed softly. A stuffed animal, a small white bear, lay beside her, its button eyes staring up in the dark. A ceiling fan turned and ruffled her hair just ever so slightly. From outside came the sound of sprinklers coming on.

It was a nice room, there were—

The door opened, briefly spilling light and silhouetting her father, John. He closed the door silently behind him and tiptoed to Graciella's bed.

My father used to come and check on me like this, when I was little. I remember pretending to be asleep, and he would watch me for a while, and whisper increasingly silly jokes until I cracked up. Then he would say, "Night, sweetheart," and—

Graciella's father kicked the side rail of her bed, hard. Graciella's eyes flew open.

"You didn't take out the trash," John yelled.

"I . . . I . . ." She tried to wipe the sleep from her eyes, blinking up at him. But it was not surprise I saw on her face, but mute dread: this was not the first time this had happened.

"I-I-I?" he mocked. "You stupid little pig. That's why you don't take out the trash, you're a stupid, fat little piggy who loves garbage, aren't you?"

"Dad, I need to sleep, I have school—" She cowered,

pulling the covers around her, trying to hold the blanket while covering her ears.

He cursed vilely, a machine-gun assault of abuse, a constant, sickening rant of filth and degradation. Then he knelt beside her, bringing his rage-transformed face down close to hers. "You don't need school, you're too stupid to learn anything. You know it's true. You're dumb as a brick, Graciella, and just as ugly. Now get your fat ass out of bed and take out the—"

"Okay, I'm coming, I—"

"Oh, please, don't start blubbering, you look like an animal, like a baboon or something when you start in with that. I can barely look at you! Filthy little waste of breath!"

I turned to Messenger, struggling to maintain my own self-control, trying to be the cool, detached Messenger's apprentice, but feeling all the while as if I would explode. "Is it always like this?"

In response Messenger waved a hand through the air, and from his fingers drifted bright silvery rectangles, each a tiny screen. And on each screen was a scene.

"Pig!"

"Worthless!"

"Fat!"

"Ugly!"

"Stupid!"

Dozens of these screens floated around me, each showing John, Graciella's father, heaping the most wounding of insults on her. I have transcribed here all that I can bring myself to say, but there were others worse. And they would not end, the screens multiplied until they threatened to fill the room like a tornado of filth and contempt.

It battered me. It was not directed at me, but it was as if I was being buried alive beneath the sheer weight of the verbal violence. It was awful to witness from the outside, to have endured it day after day, week after week, as Graciella had, to be attacked, ridiculed, subjected to this raw, unshielded hatred . . .

"No!" I cried. "No. No. Enough, freeze this, freeze time!"

Time froze. Graciella was absolutely still. The ceiling fan stopped. The sprinklers outside no longer chattered. Everything stopped.

Except for John.

The father was still for a moment, almost as if he,

too, were frozen, but then he turned his face to us. He squinted, tilted his head sideways a little. Then his eyes widened, and he *saw*.

A sound came from him. It was not a sound I had ever heard before, and not one I wish ever to hear again. It was a growl, the growl of a hyena guarding a dead prey. But there were layers within that animal growl, cries and shrieks, the sound of a lash on flesh, of bludgeon blows striking bone.

In the time I had been with Messenger, no one had ever seen us until we revealed ourselves. No one had ever moved when we froze time.

"Servants of Isthil," John said in a grating voice dripping with contempt.

I shot a worried look at Messenger. Messenger stood stony-faced, unafraid, unsurprised. "I thought I sensed your kind," he said.

John smiled and shrugged. "Well, aren't you the clever one? A Messenger of Fear, I suppose. One of Isthil's little busybodies. And what's this," he said, indicating me. "Your pet?"

Messenger did not answer.

John laughed. "Did you come to listen in? Did you enjoy it?" He turned back to the bed.

"Stop!" I cried. "Tell him!" But John did not stop, so I cried again, more insistently, "Stop him! Stop him!"

"He can't, you little fool," John snarled. "His kind have no power over mine."

"I have one power over you," Messenger said. It was said quietly, but if you imagine that he spoke without emotion, you would be wrong. I would never have believed so quiet a voice could carry so much fury. "Show yourself, incubus!"

"Oh, I see," John said. "She's a pupil, not a pet. You want her to learn, that's it, isn't it?" He focused on me, looked me up and down with a predatory intimacy.

"Show yourself!" Messenger snapped.

"As you wish, servant of Isthil."

John walked right up to me, swaggered really, and stopped within reach, facing me. He was proud of what he was about to reveal. He didn't writhe or squirm as if he were being forced to do so, he was glad of the opportunity. He smiled and then stuck out his tongue. But the tongue began to change. The pink color turned black, and his tongue grew long, longer, until it was a two-headed black snake writhing between lips that had begun to change as well, turning a dark red.

The mouth was wide and lipless, more a gash than a mouth, and within I glimpsed rows of tiny sharp teeth, shark's teeth. His eyes had migrated across his face, split apart into smaller pools, like spilled mercury. Two human eyes became six eyes that could only make me think of spiders. Not dead little doll eyes, but six active, searching, leering eyes.

His body was wiry rather than bulky, with something like skin that seemed too mobile, too . . .

My breath caught in my throat. His skin, his entire now-unclothed body was covered in barbs, like the stem of a fresh-cut rose. "Do you know what I would do to you?" he asked me. "With my tongue I would lick the flesh from you, flay you alive until you were nothing but raw, red flesh." All the while the barbs that covered him quivered, and the two-headed tongue would quickly dart in and out between words, so fast that his speech was not interrupted. Heat came off him, as if he were packed with glowing charcoal.

"Get back," I said in a voice much weaker than I intended.

"And once I had reduced you to a single vast island of pain, I would take you, I would take you!"

His tongue lashed out at me. His hands, claws now, swiped at me. He was furious. He was a single nexus of all the rage in the world. He hated me.

He hated me.

I couldn't help it, I backed away, not even conscious of what I was doing. Not conscious of anything but the monster before me.

"This one cannot harm you," Messenger said. "Nor can he physically harm Graciella. He can only pour his poison in her ears."

The demon—what else to call such a creature— nodded agreement. "Oh, it's true, sadly. But others—greater than myself—can take your precious immunity from you, little messenger girl. Oh yes, they can. And if it pleases them they can give you to me. They can give me your mind and body and your quivering soul, and then, oh the fun we would have."

He moved closer, ever closer, and I felt the door

behind me, my back pressed against it now, and panic, sheer terror possessed me.

"You want to see the demon?" he taunted me. He swung his arms wide and roared, "Here is the demon incubus!"

I panicked.

I fled.

6

FEAR TAUGHT ME TO USE MY NEWFOUND POWER. Blind panic accomplished what I had been reluctant to do. For when I fled, I did not run, but simply went elsewhere, as Messenger did so easily.

I don't believe that I thought, even for a microsecond, about where I would go. I just felt sudden animal terror and I was gone from Graciella's home, gone from the demon.

It took me a few shaking, quivering moments to realize that in my panic I had instinctively gone to where I felt safe. I was at the mall.

Not just any mall, but the mall where I had often wandered with my friends after school, or less happily with my mother who was never a great shopper, except for herself.

It was the Village at Corte Madera, just a few miles from my home in San Anselmo. The mall is really two malls, one on the west side of the 101, one on the east side, both open-air, as is fairly typical in temperate Northern California.

I was on the east side, the part with a Macy's at one end and a Nordstrom at the other. I was standing in front of the Apple store, close to the Macy's end.

The sky was dark and I sensed that it was near closing time. Accounting for the different time zones between California and Nashville, I had evidently stayed within the same time line. I had traveled through space but not time.

I don't know why my subconscious mind chose this as my destination. Why not my home? Why not my school? Maybe because this place was innocent of any association with my past misdeeds and their consequences. Or maybe it's because malls are uncomplicated and familiar.

And maybe it was because I had never seen a demon there.

There were chairs and tables outside the Peet's. I sat down in one and lowered my head to the table. Too much. Too much, too fast.

Too much.

I felt like I was coming apart. Like my head might crack open and spill filth across the metal table.

I raised my head just as an elderly couple began to sit on me, unaware, of course, that I was there. I slid out of the way, invisible.

I walked to Abercrombie & Fitch, weaving around and occasionally through kids my age, in the faint hope that I would see someone I knew. I did.

"Hello."

"Hello, Mara," Messenger said.

I did a poor job of hiding what was in my heart. The residue of shock and utter disgust was on my face.

Messenger turned off the music—well, for us at least—and did something he did on occasion, but not often: he looked at me. He looked into my eyes and I must have looked pathetic.

"I didn't know such things existed," I said.

"Nor did I before becoming a messenger," he said. "Demons can conceal themselves from human eyes."

"Are they all . . . I mean, are all evil people . . ."

"No." He shook his head. "No, humans are quite capable of evil all on their own. The incubi are a special problem. They are rare. So I am told. And they are disliked, even among demons, not because others of their kind despise their evil, but because they spend too much of their time with humans, and too little time in obedience to their masters."

I shook my head. "You've been revealing things to me slowly. You've been trying to spare me."

He nodded almost imperceptibly. "You need to understand, Mara, that your duty as a messenger gives you great powers, but your mind and soul are not protected. It is not just the wicked who end up in the Shoals."

"You're telling me I need to be strong."

Apparently that was so obvious it didn't require a response.

"I've seen the Master of the Game. I've now seen a demon incubus. Is that the worst of it? Or is there more?"

He kept up that steady stare.

"Ah," I said. I sniffed because at some point I had started to cry and my nose was running. I was in the middle of A&F, talking to a boy who should have been one of their models, and what I saw in my mind was the face of the incubus. And what I had in my heart was the knowledge of the cruelty he had inflicted on Graciella. The demon had systematically attacked her ego, her sense of herself. Each new verbal attack, each new calculated humiliation, was like an ax blow to a tree; no one blow would topple her, but with each cut she was weakened, awaiting only a stiff breeze to knock her down.

"I guess I'd better find a way to be strong," I said.

He liked that answer. No, he didn't say so, or high-five me, or even really change his expression, but I could tell.

I had the odd thought that until then I had found Messenger frightening, disturbing, infuriating, and yes, Oriax, wherever you are, attractive, but now I was starting to like him. Not like like, but as a human being. He was looking out for me. He was caring for me. And maybe that was just a part of his duty, but I didn't think so, and I flattered myself that he at least did not dislike me.

He waited, eternally patient.

"Okay," I said. "Graciella."

And without warning, we were on the side of a two-lane highway. Night was falling. There was very little around—a few scattered trees, a lot of grass, a lone trailer, and a well-composed, rustic-looking little building with what I supposed was a tin roof. There was a porch with four-by-four columns. Next to the highway was a sign with a sunburst logo and the name Authentic Coffee Company.

There was a gravel parking lot with six or eight cars and pickup trucks, and one long, white limousine.

A semi came tearing past, too fast for the relatively narrow road, and as it passed and its howl faded, I heard music coming from inside the lonely coffee shop.

We went inside by the unusual (for us) method of simply walking in through the open front door.

Inside was a remarkably pleasant room, nothing like the usual corporate coffee shop. This had wood-paneled walls, a brick fireplace, and a rocking chair in one corner. I immediately thought that this was the very sort of place I'd love to come to do homework.

But that was an unwelcome thought as it brought

a sense of loss and loneliness with it. Would I ever be able to go back to that life? Did my mother think I had run away or died? Did my friends miss me? I knew now that we had the power to move easily through time, and I told myself that when my apprenticeship, and my time as the Messenger was done, I would be able to slip unobtrusively back into my old life.

But if time was meaningless, what was I to make of Messenger's longing for his Ariadne? I had no way of knowing his circumstances, I did not know what evil he had done that had led him to be punished by being made a messenger.

Maybe in his case his old life was lost. Maybe he had somehow destroyed that old life. But my life had not been destroyed. Yes, I had done a terrible thing, for which I richly deserved this doom, and indeed had brought it on myself. But my life was intact. I hoped. I could go back.

I hoped.

It had come to this: I was pining for homework.

There was a girl playing an acoustic guitar in the corner. Her playing was not wonderful, but it wasn't terrible, either. Her voice, likewise, was too small, too tentative and untrained to be professional quality. But the song she sang . . . As I listened to the words of longing and hope, to the melody that floated so gently and insinuated itself so effortlessly into my heart, I knew I was hearing something more than a random girl in a random coffee shop.

The girl was only about sixteen. She was pretty and dressed in embroidered jeans and a peasant girl top.

She was, of course, Graciella.

I show you my bruises.
I show you my pain.
I show you the things I hide from myself.
Hope you're not frightened.
I hope that you're strong.
And pray that you'll love me,
My bruises and all.

I'm a bit of a mess.
I s'pose that you know.
Does that scare you off, or push you away?
Are you fool enough
To love me despite?

Or love me because of,
My bruises and all.

It was country music, not my usual thing, a Lucinda Williams type of song, but Graciella Jayne was laying herself out there in her lyrics and her music, and it touched me.

When she was done the half dozen or so people in the room applauded, none more enthusiastically than a young woman—no, a girl, now that she turned around so that I could see her face.

There was something familiar about that face. I frowned, concentrating, but could not place it. Had she been on television? I had only the faintest wisp of a memory of a music contest.

She had the look of a girl who'd been put together professionally. The hair, the makeup, the outfit, even the shoes, all had the well-designed look of money and Nashville taste. Then, too, people in the shop were stealing discreet glances at her. She was someone.

This someone was with a man, older, much older, who nodded, made a skeptical face, shrugged, then got up and went to the bathroom.

Alone, the well-dressed girl motioned to Graciella to join her. Graciella obviously recognized the girl, and just as obviously was startled. Graciella pointed at herself as if the girl could not really mean her. When the girl smiled and waved, Graciella set her guitar down and came over, taking the seat the old man had left vacant.

"Are you really . . ." Graciella let the question hang.

"I'm Nicolet," Nicolet said, and then the penny dropped, as the old saying goes, and I suddenly remembered. She was one of the youngest ever winners on *American Idol*. And since then her star had been rising. Had she won a Grammy? I couldn't be sure, but I was quite sure she'd become very successful. The limousine outside was almost certainly hers—she didn't look like a pickup truck kind of girl, at least not anymore.

We moved closer, Messenger and I, and heard Nicolet pouring compliments in Graciella's ears.

"Now, I don't want to offend you," Nicolet was saying, "but you aren't ready for performing. You're just not. But you can write a good song, and that's a fact. A song I could turn into a hit."

Graciella's eyes lit up. "Really? You would perform my song?"

"We'd like to see any songs you have." This from the old man who'd come back from the restroom. He pulled a chair up. "Do you have others?"

"Sure I do!" She rummaged around in her purse and came up with a dog-eared composition book. "This one's called 'Jesus Tweets.'" She fetched her guitar and sang a little.

Do not be anxious,
About tomorrow.
For tomorrow,
Will be anxious for itself.
Sufficient for the day
Is its own trouble.
Please retweet me.
And follow me back.

I follow you, Jesus.
And I retweet you.
I just want you to know,
I've got enough.
Sufficient for this day,
Are the troubles that I own,

No need to retweet me.

Just thought you should know.

A sly look passed between Nicolet and her manager as Graciella sang, the light of avarice on both parts, and a darker light of jealousy from Nicolet.

"I think we might like to buy your songs," the manager said.

"Really? Oh, my God!"

"We would do what's called a simple purchase agreement. See, that way you don't have to hire a lawyer and an accountant and a manager who will just take everything you have."

It occurred to me that Nicolet had all those things, of course—lawyers, accountants, and a manager—but Graciella's starlit eyes blinded her to the obvious fact that she was about to be ripped off.

"I think I can see where this is going," I muttered.

"Let me see if this coffee shop has a printer I can use, and we'll draw the contract up right now," the manager said. He thumped the table for emphasis and squeezed out a big, insincere smile.

"This is going to be great," Nicolet said, barely

concealing her contempt for Graciella's naiveté. "We'll be a team. Like Lennon and McCartney. You write the songs, I'll sing them."

Messenger was looking at me speculatively.

"What?" I snapped.

"What shall we do next? Learn more of Graciella's fate, or return for now to Pete and Trent?"

It took me aback. Messenger was running the show, I was just along for the ride. Right? Was he judging my readiness?

"It's not a great choice," I grumbled. "I either go with crazy bigots or with the long, slow decline of a girl who grew up being mentally abused by an incubus."

"Yes," Messenger said dryly. "Our duty seldom allows us to choose between chocolate and more chocolate."

I blinked. I blinked again. Messenger, the boy in black, the boy who pronounced terrible doom on evildoers, the servant of Isthil, my master, had just made a joke.

Not a great joke, but . . .

Of course he did not smile, that would have been too much to hope for.

"I want to see what they pay her," I said. "May I . . . Can I . . ." I wanted to ask whether I had the power on my own initiative to play with time as Messenger did.

No answer, which I suppose *was* the answer.

Could I? Well, that was up to me, wasn't it?

I didn't know how to begin. There is no magic wand in our world. No Latinate Harry Potter spells to cast. There is only will and, I suppose, imagination.

It dawned on me then, that imagination was vital to a messenger. Imagination is a tool of adaptation, a tool that allows a person to accept as real what seems impossible—what *is* impossible in the usual world.

I wanted to be a writer. It was that desire that had led me to the sin I was still paying for with this terrible duty. I had a good imagination, that much at least, if few other talents.

"Fast-forward," I said with far, far more confidence than I actually felt. And to my utter amazement, it worked. In time I would get past being surprised, but I was not there yet.

The world of the little rural coffee shop sped up to three or four times normal speed. The three of them, Graciella, Nicolet, and the manager, all began to move swiftly, hands and feet jerking, heads shifting as rapidly as a nervous bird. The guitar was lifted and set down, lifted and set down, and we heard helium chipmunk versions of songs sung at hyperspeed.

"Stop," I said.

Graciella was initialing six sheets of paper, and signing the final sheet.

I stood over her shoulder to see, but having power over time and space does not make me capable of understanding a contract.

"We need a lawyer," I said to Messenger.

"Yes." He left it like that. Just a *yes*.

But it was not a fatalistic, dead-end *yes*. It was a *yes* followed by an unspoken but implied, "So . . ."

I frowned, very unsure whether what I was thinking would work. If it didn't, I'd have made a fool of myself. Maybe humiliation was part of my duty.

"I want a lawyer," I said, trying not to grin at the way I was mimicking every police show I'd ever seen.

"Is the coffee here any good?"

This came from a woman who was standing beside me. Just standing there as if she'd been there all along. She was tall, middle-aged, attractive in a middle-aged sort of way, with large, liquid eyes, dark skin, hair up in dreads, and wearing a beige designer suit.

"I don't know," I said, staring.

"I suppose I can't drink it anyway," she said. There was a distinct islands lilt in her English. "It's a drag being disembodied."

"It's good to see you again, Ms. Johnson," Messenger said formally.

Ms. Johnson did not answer him except with a disapproving look. She took in the room and said, "I see we are in freeze frame. And who are you?"

"Me? I'm Mara. I'm . . . um . . . the apprentice."

"Really? Messenger must be nearing the end of his sentence. So, why am I summoned?"

I didn't want to answer that question at that particular moment because I wanted to ask her just who she was, what she was, how she had come here, and from where. But she did not strike me as chatty. "We have a contract we need interpreted."

"Mmm." She leaned over Graciella's shoulder and began turning the pages of the contract. As she read she would exclaim. "Ah!" or, "Ho ho!" or, "You shameless bastard." This went on for several minutes while

Messenger and I just stood there like a couple of waiters with no customers.

Finally Ms. Johnson stood back and said, "Well, that is a very fine bit of legal work, that contract."

I frowned. "So it's good?"

"It's great—if you're not that foolish girl. It gives an entity named Nicolet Productions Inc. complete ownership of any and all works produced by Graciella Jayne in perpetuity, throughout the universe, etcetera etcetera. For which she will be paid two thousand dollars and no royalty."

"And that's bad?" I asked cautiously.

"Songwriters make their money off royalties. Every time Nicolet performs a song, *cha ching*, royalty paid to songwriter. Every time Nicolet sells a download, *cha ching*, royalty to songwriter. Like that. This is an iron-clad contract that means this girl will lose all rights over all her work and never make a penny beyond the two thousand."

She said thousand as "tou-sand," which I liked.

"In short," Ms. Johnson said, "she's being screwed. Ripped off. Assuming her majority, she'll never be able to write a song again without giving it to Nicolet."

"She shouldn't sign that," I said.

"Apprentice girl, you must be new. She's already signed it. She signed it a year ago."

"Of course." I blushed. "I knew that."

"Is that all?" Ms. Johnson asked.

"Thank you," Messenger said, and the lawyer was as gone as if she'd never been there.

"This job is going to drive me crazy," I said, trying for "lighthearted."

"Don't let it," Messenger said.

7

AS IF TO PROVE I WAS RIGHT, MESSENGER TRANS-
ported us back to Trent and Pete.

"Psychic whiplash," I muttered.

It was night. Very late, I thought, because we were
in an older neighborhood of small, one-story clapboard
or brick homes, but few lights shone from the windows.

Occupying a corner was a low brick building that
looked very much as if it might once have been a small
elementary school. Blue letters on a small white sign
read, *Islamic Center of Des Moines.*

From the way the two boys staggered and kept having

to suppress giggles, I guessed that this was either later in the life of that bottle of peppermint schnapps, or another night altogether with a different bottle. But they were drunk, intent on mayhem.

Each had a can of spray paint. Pete carried a brick. Trent had armed himself with a metal baseball bat.

First they spray-painted the wall facing the street, and then the front door, with their usual unimaginative slurs and death threats.

Then came the windows.

Crash!

Crash!

The baseball bat smashed. The brick flew. The two of them turned to race back to the car, giddy, excited, yipping and howling.

And there was a man.

He was middle-aged, dark-skinned, a large man, but with a body that seemed twisted by some earlier injury. He moved as though half his body was slow to respond. I wondered if he'd had a stroke, or perhaps been injured.

He was neither armed nor dangerous. But he was outraged.

"What are you doing? What are you doing?"

"Uh . . . smashing the hell out of this place, why do you ask?" This from Trent, exercising his wit. He tapped the baseball bat against the palm of his free hand. He made no effort to run although Pete looked much less confident.

"Come on, man, let's get out of here," Pete said. He grabbed Trent's arm, but Trent shook him off.

"What are you going to do, old man?" Trent demanded.

"I am calling the police!"

The man pulled out a phone. Trent swung the bat and knocked the phone from his hand. As the man bent to retrieve it, Trent smashed the end of the bat down on the phone, shattering it.

"What are you doing, you crazy boy?" The man had an accent, not one I could identify, but it grew more apparent as he grew more agitated and afraid. "Go away! Go away from here!"

Trent grinned, a dangerous look for him. "Who do you think you're talking to, rag-head? Huh? I'm an American. I live here. I'm from here. I was born here, where the hell are you even from? Iraq?

Gabbagabbafreakistan?"

"I am from Afghanistan, I live here five years since—"

"So shut up! You're probably a terrorist. You going to blow yourself up? You got a bomb in your pocket, old man?"

When the man refused to answer Trent shoved the end of the bat in his chest. The man stumbled back. Trent hit him again and this time the man turned to run.

"Get him!" Trent yelled to Pete. But Pete was backing away, holding up his hands and saying, "No man, no man, we need to get out of here, dude."

So Trent went racing after the fleeing man. They disappeared from view in the dark, then, a yell, and a solid, sickening *thunk!*

The man screamed. "Stop! Stop! You're hurting me!"

Trent was yelling obscenities, grunting as he swung the bat again and again. The sounds of blunt force on flesh and bone were mixed with the hollow metal sound of misses where Trent hit pavement.

The man cried out for help but no lights snapped on in the windows of the neighborhood.

Finally the man fell silent.

Pete, obviously shaken, advanced into the darkness and we followed. Trent stood panting and cursing over the prostrate body. He noticed Pete and gave him a sickly, teeth-baring grin.

"Showed him," Trent said. "That's one camel-jockey who won't be talking back to a white man again. Yeah." He kicked the downed man.

"Oh, man, you have messed up bad," Pete said. "Oh, man, oh, man." He was hugging himself with anxiety, glancing all around, jumpy as a squirrel.

Far off a siren wailed.

Finally Pete took Trent by the arm and drew him away, leaving Messenger and me to stare down at the form of the battered man. He was still breathing, a fact for which I was grateful. Breathing but bleeding. His face was covered with blood. His hair was matted with blood. His breathing was choked by blood.

"His name is Abdullah Sohal," Messenger said. Then, in an aside to me, "Have you seen enough of this?"

"I guess we cannot help him," I said.

"He will survive. As you will see."

And just like that we were gone from that place and that time and were suddenly in a hospital room, looking at the same man we'd just seen being beaten. The sun was shining through the hospital window. Abdullah Sohal was having his bandages replaced by a male nurse who was attempting to make stilted, awkward conversation.

"If you have any pain, you have to tell me or one of the other nurses, you understand that, right?"

Abdullah Sohal was swaddled in bandages. There was an IV line in his arm and a thing on his finger to measure oxygen passing through his blood. His left arm was in a webbing cast. The fingers extending from that cast were clean but bruised. As the nurse peeled old gauze away from his face I saw a single mass of bruising. His face was swollen, his lip split open, teeth missing.

"Yes, I will tell you if the pain is greater."

"Okay. Same if you have any trouble passing urine. Your kidneys took a beating."

"I noticed."

The nurse winced. Then, mouth set in a grim line, he said, "This is not us. This is not Iowa. I want you to know that we all want the s.o.b. who did this caught and thrown into jail."

Sohal sighed. "It was a child. Maybe fifteen or

sixteen. The age of my own son."

"Your son? Is he on the visitors' list?"

"No, sadly. He is still in Afghanistan, with his mother. My brother looks after them."

"Ah."

And that's when Sohal asked the nurse to fetch his wallet. From his wallet he took a photograph.

Of course I knew before I saw. I knew the connection that I would see revealed.

The picture was of the woman who had wept and cried out at the funeral of the boy in the picture. The boy who had died standing up to killers.

"Oh, so *that's* what this is about," Oriax said, appearing behind me and looking over my shoulder. "Now, I see. But come on, Messenger, you can't really blame young Trent for what happened thousands of miles away."

"I blame him. He is responsible for what will happen," Messenger said. "What is *about* to happen in this time line. Abdullah was about to bring his wife and son over to America. He knows his son. He knows his son is outspoken and brave and he fears what may happen to him."

Now we watched as Sohal composed an email to his

wife and son. It was written in a text I could not begin to decipher, but because of those gifts that come with being made an apprentice to the Messenger of Fear, I could understand it.

"He's not telling them he was beaten up. Just about the vandalism and grave desecration," I said. "He's saying they'll have to delay plans to come to America. Plans that were to take effect in two weeks."

"See, he's already over the little tussle he had with Trent," Oriax said.

I had seen Oriax in action, but had never seen her attempt to halt a reckoning. The last time around she had intervened to help *doom* the evildoer. She had *wanted* him to be punished. She had enjoyed watching a boy burn.

This was different. She was trying to save Trent. She seemed indifferent to Pete, but she badly wanted to save Trent.

"It is not for this crime, but for some use I cannot see," Messenger mused aloud.

Oriax knew there was no point in denying it. "You do not have the right to punish some future misdeed, Messenger," she warned.

"True, Oriax. And neither your future-sight nor your wishes will play a part in how I perform my duty."

"No, of course not," Oriax sneered. "The ever-so-pure Messenger, idiot tool of a forgotten goddess, dupe of an absurd ancient faith." Then she turned to me. Some of her overpowering physical magnetism lessened a bit when she was angry. "Perhaps when it's your turn, mini-Messenger, you won't be quite the fool this one is."

She was gone then. I wondered where she went when she left us. Did she pass the time in some sort of hell? Was it anything like the hell conjured up by some religions? Did she spend her days cavorting with demons and torturing the damned?

Or at the end of her appearances did she retire to some impossible-to-imagine n-dimensional backstage dressing room to await her next curtain call?

But Oriax had left behind a lingering doubt in my mind. "*Is* it fair and just to take Trent and Pete to task for what happens thousands of miles away?"

I was relieved that Messenger did not accuse me of being swayed by Oriax. Instead, as he sometimes did when my question was directly related to my training, he chose to explain. "Two men decide to steal money from a store. Both vow there will be no violence. But the storekeeper resists and one of them pulls a gun and kills the storekeeper. Under the law of most nations both men are equally guilty of murder."

"Yes, but—"

"Why are they both guilty if neither intended to kill the storekeeper and only one man fired the gun?"

"Because . . . because . . . well," I admitted, "when I started this sentence I thought I knew the answer. But I obviously don't."

"Admitting ignorance is a good thing," Messenger said, sounding disconcertingly like an algebra teacher I used to have. "The intention was not to kill, but it was to break the law, to do a wicked thing. When you choose to do evil you break faith with gods and men. You declare yourself an enemy to law and morality. You choose to serve the purposes of foul creatures and forces. Trent and Pete assaulted the girl. Their school evicted them. They made matters infinitely worse, then, with violent attacks. Did they anticipate that they were setting off a chain of events that would result in Aimal's death? No. No more than the man who drives a car while drunk intends to kill a pedestrian. And yet he is held responsible."

"Do not plant a weed and pretend surprise when it grows to strangle your garden," I said, quoting from memory. "For, I tell you that to hate is to kill, for from hatred grows death as surely as life grows from love."

Messenger's mouth opened and closed like a beached trout. "You astonish me."

"Well," I said breezily, "I'm a very astonishing girl."

"Yes. At times you are." Then, he looked at me. As if he had never really seen me before. And my heart jumped.

"But a tired girl as well, I think. This day has included an encounter with a demon. That is enough. You need rest and food."

"Don't you?" I asked. I don't know why I asked that. It was impertinent, and Messenger never seemed to want me to acknowledge that he was, after all, as human as I was. Or at least I believed he was.

"Yes," he said, surprising me.

He looked weary. There were times when he seemed almost to be made of something stronger than flesh, when he would look invulnerable. But this was not one of those times. His pale skin looked like fine, bone china, translucent and fragile. He always stood strong and erect, never slumped, and I had come to unconsciously mimic that pose. But within that rigidity were gradations, subtle hints of shoulders not quite square, of breaths only half breathed, of a head carried like a balanced weight that might topple to the side.

The silence had lengthened and I knew he was seeing things not there in the room with us. He carried a burden, and though he never complained, it was painful for him. The fact that this burden was in large degree to do with the mysterious Ariadne, and that the sadness that was so much a part of him was all about lost love, did bother me, I won't deny it. Was I jealous of the invisible and thus eternally perfect Ariadne?

Hopeless, I told myself. Don't go down that path. Don't have those thoughts.

I am not to be touched.

That had been his warning to me, and when I had inadvertently touched him I had been flooded with a terrible highlights reel of his life as a messenger. I had seen things that . . .

I froze.

Those memories . . . I had pushed them away in self-defense. But they were still buried in my brain, weren't they? If I chose I could summon them and go through them. Couldn't I?

But why would I? Just to better understand the enigmatic boy in black? Would I endure that psychic pain just to know Messenger?

He was, at the moment, the only other person in my life. Somewhere in time or space my mother and my friends were there, living their lives, as I drifted through time, forward and backward. Someday I hoped, believed, told myself, I would be back to that life. This would all end someday, and with the power to move through time I should be able to reinsert myself right where I left off. Like picking up a book you've put down.

That was my hope, what I told myself, but I did not know. Nor did I ask. I rationalized that questions to Messenger are seldom answered and therefore futile, but the truth was that I wasn't sure I wanted to know. I did not want to believe that I was "missing" from the real world, that the people who loved me were suffering, worrying about me. My burden was already too great, my control over myself too tenuous. I am insatiably curious, and cannot help but wonder, yet I must, at the same time, do what I can to preserve my sanity.

Of course, in any event, I wouldn't be the same person, would I? My God, what would I even have to say to my old friends? How would I be my mother's daughter when I had known such terrors and used such power?

Part of me wanted to stay and finish with Trent now. But Messenger's instincts were right: I was starving and sad and in need of a break. Trent would be there when we returned.

"Yes, I wouldn't mind going . . . I don't know what to call it. It's not my home." That word, *home*, that word started the flow of tears that filled but did not spill from my eyes.

"It is your abode," Messenger said. "For now."

And suddenly we were there, Messenger and I. Would he immediately disappear off to whatever his "abode" was? Yet he stood in my living room, seeming still distracted. I suspected that the earlier encounter with Daniel in Brazil, and my overhearing of same, had left him feeling awkward with me. And even Messenger had to have been affected by the encounter with the incubus.

"Would you like something to eat?" I asked him. You know how sometimes you just speak without thinking? It just seemed polite. He was a visitor to my . . . *abode*. He was a guest. You offer guests food and drink.

He looked down at the floor and I was braced for a dismissive remark followed by the usual disappearing act. But when he looked up he said, "What have you got?"

"I was going to have a PB and J."

I'm pretty sure he didn't know what that was. But he nodded, and I began to assemble sandwiches. "I have mixed berry preserves and apricot jam."

"I have no fixed opinions on the matter," he said cautiously.

I made him a PB and J with mixed berry. We stood awkwardly in the kitchen, eating. On his first bite his eyebrows shot up. He sniffed at it. Took a second bite and nodded to himself.

I poured him some milk. Because let's face it, peanut butter and jelly and cold milk is perfection, really.

It was as he was drinking milk that I said, "You have some jelly on your shirt, right . . ." and pointed, which he must have thought was an effort to touch him, which caused him to recoil and in the process pour half a glass of 2 percent down his front.

"Oh, my God!" I cried while Messenger stared in confusion at the mess. I grabbed a paper towel meaning instinctively to wipe the mess, then realized that would be a mistake, and handed him the paper towel, which he used to make matters quite a bit worse by smearing the jelly and milk down his front and into the buttonholes.

"This is regrettable," he said, and I believe he may have experienced the normal human reaction of feeling embarrassed.

"Oh," I said. "You know what? You can actually go backward in time and avoid the spill." I was feeling proud of myself for that clever insight.

He shook his head. "Time travel does not change future events. And we are not given the power in order to take personal advantage."

"Do you have a spare shirt?"

He winced. "Not at the moment. My laundry is taken away and returned after a few days."

I couldn't help it: I laughed. I tried not to, but how could I not laugh at the notion that the most powerful person I had ever met or imagined meeting, the dread Messenger of Fear, had not kept up on his laundry. The mere fact that he had laundry seemed incongruous.

Messenger had been for me an object of mystery, anger, fear, and yes, desire, as Oriax had immediately seen. But he was still a boy. He was a boy with a ruined shirt and no spares available.

"Give it to me," I said, "I can rinse it out in the sink."

Messenger looked at me, down at his shirt, at me again, and said, "Um . . ." Which was the second strangest thing I'd heard him say in the last couple of minutes.

"Just . . . really. And I can dry it with my blow-dryer."

He stood, indecisive—not an emotion I connect with Messenger—so I said, "Come on," in a "no big deal" voice.

So he shrugged off the long coat he always wore and laid it over the back of a stool. Then, "My body. . ."

"Messenger, I know about the tattoos. I have one myself and will soon have more. I promise I won't be horrified."

It was a promise I could make, but not one I could keep.

He unbuttoned his shirt, including the ones at his wrists. Then, removed it and laid it on the stool closer to me.

I didn't mean to stare. But how could I not?

His bare flesh was like a Hieronymus Bosch painting of hell. Each terrible punishment inflicted during his time as a Messenger of Fear was there on him in terribly vivid tattoos, tattoos not limited to the usual colors, not limited by the boundaries of decency. Many of them moved so that rather than just being a painting, he was like hundreds of small screens, each showing a scene of terror to sicken the mind. The tattoos almost seemed at times to jostle for position, wishing to be seen, as though each was pushing its way through a crowd of other sufferers to cry, "Look at me, see what I endured."

He was watching me as I looked at his chest and shoulders and biceps. I felt ashamed, as though I was violating his privacy.

I took his shirt and brought it to the sink. I filled the sink with soapy water and plunged the shirt in. "I'll let it soak for a minute. If you want, I could get you one of my T-shirts. It would be pretty small on you."

I forced myself to turn back to him, I forced myself to look in his eyes and not at the tableau. When, inevitably, I glanced down, I struggled to ignore the tattoos and focus instead on the shape of him, on the very human shape of hard, flat stomach, of capable muscles and strong bones beneath. I imagined him without the marks of his office. I imagined I was looking at the most beautiful boy I'd ever known, stripped to the waist.

But then, I saw *her*.

She had long, auburn hair, shampoo commercial hair. Her face . . . and here I have to pause to control my wild emotions . . . her face was lovely.

But that beauty was fleeting, for the beauty was slowly devoured by a creeping rash, followed by boils and pustules that oozed blood and a clear, viscous fluid. As this disease or curse advanced, she—the tattoo—screamed silently, face all open mouth and wild eyes.

The auburn hair. The lovely face. I had had hints of them before. But it was the location of this tattoo that told the story, for it was directly over his heart.

I didn't mean to say it, I knew that it would cause

him pain, and I knew that I was seeing more than he wished to reveal about himself. But how could I not put a name to that terrible image? How could I keep from whispering...

"Ariadne."

8

ARIADNE. MESSENGER'S LOST LOVE.

Ariadne, who he searched for anywhere and everywhere.

Ariadne, whose fate had been concealed from Messenger. For his own good? Possibly. As some part of his own punishment? Perhaps.

"Yes," Messenger said at last and lowered his head to avoid my eyes.

"You . . . She was a . . . She did something wicked," I said.

"Yes," he said tersely.

"You were sent to offer her the game."

"Yes."

"And she lost."

He nodded.

"That must have been . . . That must have been the worst thing in the world for you," I said.

No response. His eyes were not seeing me but some other place, and some other face.

"Did she . . . What happened to her? After, I mean."

"All this has been concealed from me. I knew her, I . . . I loved her. Before, you understand, before I became this." He waved a hand that encompassed his body. I took it that he meant he had known and loved her before he became the Messenger of Fear. Back when Messenger and Ariadne had just been a boy and a girl.

"You must know if she survived," I pressed.

"The fates of all who endure a visit from the Messenger of Fear are few: they recover and go on with their lives however damaged and transformed they may be, or else . . ."

"The Shoals?"

He closed his eyes and kept them closed for so long I would almost have thought he slept but for the labored way he drew breath, each exhalation shuddering ever so slightly. At last he regained control of his emotions, opened his eyes, and said, "I have not visited the Shoals since. Please don't ask any more."

He was done talking about it. What could I do but respect his right to keep at least some secrets?

I went back to the sink and scrubbed the stain, working the milk and jelly out of the fabric. I drained the sink, wrung the shirt out, filled the sink with clear water, and rinsed it.

I wanted desperately to ask more. But there were limits even to my curiosity when I know that it will bring pain. I didn't need to know. He didn't need to talk about it, at least not with me, not now.

Later. Maybe. Another time.

I spread his shirt on a coat hanger, hung it from the shower curtain rod, positioned my hair dryer on the toilet seat, using a towel to steady and direct it, and turned it to "high." The gray shirt fluffed out in the loud, hot wind.

I steeled myself to seeing him again, and returned to the kitchen to find him looking in the refrigerator, like any typical teenaged boy searching for food. His back was as full of ink as his chest, but with his shirt off it was the first time I had seen his back. How can the sight of such a tableau of misery still excite something in me? Was it that I had to look longer and more closely to see the lean waist, the strained muscle, the smooth V of flanks rising to strong shoulders?

He did not know I was watching, and I took advantage of the moment. Yes, what I was thinking was silly and wrong. My excuse was that I was lonely. My excuse was that he was my whole world now, aside from the damaged and the doomed and the monsters. My excuse was that I had some slight understanding now of what he had endured and I wanted to offer him some sort of comfort.

My excuse was that he was absurdly attractive and he was after all a straight boy and I was after all a straight girl and it would have been strange had I not been drawn to him.

I wanted to touch the boy who was not to be touched.

I closed my eyes and steadied myself with a hand on the counter. I pictured myself coming up behind him, sliding my arms around him, flattening my palms against his chest, kissing the place where strong shoulder rose to elegant neck, pressing my breasts against his back.

It was almost overpowering. I think I would have done it, except for the fact that I knew what would happen the moment I made physical contact with him. Far more than the images on his flesh would have flooded my mind. I would have touched him and been assaulted by detailed memories of each horror—the wicked things done, the games endured, the punishments that could drive a person mad.

It would have been a high price to pay simply to let my lips brush his neck. And yet such was my loneliness and my sad longing for him, that it still seemed possible.

I pushed the thought aside, feeling frustrated, and with my loneliness only exacerbated.

I made him another sandwich. Meat this time. He ate it. I gave him his dried shirt. He put it on and left.

I kicked the stool he'd been sitting on, and hurt my toe.

I ate and took a bath. Normally I bathe in the morning, but morning doesn't seem to mean here what it used to mean in my old life. I didn't have a schedule.

There was no set wake-up time.

In my old life I seldom took baths per se; I preferred showers. But I didn't want to sleep just yet, I wanted to think. I wanted to soak in hot water and think about who I was now and what I might yet be.

I would become the Messenger of Fear, that much was decided. I had taken the punishment on myself, and I did not regret it. I had caused a girl's death. Yes, I had done that, motivated by spite and jealousy. I hadn't meant for Samantha Early to shoot herself in the head, but I had nevertheless caused it to happen. I had only meant to hurt her, never to kill her. Just a poison thorn, and yet her heart had died.

As hard as this new life was for me, I did not regret my decision to accept the responsibility and the penance that came with it. There are things we do in this life that are wrong but not terribly important. There are things we do that are wrong but that we can make right, mostly right at least. But this was neither of those kinds of wrong. What I had done was deadly and permanent. Punishment should fit the crime.

I was restoring the balance.

When I had completed my time, first as apprentice

and then as a messenger, I would feel that I had a right to resume my old life, though I was not certain such a thing would happen. I would never be able to undo what had been done, but I would have done all I could to pay for my sins. Beyond that . . .

The water was hot, just on the edge of painful, and there was no bubble bath to obscure from me the sight of my own body. I looked down at myself, at frappuccino flesh bent by water's refraction, and imagined myself as covered in tattoos as Messenger. It would happen, I knew that. The day would come when I would not be able to bear looking at myself this way. And no boy would ever be able to tolerate touching me.

That was what made the longing so terrible, I realized. Because it wasn't just some crush, or even desire in the usual sense of that word. It was a realization that for me the door to all of that messy, complicated, emotional reality was beginning to close. Even now any boy who touched so much as the back of my hand, or rubbed my neck, let alone kissed me, would be sickened by the images that would flood his mind.

I am not to be touched.

Never?

What did it matter? Was I still laboring under the pitiful misconception that I had some pride to defend? Was there someone I was trying to impress with my stoicism?

I was alone. I would someday be free of this duty, but I feared that I would be forever alone.

And there, just behind my closed eyelids, was the image of Messenger. No wonder I had stared at him so hungrily. No wonder Oriax had so quickly deduced what would happen between us—she had seen so clearly that a frightened, lonely girl would be drawn inexorably to the tall, mysterious boy in black.

I smashed my fist into the water.

No way out. I deserved my fate, yes, yes, I did. I did. But at the same time the less ethical parts of my mind were already looking for an escape. And such an escape had been offered, had it not? Oriax had been oblique, but it was there in her words and attitude, a suggestion that she was my way out.

Oriax.

What could she offer me? What did I want? My old life? Some entirely new life? That's what I would have wanted, should have wanted. But what I wanted now, was him, and no, not Oriax, not any creature, could give me that.

I wondered if beneath the stunning and sensuous exterior Oriax was just like Graciella's demon. Perhaps not an incubus, but some other form of demon. Maybe even something worse, if that was possible.

But I pushed that thought aside and turned my imagination to the question of Ariadne. She had done something wicked, clearly. And Messenger had been tasked to deal with her, to offer her the game, to discover and then inflict on her the most terrible punishment she herself could imagine.

What must that have been like for him? I tried to put myself in that same situation, but I had no great love in my life. I had no Ariadne of my own. The closest I could come was to think of my mother. We had all the usual teenaged daughter vs. mother fights, plus some more, since she'd started dating following my father's death.

But could I impose the messenger's fear on her if required? My God, how would I live with that? How did Messenger live with it?

That, at least, I knew the answer to. He lived with it by searching for her whenever he could, wherever he could think to look. Daniel indulged him, though Daniel clearly did not believe it was a wise use of Messenger's time.

What in fact *had* happened to Ariadne?

And with that came the dark serpent of temptation, for my mind answered the question with a possibility: Messenger might choose to avoid the Shoals, but could I not go there alone? Could I not perhaps answer the question of Ariadne's fate?

And if she were there in that place I'd heard spoken of only in the most somber of tones, would Messenger be free at last of his obsession?

I pushed the stopper knob up with my toe and the water started to drain out.

This much I was sure of: Messenger would never be whole until he knew the truth.

I slept. And I woke. And another "day" began, with no mention by Messenger or me of Ariadne.

Messenger and I appeared at a small house on a tidy lot with an impressive elm tree in the front yard and a fenced backyard.

Maybe the day will come when I feel not so queasy simply letting myself into people's homes and indeed, minds, but it has not come yet. Messenger and I walked up the steps and through the front door. As always, solid reality seemed to bend out of our way as if it was avoiding our touch. As though walls and doors and window glass found us objectionable.

And were we not objectionable? That seems the kindest way to describe our wholesale violation of privacy. We entered where we wished, like police with a warrant to serve. I have no idea where Messenger is from, but as an American it did not sit well with me.

And yet it was a duty I had taken on. I was doing penance for my own sins by making others pay for theirs.

We had, in fact, come to inflict pain and fear. Not just cops: we were judge, jury, and, with the help of the Master of the Game, executioner, all rolled into one. We had powers no one should possess.

I fervently hoped that the book of Isthil I'd begun to read was something more than mere myth, because if we did not have some great purpose, if we were not saving the world by maintaining the balance, then we were just home invaders.

A woman was in the living room, sitting on the couch, watching TV with her feet up. She wore a blue

Walmart uniform and had obviously come home from work too tired to change immediately. She was clicking through the channels with her remote control.

Did she look a little like Trent? Maybe a little.

I took stock of her, trying to find answers in her face. She was in her early thirties, not attractive, but not marked with any obvious sign of malice. She had a face that smiled frequently. Her eyes were disappointed but not angry.

Of course in the aftermath of my encounter with an incubus, I wasn't prepared to take anything or anyone at face value.

There was a nonworking fireplace, bricked up against cold winds. On the mantel were framed photos. The woman and a man, laughing. The woman and a man and a much younger Trent. They must have been at a fair—there was a Ferris wheel in the background and they were sharing funnel cake.

And laughing.

I don't know why but I have a hard time believing that full-throated laughter can coexist with evil. Maybe that's naive. But the picture of the three of them seemed utterly incompatible with the memory of

Trent slamming his baseball bat again and again and again...

It was not a wealthy family. There was a worn, tattered feel to everything. But poverty does not create evil, poverty could not explain Trent. It would not justify the hazing of Samira, far less the desecration of graves, racist graffiti, and a brutal physical assault.

"Why?" I asked, not even really intending to say it out loud because of course I assumed Messenger would not deign to answer. "Why do people do evil things?"

Messenger's answer stunned me. "Why did you?"

Now it was my turn to avoid answering. I didn't know the answer. Why had I done the evil thing that resulted in my being condemned to this life?

Why Trent?

Why me?

Silent and abashed, I followed Messenger down to the basement room where Trent was on his back on a padded bench, lifting weights, aided by his friend, Pete.

I steeled myself for my duty. I would bring fear to this place.

9

WE BECAME VISIBLE. IT WOULD HAVE SEEMED TO the two boys as if we had popped in out of thin air.

Trent lost control of one of the heavy dumbbells he was lifting. It crashed to the concrete floor. He kept his grip on the other, lowered it to the floor as well, sat up, and said, "What the hell?"

Pete took two careless steps back and nearly tripped over the bench.

"Trent Gambrel and Peter Markson," Messenger said. "You are called to account for your actions."

"Who are you? Get out of here! Get out of here right now!"

Trent had retrieved a lighter dumbbell and now stood brandishing it as a weapon.

"I offer you a game," Messenger said.

Trent cursed violently and swung the dumbbell at Messenger. The weight passed harmlessly through Messenger's shoulder. So Trent lifted it high and brought it down with all his strength on Messenger's head. It passed like a knife through butter and swept away on the bottom of its arc, hitting Trent in the shin.

He cursed again and yelled in pain.

Messenger waited until the boy's hopping around had stopped. Pete made a dash for the stairs but managed only two steps before he found himself unable to move.

"If you accept the invitation to the game and lose, you will suffer a punishment," Messenger said, not sounding blasé, but not reacting to Trent's rage, either. "If you refuse the game, you will suffer punishment. If you accept the game and win, you will be allowed to go on without any further interference."

"What is this, man?" Pete cried. "Help! Help!"

Yelling for help and shouting obscenities and threats went on for a while and Messenger let them go on until both boys were winded, and finally accepted the reality that they could neither leave, nor summon help, nor strike either Messenger or myself.

"I offer you a game," Messenger said again, in tones identical to the first time.

"What the hell, man?" Trent whined. "Who are you? Who's the chink?"

I have to admit that slur struck home. I'd listened with distaste to a long string of such slurs, but this was the first directed at me, personally. I'd never really heard anyone deliberately attack me as an Asian American before. Oh, I'd heard the sort of soft bigotry, the assumption that I must be a grind because I'm Asian, or that I must play violin and be great at math. (Neither, unfortunately.) But this was the first time someone had just come right out and called me a name in that way. To my face.

I would like to say it had no effect. But it did. It had the effect of siphoning off some of the concern I felt for what they were about to endure.

"He's the Messenger of Fear," I said.

"Yeah?" Trent looked defiantly at Messenger. "Well, I'm not afraid."

I bit my tongue and stopped myself from saying, *you will be soon*. But yes, the slur had made me spiteful and less pitying than I might otherwise be. I'm not proud of that.

"If you accept the challenge and prevail, you go free. If you play the game and lose, you will be punished. If you refuse to choose, you will be punished. You have seven seconds to decide. Play or pay? Seven. Six."

More threats, more cursing.

"Five."

Defiance and rage.

"Four."

"Who the hell are you to—"

"Play the game, you fool!" And with that, Oriax made her entrance.

"Whoa."

I was unsurprised by the boys' reactions.

"Play his game, you stupid boy," Oriax snapped. "You may win. If you refuse, you lose. And if you lose, well, then, little Trent and even littler Pete, you will very likely end up drooling and shivering, cringing like beaten dogs along the gloomy corridors of the Shoals, lost forever to your sorrowful mothers."

I admired that. The way she could just spit that out as fluently as a rapper.

"What's the game?" Pete demanded, nervous and yet reassured by Oriax, who must have seemed like an ally to him. He was staring without restraint at Oriax, barely even glancing at her eyes.

"Listen to me," Oriax snarled. She was not interested in their attraction to her, she had a goal, and she could conceal it no longer. She focused her burning-ember gaze on Trent. "You, at least, have a future. You may do . . . great things. Great and terrible things. If you survive this day. *If.*"

I wanted to ask her to explain, but doubted she would. Messenger said nothing, and something in his body language warned me to stay silent as well. But as always, curiosity . . .

"What are you talking about?" I asked.

"No," Messenger said curtly. "The servants of Malech are granted certain powers not given to us. They see further in time. But no human may be punished for what he may do in the future. Nor," he added pointedly, "for the things they say to us."

So he had heard that *chink* remark. And he had seen that it annoyed me. I fell silent.

"All right, we'll play your game," Trent said. "Isn't that right, Pete? We'll play his game. And we'll win it, too." He offered a fist for a bump but Pete was seeing very little but Oriax.

"You have accepted the game," Messenger intoned. He raised up his hands, palms out toward the two of them. It had the character of a religious liturgy, a memorized prayer. "In the name of Isthil, I summon the Master of the Game."

I tensed at this. I had not enjoyed my earlier encounters with the Master of the Game, and though I was prepared now, I was still not looking forward to it. There may come a time when that monster's appearances will seem mundane to me, but that time had not yet come.

The Master of the Game scared the hell out of me.

Something that seemed very much as if it were poison gas began to fill the room. It was a mist, a mist the yellow of fresh-bruised flesh or an aging carnivore's teeth, a sickly cloud that swirled and swelled until half the basement was obscured by it.

I had a sense that the earth-enclosed walls of the basement had been pushed out and the room itself had become huge. The weight bench and the ancient sofa on which Pete had sat all seemed smaller, almost like the furnishings of a doll's house. The low-ceilinged basement had become a vast, empty hangar with only a few pitiful sticks of furniture clustered in the middle.

Then, the random-seeming swirl of that sinister mist began to move with more purpose, forming itself around an emerging object.

The Master of the Game approached.

I thought I had encountered the Master of the Game before, and had steeled myself for his nightmare aspect, but as Oriax changed with each encounter while nevertheless maintaining her core reality, so, too, it seems the Master of the Game could change, though by what arcane rules of logic or design I could not guess.

This time as he emerged from the mist there was a fuzziness and lack of definition about the edges of his lumbering Sasquatch form. It was as if the edges that defined his fell shape were jumpy, writhing, and vibrating, like bad animation.

He still had two legs and two arms and a lump of head, but he was no longer a creature of carved wood as he had seemed to me, no longer a hideous carved maze through which trapped souls raced helpless. Now his body seemed to be made of jittery string segments all—

"Oh, God!" I cried as the truth became terrifyingly clear. The Master of the Game was made entirely of frantically whipping snakes.

It was as if someone had fashioned a mold of a very, very large man and then compressed into that mold a million serpents. They maintained the shape of a man, but the whole of him pulsed and slithered. A smell of wet copper and decay wafted toward us.

And the sound. The sound it made was hissing, rattling, the rapid sliding of scale over scale, multiplied a million times to become not the slithering of a snake or even many snakes, but that of every snake. If snakes had a god this was the sound he made.

Trent and Pete tried to run. Who wouldn't? But they found they could not move their feet. They yanked at their feet, and reached for pipes and weight stands and scraps of furniture to pull themselves away, desperate.

The effect would have been comical had it been some other place, some other time, facing something less awful than this monster from the mist.

Pete had started to weep. Trent was yelling at him, "Don't lose it, man, don't lose it!"

"Messenger, who are the players?" the Game Master asked with a voice as deep as the center of the earth.

"These are the players. Trent and Pete."

The first time I'd seen the Game Master face two players, he'd chosen one to play for both. I looked at him, wondering—and reeled in shock. The serpents that made him up were chasing tiny, desperate, crying people. Men and women, girls and boys, all so very small, so very small that the serpents' mouths were as big as church doors to them, and the fangs as big as telephone poles. They ran and dived and crawled in terror, each no bigger than a very small cockroach or very large flea.

I focused on a single one of the doomed creatures and saw a woman crawling, hand over hand, across the rapidly sliding back of one snake as another, its mouth wide, its slitted eyes fierce, chased her. The woman lost her balance, rolled onto her back, and was pinioned

between two of the serpents as the third, her preda-
tor, jerked its mouth forward and drove a fang straight
through her chest.

My hand was over my mouth, frozen in the buzzing
lethargy that so often accompanies shock.

Pete fell to his knees and began to pray, some of the
words loud, some mere guttural grunts, all desperate.

"This isn't right, man," Trent said, his voice choking with fear. "This isn't . . . You can't . . ."

"Both will play," the Game Master said. With a flour-
ish of his serpentine hand and a touch of the dramatic
in his voice, he said, "Behold."

Then the ground beneath us erupted upward, pushing the crust of cement aside like it was the caramelized
sugar on a crème brûlée. Up came the soil, vomiting
out of the ground beneath, piling up and up, and lifting
us along with it, rising and rising until it was a hill too
large by far to be contained within the basement, too
large to be contained within the house. But the house
above us had simply ceased to exist in this space that
was now a very long way from being part of a Des Moines
residential neighborhood.

And yet this was only the beginning, for now the

basement that had already grown vast grew boundless. And up through soil came rocks, and after rocks came great massive piers of bedrock, and with each new seismic thrust we were lifted up and up, now perched atop a small surviving circle of concrete balanced on a growing pillar of stone.

But even the bedrock now gave way as glowing, red-hot magma came boiling out, spilling over itself, quickly solidifying into fantastic, jagged shapes. Higher and higher it rose, swallowing the soil, swallowing the rock and the massive piers of bedrock, climbing toward us. It cooled and solidified far faster than was natural—as though anything about this could ever be natural. Soon the pillar was encrusted with fantastic protrusions.

We were far up in the air, though there was no sky to be seen. We could have seen for miles in any direction, yet there was nothing to be seen, nothing at all but the mist that now encircled the tower like a slow-motion tornado.

Finally the tower had grown high enough. My feet rested on a circle of concrete that magically let none of the magma's killing heat touch me, though the air around was like an oven.

We stood there, Messenger, Oriax, me, and the two screaming boys. Any pretense of playing the tough guy was gone from Pete, who wept and begged and bargained. Trent, too, was undone, no longer cursing, just staring in awe at what had been done, and trembling.

"The game is this," said the Master of the Game. "You will climb down this tower of stone. The one who touches the ground first, is free. The other will be judged to have lost."

I saw desperate cunning flash in Pete's eyes. He was smaller and nimbler than Trent. Trent was powerful but not quick.

Pete thought he could win. Trent, for his part, feared that Pete was right.

I looked over the edge. I am no great judge of distance, but the tower was at the very least thirty stories tall, with sides that were a barnacle-like encrustation of wild knobs and points, crevices and overhangs. Climbing down from this height would be hard and nerve-wracking. Particularly for two boys who already shook from fear and disorientation.

"Begin."

They each ran to the edge, and each looked down

as if trying to find an easy path. I doubted there was an easy path, only difficult and deadly ones. But as I'd expected, Pete was the first to sit, roll onto his belly, and stick his legs out in search of a toehold.

Trent was five or six feet to Pete's right as he, too, began his descent.

"This is trickery," Oriax muttered, and stared daggers at Messenger.

"I do not meddle in your domain, Oriax, stay out of mine." I believe that was the harshest I'd ever heard him be toward Oriax. He despised her, that was a given. He was, without a doubt, her enemy, which I supposed made her mine as well. But he rarely spoke to her, and this warning had the impression of real teeth behind it.

Oriax fell silent.

There were rules in this universe, hard to define, but real; rules that limited his role and hers as well. I wondered who enforced those rules and how it was done. I wondered what punishment could be inflicted on creatures who, after all, could move easily through space and time.

No time to consider that in any detail. For now there was only watching the descent of the two boys.

Pete had gotten out to a lead and there was no pretense on the part of either boy that this was anything but a race. I could see Trent's hands gripping an outcropping of the rock. There was already a red smear on his fingertips.

I knelt to feel the volcanic rock and was surprised at how sharp it was. I had of course seen pictures of lava fields in places like Hawaii, but I had never touched the pockmarked dark stone that seemed almost like a fossil of what had been liquid, burning stone. It reminded me of the fireworks snakes children light on the Fourth of July. But instead of ash it was an endless Swiss cheese of knife edges.

And it was down this treacherous surface that the two boys now raced, gasping, crying out in pain as soft flesh met stone, as muscle strained against gravity, as terror and the anticipation of worse to come stole their breath, robbed their hearts of vitality, and weakened their muscles.

I could see ripples of heat rising from the rocks lower down and wondered how they would possibly hold on. I wondered if this game was unwinnable. Did the Master of the Game play fair? Even if he did not, I was not going to call him out on it. I dreaded the day when it would be me, and not Messenger, who dealt with the dread creature.

They were only a quarter of the way down the rock face when it became clear that Pete would win and Trent lose—clear to Trent at least. So now he began to move crab-like across the surface of the tower, drifting sideways to be directly above his nimbler friend.

A rock came loose in Trent's hand and for a heart-stopping moment he swung out from the surface, hand waving wildly and holding a rock half the size of his head. But his strength came into play as he strained the muscles of his right arm to lever his body back to hug the vertical face. He still held the rock that had come loose.

Trent looked down, and saw his friend's head perhaps ten feet below him. He did not simply release the rock in his hand, he threw it.

Was he aiming at Pete's head? I thought so. But he missed his head and instead the rock smashed onto Pete's grasping fingers.

"Ahhh! Hey! Hey!" Pete yelled.

Trent did not even pretend to apologize. Instead he

reached far down with his left leg to find a tenuous foot-hold, then with a left hand grab, a right hand grab, and a scraping of his chest that shredded his T-shirt and left a smear of red, he halved the distance between his feet and Pete's head.

"No fair!" Pete yelled. "He's trying to knock me down!"

Oriax let loose a disgusted laugh. She at least could guess—as I, too, had come to expect—what was coming. She had seen the trickery obscured by the Game Master's bland words.

"Trent, damn it! You're supposed to be my friend!"

Trent stomped straight down on Pete's head. The blow barely connected, but it spurred Pete to action. He now saw the way his erstwhile friend intended to win the race. He saw that Trent meant to kill him if neces-sary.

Down Pete scrambled and down came Trent. Pete's wounded hand was slicked with blood and he missed his grip, wobbled precariously, found his balance, only to take the toe of Trent's boot straight in the side of his head.

In vain Pete cried out.

In vain Oriax seethed.

A second kick. A cry of pain.

"Fall, you ——!" Trent yelled. *"Fall!"*

A last kick, and this one was straight into Pete's temple. The blow stunned him. He reached for a handhold, caught only air, and for an awful moment that stretched on and on, he tottered between life and death.

Then he fell.

It took only a very few seconds for him to fall the forty or fifty feet to the ground, to smack into the crumbled concrete and rock fragments below. He had no time to scream. Just enough time to achieve momentum so that he hit the ground with a surprisingly loud sound.

Pete lay still. His skull was broken open like an egg, like some terrible real-world Humpty Dumpty. Gelatinous pink brain matter pushed up out of the rupture and oozed onto still-hot rock.

Trent hugged the rock wall, took several seconds to catch his breath, and then carefully, no longer needing to rush, finished his descent.

Before he reached the bottom, cursing furiously as his hands blistered from the heat, Messenger, Oriax, and I were there beneath him.

There standing over the gruesome body of his victim.

And the Master of the Game was there as well, still a tableau of writhing serpentine horror.

Trent, panting, pumped his seared, smoking fist in the air. "I won! Yeah! I won! Take that!"

Did he even take note of the fact that he had just committed murder? Did it even cross his mind that the body at his feet was his friend? Did he smell the sickening aroma of human flesh as the very matter that had held his friend's mind cooked?

"The game is finished, the winner decided," the Master of the Game intoned in his bowels-of-hell voice.

"Hell, yes, it's over," Trent snarled.

"The winner is he who first touched the ground." Then the Game Master extended his serpent hand and, with a rattlesnake finger, pointed. At Pete.

"Idiot!" Oriax said. "You stupid, stupid boy. We had uses for you! You could have done great things!"

Trent looked at her and his blank expression seemed to confirm her judgment of stupidity.

"He's all yours," Oriax said, her voice cold now, emptied of all emotion. And she was gone.

Trent seemed bereft. It was all beginning, I thought, to dawn on him. Oriax had been his ally, of sorts. And now she was gone in a wave of disgust and disappointment. He had won nothing. He had been only the *second* to touch the ground.

His friend lay dead and the nightmare freak show that was the Master of the Game was speaking to Messenger. "Have I performed my office?"

"You have," Messenger said. "You may withdraw."

Without a word or gesture the Game Master retreated into mist, which now swallowed the tower. When he was gone, the mist withdrew, and the tower of rock and lava was no more. The ground beneath our feet was smooth once again. We still occupied a space too large by orders of magnitude to be a basement, but the weights and the bench and the forlorn sticks of furniture were all back in place.

And Pete's head, that broken egg, was healing. The fracture was closing. The blood that matted his hair, the sizzling brain matter, obscenely reminiscent of scrambled eggs, was sucked back into his skull. There was an audible snap when the bone rejoined.

Then, slowly, Pete began to climb to his feet, he who

had been indisputably dead. He was slow and stiff, but far more spry than a person should be under the circumstances.

Messenger turned to me.

I knew what he wanted me to do.

10

ARE THERE THINGS YOU CAN DO WITHOUT really knowing how you do them? Can you explain how you can ride a bike? I mean, really understand not that you *can* do it, but how the bike doesn't just fall over?

I can enter the mind of a person condemned to punishment. I just can. I don't know how, I only know that I close my eyes and I focus on that person, and just as the physical world sort of moves aside at times to avoid my touch, so the barriers of Trent's mind moved aside so that he had no sensation of me being in there with him. In there, inside his brain. Inside his memories.

It is a terribly violative thing to do. It makes me sick to do it. I'm certain there are people who would revel in the power, but for me it is a disturbing, nauseating thing and makes me despise myself.

But that doesn't stop me, I can't let it.

So, with a deep breath, I entered Trent's world.

It was a hallucinatory experience of images and flashes and bits of dialog and strange physical sensations. It comes at you like a fire hose of way too much information.

I was not there to learn how Trent had come to blame "foreigners" for his father leaving home. I wasn't there to learn that it was a bitter aunt who first set him on the path of hatred. I wasn't there to see Trent's father's psychological abuse. Or his mother's deliberate blindness to what was happening to her son.

It did not matter that Trent had been a fearful, insecure child, or that he was struggling in school because he had undiagnosed dyslexia, or that his only sense of worth came from having a weaker boy to look up to him.

None of that changed things except insofar as they made me sympathetic. Trent had not gotten to this place alone. I suppose no one ever does. The road to hatred is lined with enablers.

But I was not inside his mind to find out those things, they were simply layers I had to pass through on my way down, down into the subbasement of Trent's fears.

There was a great deal of fear. Fear of his father never coming back, fear that it was somehow Trent's own fault. Fear of dogs, fear of flying, fear . . . and there it was.

In this spaceless space I somehow occupied, it was like a glowing, black mass, a seething melted tar pit of a thing. Fear. The great fear.

The nightmare buried deep in Trent's subconscious mind. The great fear that would shatter him.

Slowly I disentangled, dreading what would follow from revealing this truth to Messenger. Dreading what I would be forced to witness.

I opened my eyes and there he was: the Messenger of Fear.

"What is his fear?" Messenger asked me.

There was no point in evasion. "Trent is most frightened of being helpless. The image in his mind is from his childhood. He saw a man in a wheelchair, a quadriplegic. He—"

"No," Trent whispered. "No. No."

"The man was at a bus stop. It was a freezing cold day and a car came by and splashed a puddle of slush onto the man. Then, two bullies—"

"No, no, no," Trent said, shaking his head vigorously.

"—and they used the hockey sticks they were carrying to poke the man. They kept asking if he felt it. They broke the urine bag the man was wearing under his clothing and—"

"Listen, I, I, whatever you want from me . . . ," Trent pleaded. There was no bluster left. There was only fear.

I had seen this boy beat a helpless man. I knew that this boy's actions had set in motion a series of events that would lead to the death of Aimal. But now he was scared, and his voice shook, and his eyes pleaded, first with Messenger and then with me.

"Hey, I'm sorry about that chink thing. I mean, I really am sorry. I got no problem with chinks. Asian people I mean. But you can't . . . I mean . . . you guys are just messing with me."

I didn't answer. I tried to maintain a cold look. But it's not so easy doing that, not so easy to look at naked fear and remain cold and detached.

"In the name of Isthil and the balance She maintains," Messenger intoned, "I summon the Hooded Wraiths and charge them to carry out the sentence."

Now the basement was just the basement again, tight and airless. It was the smallness and confinement, and the sense of realness I think, that pushed Trent over the edge into incoherent babbling and pleading.

The mist, the cursed mist, filled one end of the room, a gateway for new horrors.

They came then, two wraiths, tall, vague of shape, faceless, but bringing with them a feeling of cold, of the cold of death itself, so that even I shuddered.

The wraiths moved closer and I heard from them a low, insistent whispering sound that contained words, but not words I could parse. Only Messenger could understand them. His face grew gray with sadness as he listened.

He was troubled when he turned to me. "Trent will live a lifetime in that condition," he said.

"What do you mean?" I asked. "It's an illusion, not

reality, he won't actually be made a quadriplegic."

"For him it will be a lifetime. Years and then decades, during which he will live out every aspect of his fear. He will remember his old life, and what we have done, but he will not be able to escape or deny, as year follows year, decade follows decade. Until he dies at last in that time and wakes again to his interrupted life."

The wraiths moved closer then, and both laid invisible, shrouded hands on him.

Trent spoke no more. His eyes rolled up in his head. His mouth hung open. He sank to the floor and sat there, crumpled. His strong arms hung limp.

Messenger frowned, but not because of Trent. He had heard or felt something. I suppose it was this universe's version of a text message. How else did Messenger know when and where to be?

It was a question I should ask him.

Add that to the list of a hundred other questions I had for him.

"I must go," he said to me.

"Where are we—"

"I, not you. I am summoned." He drew a deep breath, not pleased at the nature of his summons.

"Should I stay here with—"

"No," he said curtly. "Go. Trent will be . . ." I think he was about to say, "fine," but stopped himself. Trent would not be fine. But this location in time and space could be returned to when Messenger chose to do so.

I returned to my abode.

It felt strange to be back after so little time, a thought that drew a wondering laugh from me. Had I reached the point where what had just occurred now seemed like a short day?

I read. Not the book of Isthil or any of the other more exalted texts left for my education. Instead I read one of the novels also provided for my amusement.

I wondered idly just who stocked my private library? Was there some sort of Messenger of Library Science who selected after careful screening? Or did some unseen servant scan the bestseller lists and run down to the local bookstore?

It was an amusing thought, and I needed amusing thoughts. I read for a while on the couch and then, finding myself more tired than the mere passage of hours could explain, slipped between cool sheets. Was there a maid who came and cleaned my room and changed the linens? There must have been, for these things were done. Someone provided me with clothing and laundered same after I threw them in a clothes hamper. Someone bought me food. Someone vacuumed. And brought me the book I was reading.

Maybe I should leave a thank-you note. But I suspected I would never meet whoever this person was. Just as I was confident that I would never really know where I was, how this place came to be.

When I had opened the door to the outside, only the brooding, sinister yellow mist had met me. This place might be on the same patch of land where I had first materialized. Or it might be deep within the earth. Or suspended in a cloud.

I wondered if Messenger had the answer to all these questions. I wondered if all would be revealed to me when I at last assumed his position.

I wondered if my mother missed me. Or if she didn't even know I was gone. When I was young I'd read the story of a boy who went off on adventures but had a golem to take his place so that no one ever noticed he was gone.

Was it like that? Was there a simulation of me back

at home, back at school?

I wondered and at some point fell into a troubled sleep full of dreams.

My dreams were visited by burning boys, demons in human shape, a figure with auburn hair who alternately drifted just out of sight or appeared with flesh eaten away like a leper.

I dallied in dreamland imagining the moment when Messenger offered Ariadne a game. I imagined his desperate hope that she would prevail, and his horror when he saw that she would not.

I dreamed of the way he must have felt when he dived into her mind, invading the sanctuary of the person he loved, and found there the one thing she feared most.

My God, how had he done it? How had he done that to the one he loved?

No choice, I thought, yet had not Oriax hinted that we still had free will, at least a little?

But most of all, I dreamed of Trent in his punishment. Those dreams had a peculiar reality to them. I saw him as he was, as a boy, as a mean young sadist with a mind full of hate, but now confined to a wheelchair.

I often remain aware in my dreams, but this was on

a whole different level. I wasn't just lucidly dreaming, I felt I was observing actual events. The scenes lacked the distortion of dreams, they were clear and sequential. The level of detail, too, was most un-dreamlike, for in these visions there was not only sight but sound, and not only the obvious sounds, but the subtler ones as well. I heard the electric whine of his wheelchair. I heard the strained quality of his voice as he learned to speak with diaphragm muscles affected by paralysis.

In a public restroom I heard the closing of the door to the handicapped toilet and the sound of him emptying his ostomy bag. And then the muffled sobs of despair.

I watched as he struggled through physical therapy that did nothing but seem to magnify his hopelessness.

I saw him stare, stare for a very long time, at a place on a freeway overpass where there was a gap between railings just wide enough for him to steer his wheelchair through. Below, traffic screamed by, cars and trucks, massive steel bullets that would certainly crush him to death as he hit the pavement.

He was picturing it. He was doing more than imagining it, he was working it out in detail: This is how I squeeze through the gap. This is how I pivot to the place where a fall will land me on the road rather than just tumbling me down an embankment. This is how it will feel as I fall. This is the sound I will make when I hit the pavement. This, if I still live and remain conscious, is what the onrushing tractor trailer will look and sound like as it bears down, unstoppable, this the view I'll have of the driver's horrified face.

Would he be struck by the massive tires? Or would he be scraped along the pavement by being dragged beneath?

May the goddess Isthil protect me from ever facing such a terrible moment.

I woke to the sound of tapping. Someone was tapping on the closed door of my bedroom. Perhaps it was morning, but I was not rested. I felt like my nerves had all been sandpapered raw. The connection to Trent's punishment—a punishment that to him would last a lifetime—faded only slowly.

I went to the door.

"I made the coffee," Messenger said.

"Trent?" I asked him.

He shook his head.

"Graciella?"

"Soon, not now."

"Then . . ."

"There is a ceremonial matter. I am to attend, and so you must as well."

"I'll be ready in two minutes," I said. So that was what had called Messenger away: a ceremonial matter, whatever that meant.

I don't know what I expected. I certainly did not expect what happened.

Messenger led the way to the exterior door and opened it. But instead of opening onto the despised yellow mist, we stepped out onto a lawn that seemed to go on almost forever in every direction. It was springy underfoot, very like the grass in Brazil, giving a sense of both reality and strangeness.

I had an odd suspicion as soon as I was clear of my door, and glanced back to have confirmed for me the suspicion that my home was not there any longer. Whatever place I had just stepped out of was not visible now and had been replaced by that Brazil-quality grass, a field that rose and fell in gentle undulation. But as if this scenery revealed itself only to those who took the time to look more carefully, features arose into view: a stream crossed by a fantastic bridge; a distant volcano of impossible height, glowing at the top but emitting no smoke. And ahead of us, right where I should certainly have seen it upon arrival, was a structure that immediately reminded me of the Emerald City from *The Wizard of Oz*.

No, it was not green, but it was unworldly, composed of sharp angles that made it seem to be a single giant, multifaceted crystal shimmering in faint hues of blue and green.

"Surrender Dorothy," I said.

"What?" Messenger asked.

"Nothing. Where are we?"

"It would be difficult to explain in geographical terms," Messenger admitted. "We are nowhere specific, rather we are within the imagination of Yusil, goddess of creation and destruction. She is the great builder and destroyer, thus city and the volcano. She has created this reality for the ceremony."

"What is the ceremony?" I asked.

"A trial," he said flatly, "though guilt is already decided and only the sentence remains in doubt."

We walked with the easy gait and blistering speed that is only possible in the time distortion of this Netherworld and soon were at a gate. I felt utterly abashed by the size of the crystalline wall that loomed above us. The gate was forbidding, but in a strangely styled way, with sharp spikes of crystal on all sides. The portal itself was open, and as we walked, the spikes around us seemed to notice our presence and grew a bit larger, as if preparing in the event that we made trouble.

The gateway opened into a tall tunnel that led in turn to a chamber so vast you could have stuffed Giants stadium into it with room to spare. It had the feeling of a medieval cathedral, but was filled with light. Even the tiles beneath our feet glowed softly.

At the far end was a stepped platform that rose and rose until it melded into a series of thrones.

The thrones—I counted seven—were empty, but the space at the foot of each throne was already crowded with people, all but a very few dressed head to toe in black. No one was milling around. No one appeared to be in conversation. A hundred or more people stood in all but total silence.

"A congress of messengers," Messenger said.

This was not a particularly helpful explanation, but I was fascinated by what I saw around me as we joined that assembly. Here was every expression of the human genome—Asians, blacks, whites, and all the hues of each. There were men and women in roughly equal numbers, and ages ranging from quite old to my age. There were no young children, only teens through the elderly.

No one, not even those who by their look would be in their eighties, seemed feeble in the least. These were strong, erect people, who stood with squared shoulders and composed expressions. It seemed that messenger status conferred health and good looks—the only positive benefit I had yet discovered. Part of me wondered if I would be physically transformed when I became a full messenger. Would I have the terrible beauty of so many I saw around me now? And was that physical transformation somehow necessary or was it just the pleasure of the goddess Isthil to make her minions attractive?

Among this black-clad crowd I spotted a sparse sprinkling, who, like myself, were dressed in colors or in white. They could only be my fellow apprentices.

And these, too, were a cross-section of humanity. I was surprised that men and women in old age could be apprentices like me. I saw only two others who were close to my age, one a girl, the other a handsome boy with blunt-cut blond hair. He was perhaps twenty feet away, too far for me to speak to him, too far to overhear if he spoke. His master was also a teenager by appearance, a severe young woman who must have come from the Indian subcontinent, and who still wore the forehead jewelry called a bindi, common to her culture. Like Messenger, she appeared to be at most nineteen or maybe twenty years old. But also like him there was a sense of unapproachability about her.

The boy, the apprentice with the golden mane, turned and looked at me. He stared for a moment, then smiled. It was not a genuine, spontaneous smile, but I appreciated it nevertheless—this was not a gathering of the happy-go-lucky fun lovers of humanity, and anything warm or even polite was like water in a desert: welcome, even if the taste of it was off.

A very tall woman messenger with long gray hair strode to the front, mounted a few steps of the platform, bringing her to where we could all see her. When she spoke it was with the same eerily intimate voice Messenger used, a voice that seemed at once grand and formal, and to be a whisper made directly into my ear.

"We are called to judge one of our own," she said without preamble. No one showed any surprise. "The accused will step forward."

At that the young messenger, the master of the blond boy, moved to the front and mounted the steps to stand just below our grim master of ceremonies.

"This messenger, whose own name is Chandra Munukutla, is accused of attempting to alter the fabric of time."

Messenger sighed softly and the muscle of his jaw twitched.

"The facts of the case are these," the spokeswoman said. "This messenger was sent to address a wrong. She found a victim and rather than confine herself to her sacred office, she shifted time in such a way as to free the victim."

My head swirled sharply to Messenger. "I thought that was impossible," I blurted, though I had the sense to whisper it. The temporarily abandoned apprentice shot me a look. Not angry or even appreciative, just interested. I ignored him and hoped no one else had heard me.

"Silence," Messenger said quietly.

The gray-haired messenger went on. "We are given great powers, but those powers are only to be used to uncover truth, to understand what has occurred, to offer the game and to discover and then impose the punishment that wickedness has earned. We hold those powers in sacred trust from Isthil; they are not ours to use."

Again, there was no surprise, no whispered commentary, no pointing of fingers, just stolid, silent attention from the messengers.

"Speak, if you wish."

The Indian messenger, what was her name? I remembered Chandra only because I know a girl at school by that name. Chandra spoke.

"I acknowledge the facts," Chandra said in true messenger style, minimal yet intimate, with very little emotion discernible. "But in this case the victim was an eleven-year-old girl who would be burned by acid, permanently scarred, disfigured . . ." And now the facade of emotionlessness slipped a little and passion crept into Chandra's voice. "Her face would be a mask of horror, her lips would be so badly burned that she would be unable to eat in the presence of others. All because she had run away from home rather than be married to a man of fifty years. I saw a way to make a very small change in the time line that would save her. She would never be attacked, and thus those responsible would not need to face the game or the doom."

Now I felt tension in the onlookers. Who among these messengers had not faced a similar dilemma? If I could somehow kill the demon that had taken Graciella's father and thus cause his many sins against that girl never to occur, would it not be far better than punishing those who had wronged Graciella later in life?

"These are the temptations that come to all messengers," the spokeswoman said. She wasn't pitiless, she did not argue that it was evil to save the girl, and I am morally certain that each of us, certainly I myself, believed she had done something essentially good.

"These are the temptations," the spokeswoman repeated. "But the law that governs us is clear."

"Who saves a life saves all the world," Chandra said, an edge of desperation now all the more clear and heartbreaking for the restraint with which she said it.

I had heard the saying before. I believed it was from the Bible. But the gray-haired messenger corrected that misimpression. "Thus say many great traditions, Chandra, including the Talmud of the Jews, to which people I was born. But messengers must set aside all other faiths and serve only the balance maintained by the Heptarchy, under the oversight of great Isthil. We serve Isthil and the balance. We are not gods, we are servants. It is not ours to choose when and when not to obey."

I bridled instinctively at that. What system of morality could possibly condemn one who had saved a girl from a lifetime of pain?

I wondered, if it were put to a vote, how many of the men and women, the boys and girls present would deny the essential goodness of what Chandra had done.

I glanced at Messenger and read nothing but sorrow and grim determination on his face. My heart sank. I realized then that we were not a jury, but mere witnesses.

The gray-haired messenger waited as though she expected someone to speak. But no one spoke. The facts

11

"I ASK FOR THE JUDGMENT OF ISTHIL."

At that a beam of light so bright and terrible that it seemed to shine through each of us, so bright it might have been the eye of a nuclear explosion, shone from above, directed at one of the seven thrones.

When the light faded just enough that I could reopen my eyes, there sat upon that throne what looked superficially like a woman, but a woman who must have stood fifty feet tall. Yet how can a measurement we use to determine such mundane things as size and distance possibly describe this creature?

I can say only this: that I fell to my knees.

I am not a very religious person, and I don't think of myself as someone easily cowed or easily awed. But in Isthil's presence it was as if no other stance was possible. I fell to my knees not in fear, but because no human being could do otherwise. My insides shook. My hands and legs trembled. I felt bathed in electricity, in an energy so powerful, so incomprehensibly great, that no one, not the greatest men and women in the world, not the greatest men and women in all of human history could have done anything but kneel and be utterly transfixed.

"Isthil!" The word came from my mouth with a voice that was mine, yes, but transformed into a sound I did not know I possessed.

I was not alone in crying her name in a sort of ecstasy. The name Isthil came from every mouth, and I saw Messenger on his knees, no longer even aware that I was present, bathed in that light, absorbing that light as if he was a starving man being offered a banquet.

"Isthil!" we cried in ragged voices.

"Isthil!"

Isthil stood before her throne. In her hand was a

sword that might have felled skyscrapers or cleaved giant aircraft carriers with a single blow.

Then Isthil shrank, reducing her intimidating size to that of an ordinary woman, though no one not deaf, dumb, blind, and senseless could ever have mistaken her for anything but a goddess. It was in this reduced but still awe-inspiring form that she spoke.

"I come among you to judge a servant who has erred," Isthil said. "The penalties are these: a doubling of time owed as my messenger, isolation, or obliteration."

"Obliteration. Does she mean death?" I asked.

Messenger did not answer, but I earned a sharp, worried look from the accused woman's apprentice. He had edged closer, as though he perhaps sensed my sympathy for his master's plight.

"I will not impose obliteration," Isthil said. "There was no evil intent in this messenger's heart. Thus I choose as an act of my will to withdraw the shadow of death. But my will alone may not decide all things. Chance must have its say."

I nodded, understanding at least some of this from what Messenger had taught me as well as from my brief reading in the book of Isthil. The Heptarchy was charged with keeping balance in all things, but in all things chance—luck—must have a part. This is why we summon the Master of the Game to offer a sinner an opportunity to win and thus escape. Chance plays a role in all such contests, as it does in all our lives.

But of course Isthil had her own ways of submitting to chance. "I call upon my brother, Ash, god of peace and war."

A definite murmur swept through the taciturn messengers. My Messenger's eyes went wide. He had told me that Ash had turned against mankind, that he was an enemy to humanity, allied with Malech, the god of pleasure and denial, whose servants included Oriax.

Ash did not appear in a burst of nuclear light as Isthil had done. We all strained to see him arrive on his throne, but instead we felt rather than saw a presence behind us, and turning, I saw him.

If he was related in any way to the magisterial figure of light and stern beauty that was Isthil, that relation was very, very attenuated. Ash, god of peace and war, was large but not superhumanly so. Rather he looked quite ordinary. He was dressed like a man who might be headed out to play a round of golf or perhaps take the boat out on the lake.

Except for his face.

His face had something canine about it, a subtle pushing forward of the nose and jaw so that they evoked a muzzle. His teeth were prominent, bared in a mouth that drew back in an expression that reminded me strongly of a stray dog I'd tried to adopt once. The dog had to go, sadly, because his earlier experiences in life had left him with what animal behaviorists call "fear aggression." The dog—and this god—were hyperalert, nervous, twitchy, afraid, and covering that fear with an expression of belligerence.

The dog's belligerence had expressed itself with angry yips, snapping of teeth, and a low growl. I heard something very like that low growl coming from Ash. It was like a low note played on a stand-up bass, with the bow drawn slowly over tight strings.

His eyes were wild, darting here and there, seeking avidly for threat in each face he saw. His bare arms were strong and muscular, his movements quick. My father used to talk about fellow soldiers he'd known who walked around with a "chip on their shoulder," actively seeking trouble.

The blond apprentice must have made a face or a move that caught Ash's attention because in a blur of Flash-like speed, Ash had him on the ground with a glittering bayonet in his hand, the tip pressed against the apprentice's throat.

"Did you have something to say?" Ash demanded in a feral snarl.

"No. No, sir."

"Another pound of pressure and the tip of my blade punctures your carotid artery. There will follow a spurt of blood, a pulsing geyser of it that will weaken quickly as your blood pressure drops." Ash leaned down close and now his face was very definitely, unquestionably, a canine muzzle, teeth bared. "Do you worship me?"

"If you want me to," the apprentice managed to say between chattering teeth.

"Good." Ash slapped the boy's face not gently but not like he was looking to inflict damage, and said, "Good boy." Ash hopped back, the blade simply disappeared, and he was once again a suburban dad with a very fit and large body and scary eyes. "What is it you want, Isthil?"

"Random chance," Isthil answered, apparently not at all surprised by Ash's behavior.

"Life and death, I hope."

"Suffering of one type and suffering of another type," Isthil said, sounding disapproving.

"Mmmm. Yes. I see." Ash considered for a moment and we all waited. I think he enjoyed the suspense and the attention. "There is a symbol, half black, half white." And suddenly there was a yin-yang symbol floating in the air off to one side.

And then, just as suddenly, Ash held a tall wooden bow. The bow must have been eight feet from tip to tip, with the thickest part as big around as a wine bottle. His free hand moved and an arrow was in it; he whipped the arrow against the bow and notched it.

The yin-yang symbol began to spin, faster and faster until it was just a gray blur.

Isthil saw what he intended, arched a weary eyebrow, and said, "If the arrow strikes black, the term of indenture is doubled. If it strikes white, then the messenger who has erred will suffer isolation."

"Shall I loose a test arrow first?" Ash asked,

grinning beneath fearful eyes. "Shall I see how many of these creatures of yours I can impale with a single arrow?"

"That wouldn't be the randomness I require," Isthil said patiently. "The duty for which I requested your presence."

"No, I suppose not. But it would be fun." Lightning quick, he drew the string back to his cheek, sighted on the spinning target, ostentatiously closed his eyes, and . . .

Twannnng!

The arrow flew. It hit the target with a satisfying *thwack!* And the target's spinning slowed, slowed, until we could see that the point was almost dead center.

Almost. But clearly in the white.

"This is nuts," I muttered under my breath.

Messenger glared at me in alarm. There was no way Ash could have heard and yet . . .

In the blink of an eye he was before me. He seemed much larger up close. His breath stank of rancid meat. The low growl that came from him at all times was now loud in my ears.

To my surprise he did not stab me with the bayonet

or shoot me with the bow. He laughed and his eyes grew small, yet though smaller, I saw things there: slaughters, men and women disemboweled, children dashed against rocks. Blood and bone and spilled intestines.

"Yes," Ash said to me. "It's madness. All madness. Didn't you already guess that? Don't you know that you serve the cause of insanity?"

I didn't try to answer. I did try to swallow and tasted ashes.

"The balance," Ash sneered. "There's only one thing threatening the balance between existence and . . . non. You." He poked a finger hard against my breastbone. "You and your species. Remove man, and the balance is effortlessly maintained. What do you have to say to that, child of a warrior who died while killing?"

"My father was a soldier," I said. It came out as a squeak, a pitiful noise.

"Oh, you're all soldiers," he said with a sneer. "You will all kill, given the right motivation."

I closed my eyes, unable to look any longer into his, fearing what I might see there. When I forced myself to look again, he was gone.

Isthil remained undisturbed, waiting until the

sideshow was done. Then she stood, raised her sword in the air, and said, "This doom I impose: the messenger will endure one month of isolation. Her apprentice will take refuge with another messenger, so that his learning will not be interrupted."

She looked out over the faces turned up to her and pointed the sword directly at Messenger. My Messenger.

"You," she said, and with a lesser blast of light, she, too, was gone.

One by one the messengers began to disappear.

Chandra, the messenger who was to be isolated, said a few words to her apprentice. As she spoke, she looked at Messenger once or twice, and her apprentice just managed to stop himself from turning around to stare. Then two wraiths drifted up to stand beside her. She nodded acceptance and without a backward glance, walked away, becoming more and more transparent until she was gone entirely.

"A month in isolation doesn't sound so bad," I said.

"It will be a month in total darkness," Messenger said grimly. "A month without sensory input. Nothing but your memories and your imagination. Everyone who endures it goes mad within days. The question will be whether she has the strength to come back from madness."

Given the severity of the punishments we inflict on evildoers I shouldn't have been shocked, but I was. Isthil had just inflicted madness on Chandra? For an act of kindness?

I looked thoughtfully at the empty thrones. And I thought again of Oriax. Was she right that these gods were cruel?

I had very little doubt that Oriax's own master was crueler still, but did that justify what I was doing for Messenger and for Isthil?

I felt as if I'd been convinced to attend a cult meeting and had, without conscious decision, swallowed their doctrine. Fear and guilt had made me susceptible.

You have to think about this, I told myself.

But this was not the time, because now the blond apprentice was nerving himself up to join us. He was apprehensive, and how could he not be? But had his former master said something to him that warned him specifically to be wary of Messenger?

As he drew close he nodded cautiously to Messenger,

who did not respond. "My name is Haarm DeJaager."

He had a sort of German-sounding accent, but very slight, and his English was flawless.

"Harm?" I echoed.

"With two *a*'s." He made a tight grin. "It's short for Herman. I prefer Haarm. It's common in Holland."

A Dutch boy, then. I would have liked to ask him a hundred questions, and I wondered if he felt the same. He must be as lonely as I was, as far from friends and family. But even as I contemplated the unlikely possibility of sitting down at a Starbucks with Haarm, I felt the twinge of wariness. He, like me, like all messengers, had come to this by virtue of some terrible act. Haarm could be anything . . . a thief, a liar, a killer.

Maybe it was hypocritical to think that way, but I leaped to the assumption that whatever his sin, it must be worse than mine. Another part of my mind, the pitiless part, the honest part, said, *Worse than driving a girl to suicide?*

Still, something about Haarm felt worrisome. And yet I'd have given anything to find that imagined Starbucks and hear his story.

I didn't shake his hand. I suspected that even we

apprentices, if touched, might force upon the other person the painful memories we already carried. I would not inflict mine on him, and had no desire for the reverse.

Messenger wasn't revealing much of his feelings—if he had feelings about this—but I could sense that he was not happy about acquiring a new apprentice.

"For now simply return to your abode," Messenger said to Haarm. "My apprentice—my only apprentice, you must understand, for you remain apprenticed to your own master—and I will continue on existing issues." Messenger was feeling his way through the words, obviously figuring it out as he went along. I could imagine that this kind of situation had never come up before, or at least not that Messenger had been involved in. "Yes, for now, that's what we will do. You, Haarm, return to your abode. I will . . . at some point . . . just go, for now, and wait. I will need to seek advice."

Haarm nodded submissively, but as he did he took the opportunity to let his eyes take me in fully. He shocked both Messenger and me with what he said next.

"Master," he said to Messenger. "Have I permission

to visit your apprentice so that she may teach me what she has learned?"

Well, there we go, I thought: that's what it takes to startle Messenger. He stared. He blinked. His mouth actually hung open. Of course all of that lasted half a second, but I saw it.

"I . . . I suppose yes," Messenger said, now clearly disconcerted. "If Mara wishes."

Is it silly that I enjoyed hearing him say my name? He rarely did. Is it even sillier that I detected just the faintest whiff of jealousy from Messenger, or if not true jealousy at least a vague sense of concern that other boys would spend time with me? Probably, silly, yes. But my heart didn't care if it was silly, it skipped a beat, maybe two.

Then, before I could respond, Haarm was gone.

We were alone, Messenger and I. The landscape around us was changing. The glowing tile had turned leaden. The thrones now looked more like ancient stone carvings. The whole scene had a feeling of neglect and antiquity. And at the edges of my vision I saw the yellow mist begin to roll toward us from all directions.

Messenger's lips were pressed tight and his jaw

clenched. He was not happy with any of this. None of it.

"Graciella," he said, reaching a conclusion.

And with that we were gone from Yusil's imaginary city and standing in a much less exotic one.

12

THE MARQUEE READ, *NICOLET!* AND BENEATH IT, in slightly smaller letters, the names of two bands that would open for her. From the outside the theater was grand enough—red brick decorated with white limestone and featuring three ornate wrought-iron balconies above the marquee.

It sat on Congress Street, Austin's main drag, a street of less than a dozen blocks extending from the river-bank to the south and up to the domed capitol building at the north end. Congress Street is not the center of Austin's thriving music culture, but on nights when the

Paramount has live shows, it is the center of town.

We found Graciella across the street in a pizza restaurant. She was eating a slice of cheese pizza in the doorway and looking at the marquee through the bustle of people, young and old alike, who thronged, waiting to go in.

Where were we, *when* were we? The cars looked new enough, the clothing people wore seemed contemporary. Certainly this could not have been more than two years ago, perhaps less.

Graciella was dressed for the evening, short skirt, high heels, but not yet in the ostentatiously slutty way she would later adopt in pursuit of tricks. She did not look like a young prostitute, just like a girl dressing up.

She had her guitar slung over her back.

I glanced again at the marquee, in case I had missed her name. But no, it was just Nicolet and the opening bands. No Graciella.

Graciella stepped inside the restaurant and contemplated the bottles of water. She pulled out a change purse and counted five dollars and eighteen cents. Bottles of water were two dollars and fifty cents. It would mean half of what she had.

In the end she asked the counterman if she could have a glass of water and reluctantly he handed her a paper cup, half-filled, which she drank down greedily.

"Well," Graciella said to herself, "I'm broke with a guitar in Austin. Wouldn't be the first musician."

Back out on the street she dithered for a while, starting to cross the street, stopping herself, biting her lips.

Finally she nerved herself up to cross the street, threading her way through the slow traffic, keeping an elbow cocked back to stop her guitar from slipping off her shoulder. She passed the front of the Paramount and went down the alley to the stage door. It was conveniently painted red with the words *Stage Door* right on it. A dozen or more people, many of them younger, clustered around the door, surveyed by a large man with a Bluetooth earpiece and a clipboard.

Graciella walked straight to the stage door as if she had business to conduct and a right to be there. Given her earlier indecision her nerve now impressed me.

It did not impress Mr. Clipboard.

"Hold up there, miss. You can't go in there."

"But I'm Graciella. Nicolet knows me. I'm her songwriter."

This was a sufficiently bold claim to get Mr. Clipboard's attention. He considered the possibility that Graciella might be telling the truth. He searched for her name on the clipboard. "Any other name you might go by?"

Graciella shook her head. "I don't think so."

"Then you can't go in."

"Okay, look, can you ask Nicolet? Can you tell her I'm here? I swear, she knows me. I wrote, like, three of her hits. She knows me."

Mr. Clipboard sighed, looked skeptical, but tapped his earpiece to make a call. "I have a person here name of Graciella, says she knows Nicolet."

Graciella waited, nervous, and then Mr. Clipboard pursed his lips and said, "Yes, sir, she's right here." Then to Graciella he said, "Her manager, Mr. Joshua, is coming out."

"Good, I know him! I know Mr. Joshua and he knows me."

In a few minutes the manager appeared. He did not look happy. He brushed past the doorman, rudely shouldered some of the fans aside, grabbed Graciella's arm, and pulled her down the alley to a quieter spot.

Messenger and I followed.

"What the hell are you doing here?" Mr. Joshua demanded.

"I'm here to see Nicolet," Graciella said.

"She's got a show to do. She doesn't want to see you."

"But I wrote 'Jesus Tweets' and 'Hard By,' and they're on the charts," Graciella said.

"You wrote nothing, kid. Look at your contract. Nicolet is listed as songwriter. She owns all the rights. And you signed an NDA."

"I . . . what's an NDA?"

"The document you signed that says you can't go around making wild claims about supposedly writing those songs. That's what it is. NDA. Nondisclosure Agreement."

"But I did write them! You know I wrote them!"

"Kid, get lost. Do yourself a favor and just get lost."

Graciella stared at him. "This isn't right, Mr. Joshua, this isn't right."

He shrugged. "I don't care. It's legal. And if you make a stink I'll sue you for violating the NDA. I'll have private detectives all over you, finding out every last detail, trashing you, making you look like just another pathetic obsessed fan with delusions."

For a moment Graciella just looked blank.

Mr. Joshua smirked. "It's the music business, kid. Nothing personal, but Nicolet wants cred as a song-writer, she's going to be huge, so you are out of luck."

"I have other songs, what if I start singing them? People will see what I can do, and then they'll believe me!"

"Any and all songs you ever write—ever—belong to Nicolet. You sing, we sue. Unless I decide not to wait around for the law to take its course." With that he moved closer to her, definitely invading her space, making himself seem large and threatening.

"Are you trying to scare me?"

"You ought to be scared. You don't know who you're messing with. Nicolet is a gold mine and I am in for ten percent. You get that? Having you dragged into a dark alley and beaten up, that's pocket change. I can find six guys in six minutes who'd do it for twenty bucks each."

"I . . . Are . . ." She was rendered practically speech-less. Then she rallied. "I don't care. Go ahead and have me beat up, I'll tweet it out, pictures of my bruises or whatever, go ahead!"

At that Mr. Joshua slapped her hard across the face. Hard enough that Graciella's head snapped to the side. Then he grabbed her by both shoulders and pushed his face within an inch of hers. "Those six guys I'm talking about? They can do more than rough you up. You know what I'm saying?"

For a minute he looked as if he might strike her again. There was a violence to his expression, a ruthless determination. And he wanted to hurt her, that much was plain, he had enjoyed slapping her, had enjoyed her fear. He was breathing hard.

Graciella stood stunned, speechless now, hand to her slapped face, tears filling her eyes.

"Get the hell out of town, and if I ever see you again, or hear your name, you'll regret it. You hear me?"

When she didn't answer he pushed her, hard. "I asked if you heard me."

Graciella nodded.

Mr. Joshua made a sneering sound, turned on his heel, and walked away.

Graciella sat with her back against the bricks and cried. After a while she pulled out her little purse again and counted the few dollars and coins. A choked sob, a wiping of tears, a stiff climb to her feet, a fearful yet still somehow hopeful glance at the stage door, and she walked off into the night.

"So this is what set her on the path that led to her shooting heroin in an abandoned convenience store in Nashville," I said.

"In part," Messenger said. "There's more."

"But we're going after Mr. Joshua, right?" I admit it, I was caught up in a rage toward the manager. I would have happily summoned the Master of the Game to deal with him right there and then, and had no pity for the results. Graciella had endured horrifying mistreatment at the hands of the incubus posing as her father, treatment that I think would have destroyed me for all time. And now this.

"You no longer despise her," Messenger observed.

I shook my head. "No. I was wrong to judge her."

Messenger nodded. He looked at me appraisingly, and I think it was an approving look. "You do learn," he said.

Okay.

Okay, I know it's ridiculous to be so pleased with a simple, grudging compliment, but the truth is my heart swelled, and it was all I could do to keep from yelling, *Yes!*

Something positive, *finally*, from Messenger. I've gotten A pluses on term papers that did not give me one tenth of the pleasure of that simple, uninflected, "You do learn."

"Thank you, master," I said with all the humility I could manage which, right at that moment, was not a lot.

I do learn. Yes, I do.

Hell yes.

I would have hugged him, but that would have ended badly.

"I am leaving you to learn more about Graciella," Messenger said.

That shocked the smug self-satisfaction right out of me. "What?"

"I have another . . . something else to do. It is a simple matter: learn more of Graciella's fate. Then return to your abode."

"But . . ."

"Yes?"

"But I don't know where to . . . when to . . ."

He nodded. "True, you do not have the sight from above, but you can follow her now. And you know how to speed ahead to reach the inflection points."

"But . . ."

That second "but" was said to the air. He was gone. As was my brief period of self-confidence.

I looked in the direction Graciella had gone, and hurried after her. Before I knew it I had caught up to her. She wasn't walking very fast, and I . . . well, I could move as fast as I liked.

She wandered the streets of Austin for a while. Occasionally she cried. Twice men tried to hit on her, but she told them to go away and when one man persisted she walked into a bright convenience store and waited until he was gone.

But she had obviously not created a Plan B. It had taken all her money and resources to get her to Austin to try and connect with Nicolet. Now she was lost.

It was after midnight when the skies opened up and poured down on her. It wasn't rain, it was a deluge, water coming down in buckets not drops.

She had by this point wandered far from downtown and found herself on a road that crossed the freeway,

I-35. She climbed over a guardrail and tried to make her way down to the freeway, but the slope was steep and the ground already wet, so she fell and slid, arriving at the bottom muddy and soaked.

She stood shivering beneath the freeway overpass, hugging her shoulders, as cars and trucks roared past, their headlights blinding, throwing up sheets of water.

She climbed up the concrete slope to the space just beneath the freeway. There was a flat area, a concrete bed where she lay with her face just inches beneath the roadway. Trucks rumbled overhead and screamed by below and the rain poured unabated. But the little crawl space was dry. Hard, loud, and chilly, but dry. She curled into a ball and cried herself to sleep.

I watched this, disheartened, worried for her. Somehow not having Messenger with me made me feel more vulnerable myself and I couldn't easily shield myself from her pain. When Messenger was with me, I had his discipline to rely on. And I suppose in some way I could shift the blame for everything onto him.

But now, I stood alone, in the rain, but dry as the water simply slid past me, and knew that I could, if I chose, speak to Graciella. I could say, look, call the cops on your father—he's not just as bad as you think, he's worse and he'll never stop being a monster. And go find a lawyer to represent you and go after Nicolet and her manager.

It would be useless, of course. Useless. I had already seen where Nicolet would end up. It was like watching a terrible car accident in slow motion. I saw and could do nothing. I could not save her any more than I could save Aimal.

This was my life, I thought, me, standing helpless, watching people's lives be destroyed. I felt wetness on my cheeks and knew it was not the rain.

This was what Messenger meant me to experience. He wanted me to begin to grasp what it would be like when I was the Messenger of Fear and had no one else to lean on. It made me sad for him. He was, after all, not so different from me. He was a boy, a young man, a kid, suddenly thrust into a position of overwhelming responsibility, and such emotional torment that I was sure by the end of his service he would have suffered more than any of those who faced the Master of the Game.

"Well, this is cheerful."

Oriax. She just popped up, standing off to the side, as indifferent as I was to the water coming from just about every direction. Her arrival seemed to turn down the ambient noise, the road sounds and the rushing of water. And the lights of oncoming cars dimmed.

She was dressed for the weather, in her own way. Tall boots, of course, but no peekaboo outfit, no bared midriff or back or legs. Instead she was covered entirely in a black second skin, as if she'd been shrink-wrapped in latex or patent leather. I didn't know what to say to Oriax. The truth is, I was almost glad of her company. She must have sensed this because she moved closer, into a companionable range, arm's reach. She gazed up at Graciella, looking like a street person, which I supposed she was.

After a while I said, "What do you want, Oriax?"

For once she did not fire back with a glib answer, but seemed to consider the question carefully. Then, she said, "I want you, Mara."

It wasn't said in a seductive tone, just a simple declaration. Surely she didn't mean she wanted me in *that* way. But even this toned-down Oriax had the power to make my insides roil.

I forced a laugh. It wasn't very convincing.

"There are two kinds of people," Oriax said.

"Just two?"

"Two for the purposes of our discussion, Mara," she said. "There's the kind of person who thinks life is a grim march from birth through childhood to adulthood to old age and death. A grim march of virtue and self-denial and endless effort to do the right thing, for the right reasons. All to satisfy a god who does not exist, or in the case of our mutual friend, Messenger, a god who exists but whose demands are cruel and absurd."

I waited, absorbing this, confident that she would go on to tell me the second kind of person in her cosmology.

"The second kind of person understands that they get only one life, however long or short. That life has no deeper purpose. No great moral father figure in the sky looks down on us, or if he does look down on us, he cares nothing for our pain."

She turned to face me, and I was drawn to do the same, to stand directly before her, to meet her dark gaze, to watch with fascination as her now-green-tinged lips formed each word.

"The second person knows that life is pain, so we must seek out all the pleasure we can find. The second person knows that the only person who really matters is themselves. We are our first responsibility. Our own pleasure, our own joy, our own desire is all that really matters, and self-denial is . . . foolish."

"You serve Malech. He's only as real as Isthil," I said, not quite sure if I was right.

Oriax laughed softly. "Oh, Malech is real, all right. I hope someday to introduce you to him. Malech, who maintains the balance between pleasure and denial, and understands that there is way too much denial, far too little pleasure, and wants all humans to enjoy life a little more."

I should probably have had some clever comeback, but nothing came to mind just then. I had not felt much pleasure lately. I had seen murder. I had seen hate. I had dived deep within tortured minds to find the perfect suffering to impose on bad people who . . . who maybe didn't deserve all the pain Messenger and, yes, I myself, inflicted.

"Don't you deserve at least a little pleasure, Mara? Or are you proud of the suffering? Is that it? Are you one of those people, that first kind of person, who seems actually to get off on suffering and misery?"

"No," I snapped.

"Then what have you done to balance the denial Messenger has forced on you?"

I thought back on the time since I had joined Messenger. "I had a very nice Pop-Tart," I said at last.

To my amazement Oriax laughed. "I think you deserve more than a warm pastry, don't you?"

"I don't think it matters what I deserve," I said, not meaning to sound bitter, but sounding that way just the same.

"Give me one minute. Sixty seconds," Oriax said.

"Hah!" If I thought that monosyllabic response would discourage her, I was wrong. And to be honest, I was very lonely, and despite what I knew about her, I preferred her company to being alone.

"One minute," Oriax said. "It won't harm you. It will just be a break. A pleasure break. Like a coffee break at work, but with really extraordinary coffee. One minute, and then you'll be right back here, staring glumly at the little doomed girl up there."

I didn't answer immediately. I was thinking. But

the silence stretched on too long for me to pretend that I would automatically reject her. I was considering, and Oriax could see that I was considering.

"No," I said after a while. Just that. I didn't have the will to come up with anything more.

"All right," Oriax allowed. "But the offer remains open. You have only to call my name and I'll be there. And Mara, in that minute I can give you whatever . . . whoever . . . you desire."

I nodded dumbly. The implication was clear. There was no point in pretending that she did not know what and whom I desired.

"Before I take my leave, may I do one thing?" Oriax asked. "May I touch you?"

The request took me by surprise. I didn't know what she meant by "touch" and I'm ashamed to say that my imagination went in provocative directions.

Oriax smirked, as if she could read my thoughts. "No, not that, unless you want it, of course. For I can bring you all forms and types of pleasure, Mara. But for now, I merely want to touch your . . . face."

I licked my lips nervously and almost glanced over my shoulder half expecting to see a disapproving

Messenger there watching.

I said nothing for so long, and stood unmoving for so long, that I suppose my acceptance was obvious. But Oriax either wanted or needed more. "Say yes, Mara."

I nodded jerkily. "A touch. Yes."

She took a half step closer and now I felt again the full Oriax effect. It was as if she were a stove top and had turned the flame all the way down but now twisted the knob so that the blue flame became a flower of fire.

I was trembling before she slowly raised her hand, her perfectly manicured fingers with their green-tinged polish.

She laid her fingertips with exquisite gentleness against my cheek.

I dropped to my knees, bent forward, took a deep shaky breath, arched my back, threw back my hair, and cried, "Oh! Oh!"

Oriax's hand withdrew. She knelt before me, eye level, met my wondering gaze, and said, "Messenger serves the goddess of justice and wickedness. I serve the god of pleasure and denial. Are you really going to spend your days in carrying out grim and thankless duties without a thought for your own needs?"

At that moment I wanted two things. One, that Oriax leave, leave now, immediately.

And the other, that she touch me again.

Oriax's face was so close. It was all I could see. I forced myself to bring up memories of her mocking song as Derek burned alive and screamed in agony. I forced myself to remember that she was evil. But memory was a weak antidote to the physical reality of Oriax, and the still-reverberating pleasure that had swept over and through me at her touch.

I can barely bring myself to admit this, but at that moment, I wanted her to kiss me. And she knew it. Of course she knew it.

"No, Mara. You're not ready for that, yet. My kiss is not lightly bestowed. It cannot be forgotten. It will change you forever. Just ask Messenger about Oriax's kiss."

She gave me a lascivious wink, and was gone, leaving me alone with the fitfully sleeping Graciella.

I should have moved forward in the time line, should have learned more of Graciella. But I lacked the strength to do anything. I wanted to sleep. I wanted to push all of it away, forget everything. But I could not forget poor, shivering Graciella. And neither could I forget what had happened to me at the moment when Oriax touched me.

I did not forget her offer.

I did not forget her lips.

Her eyes.

Even much later, when I had learned and experienced so much more, I never forgot her first touch.

"What did you learn about Graciella?"

I jumped. A wave of guilt sent blood rushing to my face and neck. It was dark, though the rushing car lights were bright again.

Not much, I thought. But I learned a great deal about Oriax. I nodded toward the sleeping Graciella. "She's up there."

He nodded, not surprised. "Anything of significance?"

Did he know? I could either tell him or not. I sensed a turning point. If I lied to him a gap would be opened between us. No doubt this is what Oriax intended.

"Oriax dropped by," I said.

His eyes flickered. All he said was, "Ah." He asked no follow-up question, so I offered no further details.

Hadn't Messenger taught me to be taciturn? Wasn't I therefore justified in telling him only what he asked to know?

"We will be joined soon by the apprentice Haarm," he said. He did not say "my" apprentice.

"Yes," I said, and waited for him to say more.

"It is a very unusual situation," he said.

"Is it?" I resisted the urge to laugh.

"I will fetch him," Messenger said. "Go to your abode, we will assemble there." He didn't seem happy about it.

I had time to go into the bathroom and stare in the mirror at the place on my cheek where Oriax's fingers had touched me. There was no sign to betray me.

Graciella. Trent. Aimal. The incubus. Too much. And memories of Oriax. Way too much.

Messenger reappeared with the blond boy. Haarm said a polite hello to me, and glanced around the living room. "Much the same as my place," he remarked. "A dull and electronically deprived apartment."

"Coffee?" I asked.

"No, thank you."

I made some for myself leaving the two of them to

stare blankly into space in exquisite discomfort. I didn't care if they were uncomfortable. I was still vibrating with the Oriax effect. If I were older this sort of experience might call for a stiff shot of whiskey. I made do with coffee and a spoonful of cream.

I could see them both over the rim of my cup, the gloomy boy in black, the more cheerful yet abashed blond boy. Messenger seemed older, far older, though seen objectively the two were much the same age. But Messenger had an aura of power about him, controlled, disciplined power, but power all the more impressive for being thus controlled.

Haarm, on the other hand, looked like trouble. I've known boys like him, boys with ready smiles and charm, boys who naturally seek out the line between mere mischief and evil. I sensed that Haarm walked very, very close to that line, and of course he must at some point have crossed it or he would not be an apprentice.

"We will visit Trent so that Haarm may see how he fares," Messenger said.

"But he's . . . Isn't he . . . ," I said.

"He endures his punishment," Messenger said.

"What will seem like days to us is a lifetime to him. In a few of our days he will reach the end of his natural life, and then he will emerge from the trance that holds him."

This was said for Haarm's benefit. Haarm said, "I am familiar with the technique. My former master—"

"She remains your master," Messenger interrupted. "A messenger has but one apprentice. An apprentice but one master." It sounded like something he'd memorized. Perhaps it was in one of the books I'd been left to read. I strongly suspect that he had gone to seek advice from Daniel and Daniel had given him this formula to recite.

"I'm ready," I said, putting down my cup.

The instant the cup touched the granite countertop, we were gone from my abode and standing in the aisle of a passenger jet.

"Well, that's unusual," Haarm said.

A flight attendant came toward us, bustling and grim. She passed through us and I followed her with my eyes to see that she was rushing to help another flight attendant with a passenger.

The passenger was yelling something hard to

understand because he spoke with a slurred voice. Beside the unruly passenger was a large woman who alternated between saying, "Trent, you can't make trouble now," and telling the attendants in an urgent voice that, "He needs to go to the bathroom. His bag is full."

"Ma'am, the fasten seat belt sign is on, he will have to wait."

"I can't wait, you dumb bitch!" Trent said through gritted teeth.

Trent was no longer a teenager. He was perhaps twenty-five years old, his hair grown long, his face drawn and sallow.

"Sir, you've been drinking, and I need you to remain in your seat and—"

"I have to—"

"He can't move on his own, anyway," Trent's assistant pointed out. "I need to take him to—"

"Ma'am, I understand, and I'm sorry but—"

"Let me go!" Trent raged.

All he could move was his head, which he jerked this way and that, a frustrated, furious effort.

"The seat belt sign is—"

"I know what the —— seat belt sign says!"

The health care assistant tried again, straining to maintain a reasonable tone of voice. "I don't think you under—"

"Look, the rules are simple and everyone has to . . . Oh, God, what is that?"

Both flight attendants recoiled. One covered her mouth. Expressions of disgust radiated out from Trent.

"He has a colostomy bag," the health care worker snapped. "I've been trying to—"

"The rules—"

"I'm sitting in my own shit!" Trent cried. "I'm . . . I'm . . . I . . ." He lowered his head to his chest and sobbed. "I want to die. Just let me die. Just let me die," Trent roared. "Just someone, someone have pity and kill me!"

"You don't mean that, Trent," the health care worker said soothingly.

Trent unleashed a torrent of verbal abuse on her, on the flight attendants, on the mother who covered her children's ears.

The health care worker reached her limit. "This is your own fault! I tried to change your bag back in the terminal!"

But Trent was beyond listening. He raged and cursed and wept and demanded a drink. He called out every racial epithet he could think of and ranted in a way that must have seemed nonsensical to those around him about a messenger and a chink.

Messenger advanced the time line, causing hours to pass. The flight was a long one. After his racist, sexist, obscene rant, Trent had earned no sympathy. The flight attendants refused to try and help. Nearby passengers moved away, even sitting in the aisles by the rear bathroom rather than be within range of him. Trent's health care aide sat staring stonily ahead, probably counting the minutes until she could quit this job.

"I've seen enough," I said.

But Haarm said, "He's being justly punished according to the rules, right?"

"Yes," I said. "But that doesn't make it fun to watch him suffer."

"You have a soft heart," he said.

Messenger stayed aloof. Then we were no longer on the plane but back in the basement where the real Trent, the body that still contained the tortured mind, lay on the concrete floor as if in a coma. This Trent, the real one, was no older and was not crippled.

Haarm looked down at Trent with an expression I found hard to read. He was interested, but in a distant sort of way. I took the opportunity to look more closely at Haarm. He had extraordinary skin; peaches and cream some might say. His brown eyes were framed below lashes, darker than his hair, as were his eyebrows. He was tall, maybe six feet, maybe a little more, a little more muscular than Messenger.

Comparing the two objectively I realized that both were gorgeous, to use one of my mother's favorite words, equally so, except that some other quality shone through Messenger that elevated him to something beyond.

I wondered whether that extra something that Messenger had was supernatural. There had been no unattractive messengers at Isthil's gathering, but now I sorted through my memories, picking out individual faces and I began to see faces that were quite plain and yet had felt lovely to me.

So, it was supernatural, it could only be. It must be some power that Isthil bestowed on her messengers. Though even with that in mind, and striving to eliminate the effects of that charm, I still saw that Messenger had been a very handsome boy.

Minus the magic, though? Minus the magic I suppose I'd say Haarm and Messenger were equally att—

What was the matter with me that I was standing there obsessing over the relative attractiveness of these two males? Where had this superficiality come from? Was I really that lonely? No, I argued back, I was just a teenaged girl alone with two extraordinarily attractive boys, why wouldn't I have thoughts? Why wouldn't I compare and contrast eyes and shoulders and legs and lips?

Then how to explain Oriax?

I had no answer to that.

"This is Graciella, our other case," Messenger said, and yes, we were instantly with Graciella. She was no longer under the freeway. It was no longer raining. Was it still Austin, Texas?

Hard to say. She was walking down an empty street. It was dark. She was alone. A pickup truck passed by, then I saw brake lights flare as it stopped a block away. Then the white backup lights came on and the truck came back toward her.

I tensed and we were there beside her, the three of us invisible lurkers as Graciella, frightened, shied away and redoubled her pace, heels *click-click-click*ing on the sidewalk.

There were three men in the truck, or at least one man with a very full beard, and what might be his two sons, one in his twenties, one my age.

"This looks like trouble," Haarm said.

Strange to have commentary. I had almost wholly adjusted to Messenger's quiet and reticence.

The man with the beard, the driver of the truck, rolled down his window, leaned out, and in a thick southern accent said, "Miss? I don't mean to frighten you, but this is not the safest part of Memphis."

"I'll be okay," Graciella said, and kept walking.

The truck kept pace. "All due respect, miss, I don't think you will."

It could have been a threat but didn't really sound like one.

"I can take care of myself."

"I'd love to believe that and go on about my business," the driver said. "But I'd love more to get you to someplace where I don't have to spend the rest of the night worrying what happened, and thinking I shoulda done something."

"I'm not going to have sex with you!" Graciella raged suddenly. "I've already had like eight guys ask me. I'm not a hooker. I'm not a prostitute! I'm a musician! I'm a songwriter!"

She had stopped long enough to say that, to scream it really.

The man with the beard was annoyed and rolled up his window and drove off. But he stopped after fifty feet and came back. "Miss, my Bible says . . . well, you tell it, Perry. Matthew twenty-five, verse thirty-four and just keep going till I tell you to stop."

Perry was the youngest of the three and after biting his lip to aid his memory, began to recite. "Then shall the King say unto them on his right hand, Come, ye blessed of my Father, inherit the kingdom prepared for you from the foundation of the world: For I was an hungry, and ye gave me meat: I was thirsty, and ye gave me drink: I was a stranger, and ye took me in: Naked, and ye clothed me: I was sick, and ye visited me: I was in prison, and ye came unto me. Then shall the righteous answer him, saying, Lord, when saw we thee hungry, and fed thee? Or thirsty, and gave thee drink? When saw we thee a stranger, and took thee in? Or naked, and clothed thee? Or when saw we thee sick, or in prison, and came unto thee? And the King shall answer and say unto them, Verily I say unto you, Inasmuch as ye have done it unto one of the least of these my brethren, ye have done it unto me."

"That'll do," the father said proudly. "My boy Perry. He has the gift of memory, almost photographic, if you can believe that."

"Good grief," Haarm muttered. "She can't be such a fool as to be taken in by Bible-thumping rustics."

But Graciella had stopped walking. She was listening. Exhaustion showed in every small movement she made.

"So, here's what I propose to do," the man with the beard said. "I know of a mission that takes in kids and runaways. It's about, oh, maybe three miles from here. They'll feed you, they'll let you take a shower, and they'll give you a clean bed for the night."

"I'm fine," Graciella said, but she was weakening.

"We're about to see a rape," Haarm said. Was he

being calm and detached about it? Or was he too calm and detached?

"Now, miss, you could come sit up here and Josh could go in the back, he likes it there, but I reckon that would get your back up a little. So how about you climb in the back, and I promise I'll drive nice and slow. Sound like a deal?"

Graciella had no more will to resist. She nodded wordlessly, and climbed into the bed of the pickup truck.

They drove away slowly and we followed, three voyeurs expecting the worst. I was clenched against it, gritting my teeth, wondering how much of what was to come had to be observed by me. I had already seen a younger Graciella with her demon father, I did not want to see more.

But to my amazement the pickup truck drove slowly through nearly abandoned streets until it reached a church. There the bearded man helped Graciella down and walked her to a side door.

An elderly black woman with a bird's nest of gray hair and the wiry energy of healthy old age shook the man's hand and guided Graciella inside. The man with the beard slipped the old woman a twenty-dollar bill, the only contents of his wallet.

By the time Graciella had turned in the doorway to thank them, they were tooling away down the street.

"Okay, I admit, I am surprised," Haarm said.

"Christians behaving like Christians," I said.

"Probably decided they'd get caught," Haarm said, and his tone was condescending, as though I were younger than he and foolish to boot.

"It does not do to become cynical," Messenger said.

"How can you not, given what we see?" Haarm shot back. I was shocked at the easy way he had of challenging Messenger. I half expected Messenger to deliver a smack down.

"If there is no good in the world, then there is no hope and we are accomplishing nothing," Messenger said. "If we lose sight of good, we are lost."

Haarm rolled his eyes, but at me, with a conspiratorial wink, as though I would join him in laughing at Messenger.

"This could be . . . *could have been* . . . a turning point," I said, reminding myself that I had seen where Graciella's life led.

"The turning point," Messenger said, and without further warning the world sped by and the sun rose and rested and a fed and washed Graciella snuck from the back door of the mission. Her guitar was slung over her back, and she had a loaf of bread clutched in her hand.

We followed her through the bright streets, hoping, I suppose, at least I was, that some more good would come her way. She came to a place called the New Daisy Theater. It was a plainer, sterner-looking building than the theater in Austin. It looked as if it should have been an armory, except for the green, red, and white marquee.

Of course I knew what name I would find on that marquee.

Nicolet.

"Here we go again," I muttered.

There were alleys beside the theater, but they were closed off with tall steel gates. Beale Street is narrow, just two lanes of traffic, a long line of bars and music venues, including the original Daisy right across the street. During the day it was dead, the only activity coming from early morning delivery trucks dropping off flats of bottled beer and kegs, shrink-wrapped pallets of cans and number ten jugs, all the things that keep a bar or restaurant going.

Just a block away was the FedExForum, a massive sports arena decorated in banners for the Memphis Tigers, the basketball team of the University of Memphis. Here Graciella found short flights of stairs and stunted dividers to lean against. She sat down and began to nibble from the loaf of bread.

She was a pathetic sight there with her guitar and her loaf of bread. Time sped forward. The sun rose high in the sky. People came by in increasing numbers. People glanced at her, but I suppose she was not the first guitar-toting kid to be seen in Memphis. They probably figured she was a hopeful, looking to play some guitar, gather a crowd, maybe collect a few dollars, and catch the eye of some important music executive.

And part of that, she did. As the lunchtime crowd grew she took out her guitar. And she sang. She sang songs I had never heard, and some that I knew she had given to Nicolet.

Someone handed her a dollar and she seemed surprised and grateful. She opened her guitar case and as she sang, dimes and quarters, dollar bills, and even a five-dollar bill appeared.

Even knowing how her story ended, I was caught up in her joy at being able to perform music that people liked enough to acknowledge it with cash and applause. She had touched people. She had moved people. I saw a woman cry, unashamed, tears on her cheeks.

The afternoon wore on and the crowd disappeared. Graciella sat counting her money. It looked like twenty, maybe thirty dollars.

She stood up, bones cracking, and made her way to a coffee shop and bought herself an iced sweet tea and a ham and cheese.

As she was walking back toward the New Daisy down a narrow alley, three men followed her into the alley. Halfway down, they rushed her, grabbed her, one with a hand over her mouth, as a white van came speeding up.

Graciella tried to scream, did scream, but it was cut short and I doubted anyone had heard it.

The van took off and of course we had no difficulty keeping pace. It stopped at a grubby brick building with a faded auto-body repair sign. A steel shutter was rolled up and the van went inside.

We stood on the street, the three of us, staring at the steel door as it came down.

"The manager," I said. "Mr. Joshua. He did this."

Messenger's silence was confirmation.

"Aren't we going in?" Haarm asked.

"I don't want to see," I said through gritted teeth.

"I do," Haarm said. Then, realizing how that sounded, he added, "I mean, that's what we do, isn't it? That's what Messenger—my messenger, my master—taught me, anyway. We are to witness and understand. Right?"

I saw that Messenger was looking to me as though it was my decision. "I don't want to see this," I said, not as firmly as I meant to say it, but meaning it just the same.

"There are worse things," Haarm said, though not flippantly.

"Not many," I snapped.

Messenger decided the issue by rolling us forward in time. Judging by the lengthening of the shadows, hours had passed. Without a word, Messenger passed through the steel door, and we followed.

13

IT WAS DARK INSIDE, DARK IN THAT WAY THAT places that never truly see daylight are dark. Old and musty darkness. Darkness smelling of grease and dust and abandonment.

The three men sat on a stuffing-busted couch and a rickety wooden rocker watching a television, which supplied the only light. They were surrounded by beer bottles and overflowing ashtrays.

We found Graciella lying on bare concrete, beside an old steel tool bench. She had been badly beaten. Her clothing was shredded. But the detail I focused on was her guitar, which lay in splinters.

I closed my eyes.

I stood there refusing to open my eyes again, swaying slightly, feeling as if the ground was moving beneath me.

"She should get out of this place," Haarm said.

"They aren't done with her," I said. I don't know how I knew that. Maybe it was something in the men's voices, the loud way they cheered the game on TV, the aggressive way they slammed their bottles down when their team scored. I don't know. I only knew that they had not finished with her.

"I don't want to see," I said.

"You better toughen up, sweetie," Haarm said.

I did not plan what happened next. I'm not proud of it.

But I'm not ashamed either.

I turned and punched the blond boy in the stomach. It wasn't a very hard punch, I'm not very big, and I've never punched anyone before.

Haarm yelled something in Dutch, then switched back to English, and tried to laugh it off. He shot a look at Messenger as if expecting Messenger to discipline me.

Messenger might almost not have noticed, except that Messenger notices everything. He did not smile, but neither did he frown or show any concern.

I don't think he liked Haarm very much. And just then, neither did I.

"Sorry," I lied.

Time sped forward and now we were outside the shop as Graciella stepped out onto the street, holding her clothing together with her hands, shuffling like a very old woman, makeup a black smear running from her eyes, blood caked in her hair.

I hoped she would go to the police. I was disappointed when she did not. She borrowed a woman's cell phone to call her parents and I listened to only one side of the conversation with her mother. Her useless, blind, clueless mother who had done nothing to save her from the demon that was her father.

"It's me. I need to come home. I really need to come home."

A pause.

"I spent all the money I had. Mom, I need to come home. I really, really need to come home, okay?"

A longer pause. Graciella was weeping, sobbing into the phone.

"No, I don't want to talk to Dad. No, no, Mom, no, I—"

She swallowed hard and squeezed her eyes shut. Her voice was cold now. Emotionless.

"Dad, I need money to come home."

Pause.

"Will I behave myself? I . . . What do you mean? What do you mean by that?"

The woman who had loaned her the phone was looking sympathetic but also impatient. She stood a few feet away, trying to give Graciella privacy, but also obviously worried that this damaged young woman would steal her phone.

"Dad, I . . . I just need enough money to . . ."

This time the pause went on for a long time. Only slowly did I realize that her father had hung up on her.

Graciella let her hand drop to her side. The woman who owned the phone gently took it from Graciella's hand. Then she opened her purse, pulled out a ten dollar bill, and pressed it into Graciella's hand, mumbled something kind, and walked away, using her sleeve to wipe Graciella's tears from her cell phone.

"Yes, there is good in the world," Haarm said, "but it's not enough."

He looked warily at me like I might punch him again. But honestly, he was right, wasn't he? The man with the beard, and the old woman at the mission, and now this woman with the phone and the gift, they were powerless to stop the destruction of this young girl.

Was it partly Graciella's fault? Had she been foolish? Had she made mistakes and taken wrong turns? Yes. But she was just a kid with talent wanting to find a way to express that talent. She wanted to be someone, someone other than the object of her mother's guilt and her father's insidious abuse.

She wanted to be a musician, a songwriter, a performer, not the bruised and bloodied victim of brutal rape carried out on the orders of a greedy man in the employ of a ruthless Nicolet.

I felt sick and sad and helpless watching Graciella walk away. Somehow she looked so much less of a person without her guitar. Just another sad street kid.

I hated the world. I hated what it did to gentle people.

Blessed are the meek? Maybe in ancient Israel, not on the streets of Austin or Memphis or the shooting galleries of Nashville.

"You can't help people who won't help themselves," Haarm said. Maybe if I'd had the energy I would have punched him again. But he wasn't wrong.

"Maybe we can't save her," I said, "but we can hurt for her."

"What?" Haarm seemed to be trying to tone himself down, and tried to make himself sound as if he was concerned for me, but the mockery came through. "Seriously, you have time to feel the pain of everyone you're going to encounter in this job?"

"We are meant to feel their pain," I said. "That's why we wear the marks."

"The marks? What marks?"

I stopped walking, tilted my head to get a better look at him. "Do you really not know?" I glanced at Messenger, who seemed content to attend passively. Of course he was judging me, it's what he did, watching his pupil to see whether I had learned the lessons he taught me. I didn't know if I had or not. I was sure that Haarm either had learned nothing from his master, or learned a very different set of lessons.

I rolled up my sleeve, and when that didn't work, I tugged down the neckline of my shirt to reveal a bra strap and the tattoo.

Haarm stared at it, fascinated. "It . . . I think . . . It almost looks like it's moving! Where did you get that?"

"You really don't know," I said. "He doesn't know," I said to Messenger, seeking some guidance.

"Teach him," Messenger said.

"This is the mark I received for my first case. Derek Grady. He had a deeply buried terror of burning alive. I watched him burn. I smelled him burn."

Seeing disbelief in Haarm's eyes, I did something I probably shouldn't have done. But he looked smug and so sure of himself. So I reached over and in unconscious imitation of Oriax, laid my palm against his cheek. Flesh to flesh contact.

I am not to be touched.

His eyes opened wide, he gasped, sucked in air, batted my hand away, took several stumbling steps back. "What? What? What the hell!"

"You don't know that physical contact between our

sort causes memory transfer? Didn't your master teach you—"

Haarm, for the first time in our brief acquaintance, seemed genuinely horrified. Something had finally penetrated that wall of smugness.

"He is new to his apprenticeship," Messenger said blandly. "He has not yet reached beyond the earliest training." He narrowed his eyes and looked at Haarm as if weighing him up and finding very little of substance there.

But when I saw the shock in Haarm's eyes, I admit to feeling a little guilty. I reminded myself that this is a strange world we now inhabit; the messengers and the apprentices and maybe Haarm was just raising defenses against all the pain that comes with the job.

"Let us witness the final turning point for Graciella," Messenger said.

Once again, I did not know where we were. It was a city. That much I could see around me, but which city, and when? I never did find out. It didn't matter, I suppose. Maybe it was Nashville, where I had first seen Graciella OD. Maybe not.

Loud music throbbed from a row house on a street of row houses. It was not a gentrified neighborhood, rather one of those places with serviceable old buildings that might someday attract the young professionals and the retired couples looking for something with an urban edge. Someday all those folks would arrive and begin remodeling kitchens and painting facades and parking their Priuses and BMWs on the street, but that had not begun yet, not on this block.

Graciella, wearing clothing that marked her as what she had by this time become, approached the door, trying for swagger and achieving only an awkward balance on too-high heels. She knocked on the door, too softly to be heard above the insistent bass. She knocked again, more forcefully this time, then stuck her knuckles in her mouth.

The door flew open. Inside was an obviously drunk and way too happy boy in a T-shirt, shorts, and flip-flops. He looked no older than Graciella, but something about him, maybe just the way he carried himself, the confidence that escaped past the blur of drink, marked him as a boy who came from privilege.

"Hey there, young lady," he said.

"I heard there was a party and, and, and you were looking for . . . girls."

"There is indeed a party, and we are definitely looking for girls," though he used a much cruder word. "And you are a fine specimen."

"A hundred dollars, up front," Graciella said.

It was a phrase she had used before, I heard it in her voice, and it sank my heart in my chest.

"A hundred dollars?" The boy shook his head as if this was news to him. "That's a lot of money. What can you do to earn a hundred whole dollars?"

"I can do whatever you want," she said defiantly.

"That's exactly what I was hoping you'd say," he answered with a wicked leer.

A second male appeared, maybe eighteen, maybe not quite. He reached around the first boy and stuck a lit joint in his mouth. "Another hooker?"

The frat boy took a long drag on the joint, held it, and with smoke seeping out said, "Come on, Tony, we don't say hooker. We say 'professional sex worker.'"

"Uh-huh. Get her in here, because Oliver has some dudes needing some professional sex work."

The first boy drew Graciella after him and shut the door. I had a pretty good idea what I would see happen at this party, and though I dreaded it, I felt I had shown weakness earlier, and now that I was established as the more experienced apprentice, I wanted to show Haarm that I was tough enough to see and do what was necessary.

I led the way through the door.

Inside the lights were low, the walls dirty and scrawled with graffiti. Ancient wallpaper hung in tatters in places, and the paint on the ceiling was bubbled and scarred.

There was a depressing familiarity to the environments in which we saw Graciella now. This room smelled more of mildew and less of grease than the abandoned Memphis garage where Graciella had been raped, but the sense of decay was identical.

Two battered couches, a coffee table with one leg replaced by cinderblocks, a mattress, four men, two other women, if you could call these dead-eyed young girls "women."

There was one difference from the previous scene: on the table was an array of drugs and paraphernalia.

The boy who had answered the door was not the one in charge. Neither was the second boy. The person in charge was younger than both, but his dominance over the room was expressed in the way he occupied an entire couch by himself, arms spread wide over the back, legs up on the coffee table, laptop open, a small pile of cash resting beside him.

"Hey," this boy said. "My name is Oliver. Who are you?"

"Candy," Graciella lied. She did it in an easy, practiced way that made me think we had leaped ahead at least a few weeks in time.

Oliver was handsome and charismatic, with a lush mane of black hair, dark, dreamy eyes, and a body that had spent significant time in a gym, probably with the help of some steroids.

There was relief on Graciella's face. This was better than what she had recently endured, it was clear on her face. Her eyes darted to the money and Oliver saw it and smirked.

"Let's take one thing off the table between us right now, Candy," he said. He shuffled through the money, pulled out two twenties, and handed them to Graciella.

"You can keep that. That's just for walking in here. You can walk right back out with those two twenties. Or . . ."

"Or?"

Oliver shrugged. "Or"—he patted the couch beside him—"you can sit here with me and chill for a while, smoke a little weed, and we see what's what."

Graciella hesitated with the money in her hand. Forty dollars would buy her a meal and maybe a place to spend the night. On the other hand, more of that pile of money might mean finding a steady place, maybe a place she could stay in long enough to find a job. The calculation was all over her face.

She sat down beside Oliver, who nodded and lit a joint that he handed to her without inhaling himself. Graciella took a hit and coughed out a cloud of smoke.

"Would you like a beer?"

Graciella nodded. One of the other boys, now clearly subservient to Oliver, fetched a bottle from a cooler full of mostly melted ice.

"So, tell me your sad story, Candy."

"I don't have much of a story," Graciella said. She sat almost primly, perhaps clinging to a hope that no more would be asked of her.

"Oh, come on, we both know that's not true. A pretty girl like you does not do this unless there's a story. And we both know it involves some bad shit happening to you."

Graciella told Oliver her story. She smoked some more pot, drank a little beer, relaxed enough to put her feet up. The other two girls were now shooting her looks of poisonous jealousy.

Oliver gave every impression of listening intently, nodding at times, making small noises of sympathy at other times.

Finally, he said, "Yeah, there's always a father involved, isn't there? A father, a stepfather, one of those. It's tough, isn't it? My father's no better."

"I'm sorry," Graciella said.

"Well, it happens, doesn't it? Some people get the easy life, some people don't. Those people, the people like you and me, Candy, we have to make our own way in the world. We have to survive. Right? And that means doing what has to be done."

Graciella nodded. She was, by this time, noticeably high.

"Now, here's the part where I tell you what I'm

about," Oliver said. "I am what is commonly known as a pimp. I also occasionally sell a little weed, and even a little smack. You know what that is?"

"Heroin?"

"Heroin. It kind of goes with the whole lifestyle, you know? Some of my girls find it makes it easier doing what they have to do to survive." He smiled, shrugged, all very casual.

"Are you asking me to . . . to work for you?"

"Look at it more like I'd be your agent. Let's face it, what are you getting? Twenty, thirty bucks? I mean, come on, that's no life for a girl who looks like you. I can set you up on dates where you charge three hundred, four hundred bucks. You keep sixty percent. And I'm a straight shooter about that, isn't that right, Buffy?"

One of the girls nodded. "Oliver isn't like some guys. He's more like a manager."

"For example, right now we're waiting on a party that starts in, what, an hour and a half. Older guys, but respectful. And they're rich as hell. They want three girls, and look at me with only two." He waved a hand toward the other girls, a salesman showing his wares. "It's a party on this dude's boat. They'll take it out on the river, drop anchor or whatever it is they do, I'm not exactly an expert on yachting, have a little party, and drop you back at the dock. The whole thing is two grand. I keep eight hundred of that as my commission, and the three of you split the rest. That comes to four hundred each. Tax-free cash."

Graciella looked toward the front door and her fingers rubbed the two twenties she had been given. A sick look of dread came over her, but she pushed it down and forced a desperate smile.

"Good girl," Oliver said. "Tony, get cooking. The girls are going to want to be relaxed."

Graciella stiffened but did not bolt as Tony opened a small packet of white powder into a big soup spoon. He lit a Sterno, the kind of thing caterers use to keep chafing dishes warm. He added a little water to the powder and stirred carefully with his little finger.

Then he placed the spoon over the flame until the liquid began to boil just a little at the edges.

"I don't think I want to—"

"Oh, stop that," Oliver said in a teasing voice. "We're not mainlining, we're just chipping. You can't even get hooked from a little skin pop."

The other girls drew closer now, drawn like moths to a flame. When Graciella looked away Oliver's expression grew hard and contemptuous. The mask had dropped and although what I saw beneath it was nothing as horrifying as the demon's hideous face, it had about it some of that same hunger and greed. And in some ways it was worse for being a young face, a face you'd expect to see smiling from the pages of a high school yearbook.

Tony used an eyedropper to measure the cooling liquid into a syringe.

"Buffy, you have seniority, so you go first," Oliver said. "I run my business like a business," he added as an aside to Graciella. "You work your way up in the ranks. Fair is fair."

Graciella watched in fearful fascination as Buffy took the syringe, bared her arm, and stuck the needle just beneath the skin.

Buffy squeezed the plunger slowly. A small bubble like a skin blister formed, but the expression on the girl's face was not one of pain.

The other girl, Kitty, did the same but added in a

whisper, "More later, right?"

"After you get your work done," Oliver said sternly. "Your turn, Candy. Here, I'll do it for you."

I already knew the end of this story. I knew Oliver was lying. I knew from a shocking glimpse of Kitty's arm, with veins that looked too black beneath her light skin, that she had been using for some time, and almost certainly mainlining. Kitty was a confirmed junkie and could barely pull her eyes away from the scattering of plastic bags on the table.

"Like a vampire at a blood bank," Haarm said. "But maybe, if she just does it this once . . ." He looked at me and saw the answer on my face. "Ah. So. This is the one we want, isn't it?"

Messenger said, "His name is Oliver Benbury."

Oliver now poked the needle into the delicate skin of Graciella's inner arm.

A look of surprise, followed by shock and then utter, profound bliss, transformed Graciella's face.

"See?" the pimp said. "Doesn't that feel great? That high will last until you're all done with your work tonight. And who knows, the old dudes may have other stuff for you. Maybe some coke. Booze for sure."

Graciella smiled and lay back, relaxed and careless, on the couch.

"Bring the van around," Oliver said with a knowing look at the two boys. "You know where they're going."

14

TO MY SURPRISE, MESSENGER MADE NO MOVE TO follow Graciella, nor to advance in her time line. Instead, we waited, watched, unseen, as the boy who had answered the door and the three girls departed, none walking too steadily.

When they were gone so was the pimp's mellow act. He stood up and snapped, "Clean this up, Tony. Like we were never here. Find me another squat. Text me when you have it. I'm going home."

It was Oliver we followed, out of the ramshackle building, and two blocks away to a covered pay parking garage where he slid behind the wheel of a very new Mercedes.

Rather than follow him on his drive, Messenger took us to his destination. I suppose the house should not have shocked me, not after seeing the car. I don't know what the exact definition is of a mansion, but the house was set way off the road, down a long paved driveway. It was two stories, brick and stone, with expensively dressed windows pouring buttery light across a manicured lawn big enough for a game of field hockey.

What did we see when we followed Oliver inside? Nothing in particular. His parents were both at home. His mother was doing some sort of paperwork that involved piles of documents and envelopes spread all over the dining room table. When Oliver came in she smiled, asked him about his day and about the study group where she'd thought he was. She offered him a snack. He declined.

It was all very average, very normal.

Oliver's father was in an easy chair in front of the TV. He had dozed off and woke only when Oliver patted him on the shoulder.

"Hey. Oh. Hey, Oll. Did I fall asleep?"

"Nah, you were snoring while you were awake," Oliver teased.

They had a five minute sports conversation and then Oliver went up to his bedroom, quickly blew through some homework, grabbed a bowl of ice cream from downstairs, brushed his teeth, and fell asleep.

There was no demon. There was no evidence that this was anything but a normal, loving home. Oliver had just recruited an underage girl for his prostitution ring, and in order to ensure his grip on her, he had started her on the road to heroin addiction. There was no obvious explanation for his moral blindness that I could see in this home.

"I want to see more of his past," I said.

I'm not quite sure when I had started to have an opinion about what we should see next. I'd always just followed along with Messenger. But there was something about this case, this girl, Graciella, and the cold-blooded way she'd been destroyed by Nicolet and by Oliver that got under my skin. Maybe it was guilt over my earlier arrogant dismissal of her as a loser. Maybe now that I had seen what she endured, and seen my own callousness exposed, I felt an obligation to her.

Or maybe she reminded me of an earlier guilt, of Samantha Early, the talented young writer that I—yes, I—had cruelly driven to suicide. Maybe I saw too much of myself in Nicolet and Oliver both.

"You are looking for an excuse?" Haarm asked. "For this drug-dealing pimp?" He sounded incredulous.

Messenger answered, "We are the eyes of Isthil. We must understand, so that she understands."

It was the first time he'd said that and I was a little surprised. I had not thought of myself in those terms. It suggested that Isthil, or some arcane mechanism involving Isthil, decided the outcome. But it was the Master of the Game who created the contest, and the mind of the guilty one that supplied the punishment.

We spent some time figuratively leafing through Oliver's life, searching for the precipitating event, the abuse, the parental neglect, the addiction, the brain injury, whatever, whatever excuse might possibly explain Oliver's descent into evil.

But there was no easy explanation. Oliver had had a good life. He had once been a seemingly good kid. Then, for reasons I could not uncover, he had started down the path of arrogance, of contempt for everyone around him, of indifference to right and wrong, blindness to the pain of others.

What had been his excuse for ruining the life of an innocent girl?

What had been mine?

I felt sick inside, disgusted by the Trents and Olivers and Nicolets of the world, hating them for what they did. What people like them did. What people like me did.

"There's nothing," I said at last. "He's just rotten. A rotten human being. He doesn't even need the money."

We went from there to pay an unseen visit to Nicolet.

Nicolet did not have Oliver's money, nor his stable family. Her mother was an alcoholic who was in prison for a drunk-driving accident that killed two people.

Her father was a hard-working baker, up every day at four a.m. to go to a commercial bakery and make bread and rolls. It was repetitive work, but he loved it. Mostly they used big mixers, but Nicolet's father would sometimes pull out a wad of dough and knead it in his hand, just for the pleasure of smelling the yeast, and feeling the elasticity of the living dough under his floured palms and fists.

Growing up, Nicolet was alone a lot, and I felt some

sympathy for her. Her father would come home while she was at school, take a nap but set the alarm to greet her as she got off the afternoon bus. Then he would help her with her homework until she reached eighth grade and he found he was no longer able to keep up. He was not an educated man himself and felt ashamed of it.

He would stay awake long enough to make Nicolet dinner, and on occasion drive her to after-school events. At eleven he would go back to sleep, catch five hours, and start the grind all over again.

It wasn't a great life, but as I watched him with his daughter I felt acutely the loss of my own father.

"A good man," Haarm said.

I found his commentary irritating. It brought home to me the unseemliness of what I was doing, peeping into people's lives, weighing them up, deciding on the basis of a few minutes of their lives whether they were good people or bad, and whether their actions had contributed to the tragedy we were there to understand.

Haarm seemed untroubled by the moral complexities. Of course he was even newer to this life than I, and perhaps his master had been even less communicative than Messenger. But I judged Haarm, as I judged everyone, and found him lacking. I was aware of my own hypocrisy, judging him for being judgmental, but I told myself that I was a better person than he because at least I cared. At least I had not shut myself off from the pain. And at least I recognized my own hypocrisy.

Humans really are geniuses at excusing their own behavior while condemning others—especially those others they don't really know.

Haarm, I decided, was unfeeling and harsh and I resented his presence. He confused me. He unsettled things with Messenger. He was a third wheel, as the old saying goes, one more person than was needed in the tight little world of Messenger and Mara.

I hoped he would return to Chandra soon.

But what if Chandra did emerge from isolation with her mind gone? What then? Messenger had said that there could be only one master for each apprentice, so presumably he would go, eventually.

We followed Nicolet as at age eleven she suddenly began to take her music lessons seriously. She was never more than able on a piano, and the guitar was beyond her, but as she progressed into puberty her voice, which had been shrill and unsteady, deepened and widened and began to be a really extraordinary thing. By the time she was fourteen she was singing with a cover band, sneaking out to late-night jams while her father was sleeping, and rushing home to be in bed when he woke before first light.

"It is almost dull to watch," Haarm said. "But her voice . . ."

I nodded. Yes, her voice. The girl had a gift.

Once a month Nicolet and her father would drive to the prison where her mother was finishing a seven-year sentence. And I saw that for both the father and the daughter, the impending release of the mother was fraught. They both made the right noises about wanting her home, but they had achieved a stability, the two of them. It was a lonely stability, a dishonest one, too, since Nicolet was sneaking out most nights and so sleepy that she often ditched school. But they had found a way to survive, to be happy, and that's rare enough in this world.

Within two months of the mother returning home from prison, she was dead of alcohol poisoning.

We watched the funeral ceremony.

I'd only ever been to one funeral before becoming

Messenger's apprentice, my father's. That had been a military ceremony, with blanks fired by crisply uniformed soldiers, a bugler, and something like a hundred people in attendance, many of them his fellow soldiers. There had been comfort in the formality of it all. I can never forget the ceremonial removal of the American flag that had covered his coffin, the careful folding of it into a neat triangle, the handing of it to my mother who passed it to me.

The ceremony made it more than just the death of one sad girl's father. By that ceremony my father was inducted into the honored ranks of men, and some women as well, who had worn the uniform and died doing what they had been ordered to do. Even though I was young at the time of his death, I knew enough to feel the spiritual presence of long lines of brave soldiers and felt that perhaps, if there was any truth to our fantasies of an afterlife, my dad would have company and plenty of guys to swap stories with until the day when I would join him again.

But this was not that funeral. Four people attended this funeral. The father, the sister-in-law, the clergyman, and Nicolet.

I saw in Nicolet's eyes the moment she shut down the pain and pushed away all feeling, not just for her mother but her father as well. On that day the struggling remains of Nicolet's family had died.

Nicolet had an excuse. Not enough of an excuse, for nothing is ever enough to excuse ruining a person's life as she had ruined Graciella's life. But there was at least some event we could point to and say, "Ah, it started here."

The odd thing was that the coldness that now filled Nicolet did not hamper her talent. If anything she found a new depth, so that when she sang songs of love betrayed, she didn't sound like a girl who knows little of life. There was an honesty to those kinds of lyrics now.

And this was how Mr. Joshua discovered her. He joined his greed and ruthlessness to her unsparing pitilessness, and a grim partnership was formed.

I saw that Messenger was watching me.

I said, "The title of this week's lesson is monsters."

Haarm laughed quizzically. "What's that mean?"

"Demons and pimps, greed and ambition," I said, not really caring if Haarm understood, knowing that Messenger would. "They come with excuses or come with none. Rich and poor, male and female, every race, every religion. Evil is an equal opportunity affliction."

Haarm shrugged uncomfortably. "And we do what we can, yes? We stand up for the victims."

I shook my head. "No. We just protect the balance. We push back against evil so that it will not tip us into nonexistence."

"That's a dark way to put it," Haarm said. "You make it sound as if we're just limiting the damage. Come on, little Mara, we're the good guys, right?"

I know he was just trying to break me out of my funk. Or maybe he was just being a smart-ass because he's a smart-ass by nature. I probably should have said something lighter, something generous to improve the mood. I didn't.

I said, "What deed of yours made you a messenger's apprentice, Haarm?"

Haarm actually took a step back. His pale skin flushed.

"Good guys," I said with more aggression than was kind. "We're monsters, too, the three of us. Monsters being punished by being made to punish monsters."

15

I STOOD ALONE IN THE NEARLY FEATURELESS blandness of my abode. I just stood there. The silence buzzed in my ears. The full weight of my loneliness came down on me hard.

I missed my friends and school. I missed my home and my mother. I missed the weekly pilgrimage to place flowers on my father's grave.

I wanted so desperately to be in my own room. I wanted so desperately to sit at the kitchen table with my mom and gossip over a plate of brownies. It wasn't a feeling, it was a physical craving, a *need*.

On a lesser level I missed the internet and my phone. I hated not knowing what was happening in my own little world, back in San Anselmo.

I wanted to cry but they would have been empty tears of self-pity, and I suppose my subconscious understood that I had no right to feel sorry for myself. I was alive. Samantha Early was not.

I don't know how long I stood there staring at nothing, feeling alone before my eyes came to focus on the book of Isthil.

I picked it up and sat down on the couch. The sound of air escaping the cushions as I sat was loud to me. So was the sound of paper pages being turned.

In my head one of Graciella's songs was playing.

I'm a bit of a mess.
I s'pose that you know.
Does that scare you off, or push you away?
Are you fool enough
To love me despite?
Or love me because of,
My bruises and all.

I had begun by being skeptical of Isthil and the Heptarchy and all of it. But I had seen Isthil myself now, and maybe she wasn't God in the way I'd always thought of God, but she was something, some creature of great power. Her mere presence had weakened my knees so that I had knelt most willingly to her.

Now I needed her to be real, to be something more than a very imposing creature who had earned Messenger's devotion. I needed her to be wise.

I needed her to be *right*.

Into existence came the Seven.
Summoned by the will of existence itself.
Summoned to serve existence.
Summoned to ensure that this time,
Existence should not fail.
Summoned to maintain the balance,
Of the guppy, the feather, and the pebble.
Summoned to extend the length of that blink.

And thus was Isthil born.
She traveled the world and saw,
Traveled the world and listened,

Traveled the world and felt.
And thus spoke Isthil when she had come to understand:

Here is the center of the balance.
Here on this earth existence hangs.
Here the Seven balances must be maintained,
Else all should perish.

So she said to her brothers and sisters:
We are not called to idleness,
We are called to a great work.
We have been called into existence by the Source,
So that this universe shall not perish,
So that life will not cease,
So that beauty and joy may live on.

At some point I had started to read aloud. "So that what is may go on being; so that this time the will of existence shall not be thwarted; so that the eye of consciousness will not be closed again."

I heard the sound of someone clearing their throat politely. I looked up expecting to see Messenger, dreading where he would take me next.

But it was not Messenger. It was Haarm.

"Haarm?"

"Who else?" he asked, smiling and spreading his hands in a gesture of innocence.

"What do you want?"

"You're getting into that, huh?" he asked, nodding at the book.

"I don't seem to have cable or Wi-Fi," I said. "I have these books."

"Yeah, me, too," he said.

"Have you read them?"

He snorted. "Why, so I can understand?" His tone mocked the very idea.

"You don't want to understand?"

He shook his head. "We're trapped. The messengers are our jailers. The books are their way to convince us to accept our fate like it's all part of some great, cosmic plan."

"You have an alternative?" I asked, closing the book.

"You have anything to drink? I'm parched."

Wearily I rose, walked to the kitchen, found a bottle of sparkling water, and brought it to him.

"Shame there's nothing stronger," he said. "If anyone

deserved a glass of, I don't know, something, it's us."

"I'm not feeling deserving," I said shortly.

"I hope I'm not intruding," Haarm said. "I wasn't sure what the protocol was. No phone, not even a front doorbell to ring..." He grinned in what he surely meant to be a winning way and said, "I was half afraid I'd pop in here and you'd be changing clothes or just getting out of the shower. Well, half afraid, half, you know . . . hoping."

I stared at him. I had a feeling I knew where this was going. Sure enough . . .

"You're a very pretty girl," he said.

"You're kidding."

"No, you are. You really are. I've always had a thing for Asian chicks."

"Are you seriously hitting on me?"

"Look, we're together, right, and it's not like either of us has a lot of other options."

I was having a hard time believing he was actually doing what he was clearly doing. Until he got up and came over to sit beside me on the couch. And then turned to face me.

"Are you seriously hitting on me?"

"Don't be so hard on yourself, you're really cute and—"

"Are you insane?"

He drew back.

"What? Seriously? You're going to fix my loneliness, are you? I've had better offers," I snapped.

He laughed again. "From him?"

"From Oriax," I said. "And believe me, whatever this is that you think you've got"—and here I waved a contemptuous hand in the general direction of his body—"however amazing you are in your own mind, believe me, Oriax is all that times a thousand. And I'm not even into girls."

He stood at last. "Who's Oriax?"

"You haven't met her?"

He shrugged. "Maybe I did, I don't always remember people's names."

This time it was my turn to laugh. "Believe me, Haarm, if you'd met Oriax, you'd remember. Now, get out of here. Really. Now."

He shrugged, shook his head as if amused by my resistance, and disappeared. I retrieved Isthil's book and though there was no mark on it, I brushed it reverently with my fingers before placing it carefully back on the table.

After the obnoxious apprentice was gone did I feel the silence and emptiness around me even more keenly? I am embarrassed to admit that I did.

16

NO, I DID NOT TELL MESSENGER WHAT HAD HAP-
pened between Haarm and me. Later, in hindsight, I
would see that this, too, was a mistake.

But when Messenger came to collect me I knew we
had the worst of duties to perform, and it didn't feel like
a time to complain about a "coworker."

"So, it's time?" I asked him.

"Let us collect Haarm, and then we will begin."

He noticed that the book of Isthil was gone from
the coffee table. He didn't ask, but Messenger doesn't
always need to give voice to his questions.

"It's on my bed. I fell asleep reading it."

He nodded slightly and I think he was pleased.

I wanted to tell him that I was beginning to really understand what he had endured in his time as a messenger. I wanted to confess that I dreaded my future having seen something of what was in store. I wanted to tell him that the reading had helped calm my worries, but only a little.

I wanted to tell him that Haarm was . . . what? Immature? What exactly was the word for a boy who came away from what we had witnessed and found it stimulating?

I wanted to tell him that I wasn't sure I was going to make it, that the isolation, the empty times punctuated by horror, were wearing me down to the point where I could see a day when I would welcome even Haarm. Or worse. But there is no therapy for messengers.

Messenger took me and we collected Haarm. Haarm looked tired, as if he hadn't gone to sleep. He was wearing the same clothing, his hair was a mess, his eyes were bleary, and he blinked too much.

Haarm avoided looking at me, and his carefree

way was decidedly more subdued. He seemed nervous. Maybe, I thought, he had had time to think about what had happened, what he had witnessed, and the inappropriate way he had spoken to me. Maybe he was embarrassed. If so, good.

For the sake of honesty, for I have promised myself that I would be truthful in all things, I will admit that Haarm's attentions weren't *completely* disliked by me. It was more a matter of timing than anything else. Had he seemed like a nicer guy, had he been a little less crude and indifferent . . .

But I wasn't Mara the high school girl, I was Mara, apprentice to the Messenger of Fear. I had duties to perform, a penance to do. And yet . . . And yet didn't Messenger allow himself the bittersweet pleasure of pursuing Ariadne?

I don't know why this particular thought had not occurred to me earlier. No, that's not true, I do know why: because Haarm's silly advances had forced me to think. Haarm, looking at me as desirable, had brought home to me that my desirability had a short shelf life. Soon Trent's misery would join Derek's on my body, a permanent reminder. And what would Nicolet and

Oliver endure? What horrors would their suffering etch onto my body and soul?

A year from now it would require an act of deepest and most passionate love, as well as the courage to endure agonies of mind, just to brush a fingertip against my collarbone. A year from now, holding my hand would be the most awful experience of a boy's life.

The full depressing reality of my life came clear to me. My God, to be a messenger meant a life without love, at least without romantic love, physical love.

No wonder Messenger was so desperate to find Ariadne. He had lived this loveless life. He craved relief. He was like a plant slowly dying from lack of water. He was starving before my eyes.

We were a sort of celibate priesthood, we messengers and apprentices. We were like monks and nuns. In medieval times, women who became pregnant outside of marriage, or women who were unruly, difficult, opinionated, or merely inconvenient, were often shut away in nunneries, there to live out lives of quiet despair. That was me now. I was being shut away. And with each new descent into a wicked mind, I was deepening my isolation, obliterating my chance of ever . . . of ever . . .

"Are you unwell?" Messenger asked me.

I shook my head, not ready to speak.

I prayed, not to Isthil, but to *my* God, that Oriax would not appear this day, for I was feeling weak and did not wish to face temptation.

To my surprise, Messenger took us first to Trent, still as we had left him, curled up on his basement floor. His mind was elsewhere, enduring the time punishment, living an entire life as what he feared: a weak and defenseless cripple.

How could I not pity him? He was being forced to live a life without power over himself, without any likelihood of love. How could I not identify with that now?

"I don't want to . . . ," I said. "I know I will be delving into Nicolet and Oliver, isn't that enough?" My tone was ragged. I felt as depressed as I have ever felt. I looked at Haarm's hands, I couldn't help it, I wasn't even really thinking about him except as a boy who could never touch me. They weren't his hands, but every hand.

I am not to be touched.

God in your heaven, can't you save me?

"I will perform the witnessing," Messenger said. He

made no comment, offered no argument. Did he know that I had glimpsed my future?

"Sorry about . . . ," Haarm whispered.

"It's okay," I said.

And of course, being the perverse person I can sometimes be, I felt an almost overpowering desire to reach for and hold his hand. I resisted, and the decision to do so felt as if I were now pounding the nails into my own coffin.

I am not to be touched. Haarm is not to be touched.

Messenger is not to be touched.

But Oriax . . .

Messenger blinked, nodded once briskly, seemed almost amused for a second, then slipped back into his usual taciturnity, and we next appeared amid the bustle and excitement behind a large stage.

Music was playing, very loud, very close. It took me a minute to assemble the pieces into a coherent framework and to realize that we were backstage at a live show. Costumed performers were rushing around, men and women with headsets were speaking terse instructions, crew were moving instruments and painted Styrofoam sets. There were cables snaking across the floor, and bright computer monitors everywhere as well as the glow of iPads carried by people whose jobs I could not guess but who were very busy and moved with the swift efficiency of long practice.

I heard a booming voice yelling into a microphone, "Now, how was that for some banjo picking? Ladies and gentlemen, I believe that was worth another round of applause before we bring out our next act!"

Beyond the edge of a drawn curtain a large audience clapped and whistled, and women's high-pitched voices shouted, "Woo!" and men's voices yelled, "Yeah!" I looked out toward the audience but couldn't see them clearly because the lights shining on the stage, and therefore in my eyes, were too bright.

A three-piece band came off the stage, grinning and sweating, to hear voices crying, "Kicked ass, brother!" and, "That was the stuff, man, you brought it!"

The band walked through us carrying their instruments, and raced to a table set up with food and bottled water and beer.

"And noooooooooow," the announcer cried. "Here she is, the newest country music sensation, she is taking over the charts, folks, a real talent, the real deal,

give a big Grand Ole Opry welcome tooooooooooo . . .
Nicolet!"

Two facts. One: this was the Grand Ole Opry, the
ultimate venue, the greatest stage for country music
anywhere.

And two: Nicolet had been standing in the wings,
just a few feet away without my noticing it.

Nicolet's face split into a huge, toothy smile, and she
strode toward the spotlight.

Messenger stepped in front of her. Nicolet saw him,
tried to brush past, and found her feet were fixed to the
boards.

"What the hell?" she demanded.

But no one was listening. Nor was anyone speaking.
Everything, everywhere in the Opry, had stopped.

Nicolet looked around wildly. "Hey, what's going
on?"

Frozen stagehands. Frozen electricians. Frozen
band members. A silent audience.

Silence everywhere.

Messenger held his hand up, silencing Nicolet as
well, who continued to try to escape, but could not move
from her spot just outside of the spotlights.

To me, Messenger said, "Bring Oliver here."

Now I felt as frozen as everyone else. This was by far the biggest independent responsibility laid on me yet. I blurted, "Me?"

"Yes," Messenger said.

In reality I probably stared blankly for no more than a few seconds, but it felt longer. But what was I going to do, refuse? So, I nodded. "Okay."

I pictured Oliver in my mind, and when I did I saw a place as well. He was at school. He was in class, seated in a circle of desks around a teacher.

I imagined myself there, and then, I was.

He did not immediately notice that everyone and everything around him was still and silent. He was taking notes on an iPad and the soft impact of his fingers on the screen went on for a dozen words before he looked up with a quizzical look on his face. He saw his frozen teacher.

Then he saw me.

"What's going on?" he asked, as if he was arriving late to a practical joke of some kind.

"You are to come with me," I said.

"What are you talking about?" he demanded, not

frightened, just puzzled.

"I'm talking about filling a syringe with heroin and shooting it into a girl's arm," I said.

The smile that had lingered now dropped from his face. "I don't know—"

The last part of that sentence, "—what the hell you're talking about," was spoken to the frozen audience of the Grand Ole Opry.

I am certain Oliver was surprised.

Five people stood at the back of that stage—Oliver and Nicolet, Haarm, Messenger, and me. There were hundreds, maybe thousands of people around us, but they might as well have been statues. They stood or sat, laughed, spoke, or muttered into microphones, all utterly still, as still as the people in a painting. The stage lights were purple, giving the scene an extra layer of surrealism.

Oliver was dressed in jeans and a T-shirt. Nicolet wore spangled boots, a cutaway skirt, and midriff-baring top.

Many unusual people and things had appeared on the fabled stage, but this was no doubt the strangest.

"Who are you people?" Nicolet demanded.

"I'm not with them," Oliver said. "I'm . . ." He failed to come up with a way to introduce himself and fell back on, "This is one weird dream."

"You have done wrong," Messenger said. "You must first acknowledge the wrong, and then you must atone."

"I don't acknowledge anything without a lawyer," Oliver said.

This brought a grin from Haarm. "Just like on American television shows."

Really? He was making wisecracks?

"You have each helped to cause the degradation, victimization, addiction, and infection of Graciella Jayne."

That got Nicolet's full and undivided attention. "I don't know what that little bitch has been telling you, but—"

"Nicolet and Oliver, I offer each of you a game," Messenger began.

"—she's not . . . Wait a minute, what the hell is this about?" Nicolet demanded, her anger growing. "You can't do this to me. Do you know who I am?"

It was not my turn to speak, but I couldn't help it. "Do you know who Graciella Jayne is?"

"I . . ."

"And you would know her as 'Candy,'" I said to Oliver.

"The little whore?" he blurted. "I don't even know where she is! She's not working for me anymore."

Messenger shot me a look that was not approving of my interruption and just stopped me as I was about to say, *She's in the hospital, thanks to you.*

"Nicolet DeMarche and Oliver Benbury, this wrong demands punishment. I offer you a game. If you win, you will go free, unbothered by me or my apprentice."

Nicolet and Oliver exchanged a look, realizing that whatever this dream was, they were both in it together. But what could they do? They were each in their own way powerful and used to getting their way. But their power was nothing to Messenger.

"What game?" Oliver asked.

Give him credit: he recovered quickly.

"I'm not playing any game," Nicolet snapped. "Mr. Joshua! Where are you? Get your ass out here and deal with this!"

Messenger let Nicolet go on for a while longer, demanding and threatening, until she seemed to run out of steam.

"You must choose whether to play the game," Messenger said when her personal storm had blown past.

"I asked what the game is," Oliver said, definitely scared, but wily as well, smart and determined not to be overwhelmed. "I have a right, don't I?"

"Play or do not play," Messenger said. He spoke the words softly, but of course they heard him. "I give you seven seconds to decide. Six. Five."

"Whoa, hold up," Oliver said, and made a move toward Messenger as if he was going to shove him.

Messenger did nothing, just stood there and met Oliver's angry gaze. I had no doubt that Messenger had more than enough power to do as he wished with Oliver, and I think he was tempted. But Messenger's power is so great that even thugs like Oliver can feel it. The power surrounds Messenger like a force field. You feel it, and never more than at the terrible moment when Messenger performs his duty.

Oliver, pimp and drug dealer, raised his hands and tried to take a step back, but was held rooted. Nicolet had tasted enough of the privilege of her new fame to remain unintimidated. The diva in her was not yet done making threats.

"Go screw yourself."

"Decide now," Messenger said.

"I'll play your game," Oliver said.

"Do you work for Graciella? I don't know what lies she's telling, but that's what they are: lies. Is that what's going on? Mr. Joshua! Damn it! Where is my manager?"

"Since you refuse to state your preference, I will judge that you have declined the game," Messenger said.

"Take your game and shove it right up your—"

It makes it a bit easier when they remain belligerent.

Messenger nodded to me.

I steeled myself for what was to come. Despite her fame and talent, Nicolet was not so very different from me. She could have been a girl at my school. Was her sin so different from my own? Had she even known what Mr. Joshua was doing to Graciella? A horrible person, yes. But perhaps not quite *that* horrible.

I stood behind Nicolet and placed my left hand over her heart, and pressed my right palm against her head. This was ritual and I knew the words I must speak. "By the Source. By the rights granted to the Heptarchy. By Isthil and the balance She maintains. I claim passage to your soul."

My first entry into her mind and memory put that thought to rest. I saw the conversation between Nicolet and Mr. Joshua. It had taken place in a hotel room.

Mr. Joshua: Gonna have to lean on her, that's the thing.

Nicolet: Can't we do something legally? You know, sue her or whatever?

Mr. Joshua: Look, Nicky, the thing is, I checked and she is a minor. We take her to court that contract gets thrown out. So it can't be legal, what we do.

Nicolet: I don't want any of this coming back to me.

Mr. Joshua: Obviously. I mean, I am here to protect you. After all—

Nicolet: After all, you make your money from me.

Mr. Joshua: Exactly. So this'll be the last time we talk about this. But if Graciella won't shut her trap, I'll have to teach her a lesson. And it has to be a harsh one.

Nicolet: Has to be. She's the one to blame.

Mr. Joshua: I'll take care of her.

Nicolet: Her own damn fault.

This conversation was right at the top of Nicolet's consciousness, being actively recalled. The confrontation with Messenger, and no doubt my own accusatory words, had brought it bubbling up out of her memory.

But proving her guilt was not the duty I was there to perform. I was not searching for guilt, I was searching for fear.

It is like what I suppose a hallucination must be. Images rose to me, floated by, twirled away, as if I were swimming underwater and these memories were bubbles drifting up from some scuba diver below me. Some passed quickly, too quickly to really see. Others lingered long enough for me to see patterns and events, to feel secondhand emotion, to appreciate scenes of beauty or moments of hilarity.

Bad people do not have only bad memories. There were many interesting, joyful, exciting memories floating by. But fears are different. If normal memories are shimmering bubbles, fears are like those deepest of sea creatures that come in fantastic, otherworldly shapes and must create their own sullen and sickly light.

It was these that I followed down, chasing them as they tried to evade me. I caught them each in turn: the fear of failure, the fear of amputated limbs, the fear of losing her voice. But one terror slipped my grasp again and again until, at last, I had it.

It was prosaic, really, nothing terribly original. But as I rose back through the layers of Nicolet's mind, I saw memories that confirmed that this fear had a powerful hold on Nicolet.

I blinked and was out. Messenger waited patiently. Nicolet cursed a blue streak and Oliver was clearly looking for an exit, any exit, hoping that we were too distracted to notice him.

Haarm was watching me intently, curious I guess. And, as earlier, I could not help feeling that something about him was more off than previously. I did not know Haarm well, but he had from the start exuded a cocky self-confidence. Now he seemed wary. Was this just a result of me refusing his advances? Or had Messenger or perhaps even Daniel had a little talk with him?

"What is Nicolet's doom?" Messenger asked.

"Her greatest fear is pretty common," I reported. "Nicolet is terrified of flying."

Nicolet confirmed this by blanching. Her abuse and endless shouts for Mr. Joshua stopped as suddenly as if I had thrown a switch.

"So, what are you going to do, force me onto a plane? Security will stop you. No way. Uh-uh. No way. No. Way."

I resisted the urge to answer, *Way*. But honestly, I was wondering how it would be done.

Messenger finally lost patience with her renewed yammering, raised a hand, and while she continued to move her mouth and tongue, no sound came from her.

"Oliver Benbury," Messenger said. "You have chosen to play. And so, in Isthil's name, I call upon the Master of the Game."

17

I STEELED MYSELF FOR WHAT WAS TO COME. I wondered if the time would ever come when I would not dread the approach of the Master of the Game.

The foul yellow mist, that harbinger of supernatural terror, rose now. But it came in a way unlike any previous appearance. I stared in fascination as the hundreds of still-life people in the audience opened their mouths wide. It was an eerie thing, no question, to see men and women, young and old, each insensate, oblivious, and unseeing, open their jaws to the point where I heard jawbones crack.

From these open mouths, and from nostrils as well, rose the yellow mist, as if these orifices were pipes. The mist first drifted then streamed and finally seemed to blast like steam, until it concealed all those distorted faces and circled around us on the stage. The purple lights still shone down on us and where the light touched the mist, took on the color of excrement.

I had seen the Master of the Game in several guises, and I expected some new nightmare shape. But the Game Master is endlessly inventive, and capable of becoming corporeal in many shapes.

This time he was no maze of doomed humans, no nest of snakes formed into human shape. He emerged from the mist and he was not a he. The Master of the Game came in the shape not of a fantastical monster, but of a girl.

It was Graciella who stepped slowly into view. Graciella. I saw the recognition in the eyes of the two accused. I saw concern, but not abject terror.

Until this embodiment of Graciella began to change.

She approached as she was in real life, but with each lessening of the distance between us I saw details that defied the overall impression of a young girl. It first became apparent in the way her flesh seemed to undulate, as though her bones did not quite provide the rigidity her body needed. As though she were a sort of water balloon, a sack, a plastic bag in the shape of a girl but containing a sluggish liquid. This suggestion of a viscous fluid just beneath her skin became ever more real as the flesh grew first translucent, and then ever more transparent.

Her arms. Her legs. Her neck and face. Sheets of clear plastic film over some seething corruption beneath.

"No, no, no," Oliver cried. "That's not . . . This is all just special effects, hah hah, you almost got me, almost!" And that shrill verbal denial lasted until the Master of the Game had stepped all the way clear of the mist and stood bathed in the stage lights and Oliver could see, as I could see, that what lay pulsating beneath the fragile flesh was not muscle or bone or blood.

Have you ever seen a scanning electron microscope picture of disease organisms? Bacteria and viruses, proliferating amoebas, voracious worms, and the clanking spidery creatures called mites? They say there are something like five pounds of bacteria and other parasites alive in and on the human body. This body, this accusatory vision of Graciella, was a hundred pounds more, all magnified to visibility. She was nothing here but the filth of human existence, all roiling madly beneath a surface that threatened to burst open from the pressure like rotting fruit.

And then, unable to look away, unable to save myself from the full horror, I saw that these creatures of disease, these invaders, were feasting on a million tiny Graciellas, burrowing into microscopic iterations of her, writhing in silent agony as spirochetes corkscrewed their way into her.

Later I would wonder at the artistry of the Game Master, at the vibrant but sadistic imagination he brought to his duty. But seeing this creature, seeing this embodiment of disease and corruption, I could only wish that I might somehow stop the images from imprinting themselves on my memory. Later I could achieve a shaky objectivity, but not now, not now.

Still muted, Nicolet screamed in silent terror. She screamed until her face was red and bathed in sweat. She screamed until I thought her eyes would be forced from their sockets.

Oliver vomited. Haarm was almost as badly affected.

I wondered if he had ever encountered the Master of the Game, and if so in what guise he had appeared.

Messenger and the Master of the Game spoke the ritual words that consigned Oliver's fate to the game.

"This is the game," the Game Master said in a voice that was so perfect a re-creation of Graciella's own soft alto that it sent a chill up my spine. "The game is called Hangman."

"Hangman," Oliver said, wary of believing his luck. "You mean, like guessing the letters in a word?"

The Master of the Game waved a hand and from the surrounding mist appeared a set that was reassuringly familiar, a large chalkboard with nine short horizontal lines for letters.

"A word," the Game Master said. "Nine letters. Each time you miss, a body part is added. There are seven portions: head, shoulders, left arm, right arm, torso, left leg, right leg. You may guess only consonants. Each wrong guess adds a part. You may purchase a vowel, but doing so will cost you a body part."

I saw Oliver relax a little. He was an intelligent boy and thought he would win. An intelligent boy, but not one familiar with the ways of the Game Master.

Unlike Oliver, I was not terribly surprised when rather than a glittery wheel, a shape that has terrified the wicked for centuries appeared at the far end of the stage.

It was a platform made of rough wood. It was raised atop thirteen steps. And on that high platform stood two stout upright beams buttressed at the base. A crossbeam connected the two uprights, and it, too, was strengthened by short angled segments. In all it formed a wide, upside-down *U*.

It was a gibbet. A gallows, lacking only a noose.

"Okay, my first letter is—"

But the Master of the Game was not done and Oliver fell silent as he saw "Graciella's" mouth open wide, wider, too wide so that if she were real her jaw must have come unhinged.

A blue-black tongue, split at the end, shot from that mouth, and withdrew as though it had tasted the air and not liked what it found. The next details visible were eyes, one on either side of the tongue that now tasted again and withdrew, again and withdrew. These eyes were dully polished brass balls, split by pointed vertical ovals, forming the irises.

Snake's eyes.

The head of the snake now pushed out, as big as "Graciella's" distended mouth could accommodate. Inch after inch the scaled body followed, and then foot after foot, until the snake's head drooped to the stage floor. Four feet. Six feet. Eight feet. More. It was impossible, of course, the snake in all its glory was bigger than the body from which it had emerged. But we were in a world not limited by the possible.

At last the tail appeared and the snake slithered quickly to the platform, slithered sidewinder style up the thirteen steps, curled itself around one of the uprights and maypoled around it till it reached the crossbeam.

By now Oliver could see where this was going. He tried to make a joke of it. "What, you couldn't just buy rope?"

The Master of the Game was not bothered by the quip. The truly powerful do not need to insist on their power, they have merely to possess it.

The snake crawled out onto the crossbeam, looped its tail around the beam, and dropped its head. It writhed a little, but otherwise seemed content to hang there.

"Begin," the Game Master said.

"Okay, no vowels, right?" Oliver licked his lips and I could see him sounding out various possibilities. "*T!*" he cried at last.

On the chalkboard the fourth line sprouted a letter *T*.

_ _ _ T _ _ _ _ _

"Yeah. Okay," Oliver said, feeling a possible escape ahead. "Okay, next letter, *D*."

What happened then was too sudden and too swift for human eyes to follow. The snake shot forward as fast as its own flicked tongue, it extended well beyond its own length. It moved so fast that it created a loud crack, like a bullwhip. It wrapped around Oliver's neck and sliced bloodlessly through his flesh and bone.

The snake withdrew as fast as it had flung itself forward, and when it came to rest, Oliver's head and neck hung in a living noose.

This at last brought a shocked cry from Haarm. I was proud of the fact that I did not react: I had already guessed the nature of this particular game of Hangman.

Oliver's headless body remained standing. I might

not have recoiled in shock, but I stared in fascinated horror at the sight of a still-living body, minus its head and neck, standing. Even more than the sight of Oliver's head hanging from the noose, this fascinated me.

It was even more disturbing to Oliver who shrieked, somehow still able to speak though his lungs were now ten feet from his vocal cords. His eyes stared, incredulous, at his own body.

"This can't be," he said.

It's the sort of thing I used to say when I was still new to the powers of Isthil's servants.

"This is a nightmare. I'm just having a dream. This is all—"

"Next letter," the Master of the Game urged blandly.

"This is bull!" Oliver yelled. "This is insane! I'm waking up now. I'm waking up now! Now!"

It could have been comical. It was like something out of an old cartoon: a head entirely apart from its body, hanging from a snake's noose, and ordering himself to wake up.

When he kept yelling and ignoring the order to choose a letter, the Game Master summoned an hourglass with swift-falling sand. "Choose before the last grain falls or a body part will be added."

"Um . . . okay, okay . . . um, um . . . *E!*"

In his panic, Oliver had chosen a vowel. The *E* appeared on the chalkboard in the second spot. But in payment a line of light sliced across his standing body from shoulder to shoulder, and all that was above that line appeared now, attached to the hanging head and neck.

_ E _ T _ _ _ _ _

Oliver's arms remained behind, attached now to nothing, but still in their place.

The weight of his shoulders added to his head dragged Oliver downward. The snake noose tightened. Oliver tried to scream but his larynx was being crushed and the sound that came out was a pitiful croak.

The hourglass turned of its own accord.

"This isn't a game," Haarm said. He looked more anxious than horrified.

"*L!*" Oliver managed to say, and with that his left arm flew to attach itself to his shoulder. The additional weight was cutting off the flow of blood to his brain, and he grabbed the snake noose with his one arm and managed to lessen the pressure enough to say, "*N.*"

Here followed one of the more unusual moments I've ever experienced in one of the Game Master's games. The Game Master, still in Graciella's young voice, asked, "*M* or *N*?"

"*N*!" Oliver grated.

"Like Netherworld? Or like Malech?"

"Like . . . like . . . nine!"

"Mine?" the Master of the Game repeated.

I do not believe for a moment that the Game Master had a sense of humor. That would be impossible. And yet . . .

"Or like never?"

"Never! Never!"

And with that Oliver found his other arm. Both hands now gripped the noose and this was enough to allow him to scream curses for several seconds as sand rushed too quickly from teardrop to teardrop in the hourglass. Seconds before the last grain fell, Oliver gasped, "*H*!"

Without comment, two letters appeared on the board. It now read:

H E _ T _ _ _ H _

I solved the puzzle. But the audience must never

shout out answers. So I kept my peace.

"*R!*"

And yes, there was an *R* in the sixth place. But a wrongly guessed *S* added his torso, leaving just his legs still standing in place.

The weight doubled as his body, from pelvis upward, joined the rest of him and dragged him down. He strained with both hands, biceps quivering, neck a twist of arteries and distended tendons, face shining from sweat, eyes bulging.

Oliver was very frightened now. Nicolet no longer looked as if she regretted not playing.

And Haarm was becoming agitated. He kept looking over his shoulder as if expecting someone to arrive and put a stop to this vicious game.

I glanced at Messenger, wondering whether he had noticed Haarm's distraction, but Messenger refused to meet my eyes and instead looked fixedly at Oliver. At what was now most of Oliver.

"I . . . ca . . . I . . ." Oliver was choking as his arms weakened.

"Are you choosing the letter *I*?" "Graciella" asked innocently.

"Chhh . . . chhggr . . . no . . . letter . . . *P!*"

And yes, as I had guessed, there was a *P* in the third slot.

H E P T _ R _ H _

It seemed obvious to me now, but then I had heard the word frequently since adopting my new duties as apprentice. It was not otherwise a common word, not a word Oliver was likely to have on the tip of his tongue.

That tongue now bulged between his lips. It had turned a dark red color. The muscles in his body strained to hold the choking weight.

With a supreme effort Oliver pulled himself up just enough to gasp, "*B!*"

His left leg now hung from the rest of him and kicked at the air, seeking something to rest upon. It hung just eight or ten inches above the platform. Too far for Oliver, and too heavy. The additional weight caused him to lose his grip on the noose and he swung, voiceless, airless, while the sand fell through the hourglass.

One more wrong letter and he would lose.

But he could not speak. His hands had been dropped to his side so that circulation could be restored, but I doubted he would have strength enough to rise for the last letters, the letters that might save him.

Yet I had underestimated the drug-dealing pimp, for he found a last reservoir of strength and managed to gasp, "*C!*"

H E P T _ R C H _

He had it now. I could see that he had it. There was desperate awareness in eyes now bulging out of his face above tongue turned black.

He saw the answer, but he saw it too late. He clawed madly at the noose, but the strength was gone from his fingers. He clawed, clawed, weaker, less focused. His eyes glazed over.

The sand ran out.

With one leg attached, the last of Oliver was no longer able to lift himself to speak.

"Heptarchy," the Game Master said. And with that, the snake noose released its hold and Oliver fell to the platform in a heap.

But he was not dead. The game is never fatal, not really.

Oliver remained bent over on his hands and knees, gasping for air.

"The game has been lost," the Master of the Game said.

"Yes," Messenger agreed.

"Have I performed my duty, Messenger of Isthil?"

"You have," Messenger said. "You may withdraw."

Oliver was sent tumbling down the thirteen steps to land, still sucking desperately for air in a throat that was half-crushed.

The Master of the Game withdrew and took with him the gibbet and the snake and his vile simulacrum of Graciella, and faded into the mist.

"Oliver Benbury, you have lost the game," Messenger said. "And now you will endure the Piercing to determine your punishment."

"Let *me* do it."

Haarm.

I spun toward him. "What?"

"I may not be *your* apprentice," Haarm said to Messenger, "but I am still *an* apprentice and you have been charged with my training for now."

Did Messenger suspect something was very wrong with this bold request?

"I can do it," I said, peering closely at Haarm.

"You've already done the girl," Haarm said. "It's my turn."

I had not thought of the ritual of the Piercing as something to be fought over, and I admit I was baffled, though suspicious.

"Haarm will perform this duty," Messenger said.

Haarm roughly dragged Oliver to his feet. There was no fight left in Oliver. Oliver was a whipped dog, cringing and subservient.

As I had done with Nicolet, Haarm now moved behind Oliver and placed his palms against heart and head. For perhaps two minutes I watched and waited, splitting my attention between Haarm and Nicolet and Messenger.

Something was not right here, and if Messenger didn't sense it then he was not the person I believed him to be. But he said nothing and did nothing.

At last Haarm blinked, and wiped his hand over his eyes as if waking from a nap.

"He has many fears," Haarm said, steadfastly refusing to make eye contact. "But his great fear is of . . ." Haarm swallowed and his eyes flitted left and right.

"He has a strange fear of plush animals. Teddy bears."

I was looking right at Oliver as Haarm said it. I saw the surprise. I saw the mystification. And the relief.

Fear? Not even a little.

Haarm, on the other hand, looked nervous and belligerent.

I was still trying to make sense of what had happened when the answer appeared, looking, as always, like the girl who was actually too hot for the Victoria's Secret catalog.

"What are you doing here?" Haarm cried.

"Where else should I be?" Oriax asked innocently.

"But—"

Oriax waved him off dismissively. "Oh, don't be dull, Haarm. Did you really think they wouldn't figure it out? Little mini-Messenger here isn't stupid—sexually repressed and frustrated but not stupid." She slinked her way toward Messenger, grinning with her too-sharp teeth. "And Messenger? He's not just a pretty face." She sighed theatrically, enjoying her moment of victory. "Although it is a very, very pretty face."

"It's my fault," I said. "I mentioned Oriax to Haarm. He came to see me and he made me angry and I blurted out her name. He must have—"

"Oh, please, mini, don't disappoint me," Oriax said. "The big dumb Dutch boy here has been mine for a long time."

Messenger nodded slightly, almost a token of wary respect. "The timing was less than perfect," he said.

Oriax shrugged. "Yes, true enough. I was hoping to get Haarm into your little circle earlier."

"It was Trent you wanted to rescue," Messenger said.

"Trent," Oriax said wistfully. "He was on a very useful path. There's never really a bad time to add another hater, but Trent, well, there was a particular role he could have played. He would have been just the right thug at just the right time. My lord is not happy with me for failing to save Trent."

Haarm had begun to edge away from me and from Messenger.

Oliver just looked scared and wary and still badly shaken from his encounter with the Master of the Game. But he responded to Oriax the way people do, eyes taking in every detail, and then taking in those same details again.

"Yes, Trent would have been useful," Oriax said, and

pretended to wipe away a tear before laughing gaily and saying, "But a sixteen-year-old who is already pimping and pushing heroin? We'll find something useful to do with him."

"Let me redo the Piercing," I said. "I can find out what he's afraid of."

Messenger shook his head slightly. "That ritual may be performed only once. Oriax knows this."

"Yes, *she* does," Oriax said, mocking his seriousness.

"You set up Chandra," I said to her.

"Not quite," Oriax said. "I just seduced her apprentice. See, I'll tell you a little secret." She came to me, close enough, too close, and though at that moment I raged inwardly at her, I could not resist entirely the gravitational pull she exerted over me.

"All are sinners," Oriax said. "All fail to do their duty at some point. Everyone falls, even Messengers of Fear. Chandra had a soft heart. I had seen her intervene in the time line before and I knew she would do it again. But I needed someone to inform Daniel, and, well, Daniel doesn't listen to me. So I had a charming . . . discussion . . . with this great blond lump here, and he was not hard to convince. He ratted out Chandra. The law of averages made it reasonably likely that he would be temporarily assigned to Messenger—he's very well thought of, you know. Oh yes, he is the Golden Boy. Once assigned to Messenger, Haarm would be in a position to help me with Trent. That didn't work, but I did manage to salvage a few things: Chandra is out, and I saved this potentially useful creature." She waved an elegant hand at Oliver. "Unless of course you intend to attack him with plush animals, Messenger. And even now, there's still hope for Trent. Who knows what he may do when he returns to his life? You may not have broken him entirely. He may yet be salvaged."

Messenger did not answer her. Instead he said to Oliver, "You have escaped your due punishment. You are free to go."

"He'll go with me," Oriax said.

"He cannot be forced to do so," Messenger said. "He is free to make his own decision."

Oliver perked up at this. He climbed to his feet, shaky, traumatized, but recovering his wits. "What's the deal?" he rasped.

"Go back to your life," Messenger said. "Consider

what has happened. Take stock of what you have done, of the damage you have caused. Change your life. Be a better person."

Oriax laughed delightedly. "Oh, that's so very Messenger."

She stepped to Oliver. Without looking at him, but keeping her eyes on Messenger, she stroked her hand down Oliver's cheek. "Did the bad, bad Master of the Game scare you, little Oliver? Did the bad Messenger hurt you?"

Oliver's knees buckled and he knelt, gazing up at her, his face no longer ravaged by fear. His mouth was open and his eyes ecstatic.

"Yes, I think he'll come with me," Oriax said, her voice dripping contempt. "I'll find uses for him. Isn't that right, Oliver? You want to come with me. You want to serve me. You want to swear eternal allegiance to Malech. Don't you?"

"Yes! Yes!"

She bent slightly at the waist and just brushed his forehead with her lips. I thought he might faint.

"Now there is one last question to be decided. You. You mini . . . I mean, Mara."

I managed to shake my head but words did not come. They didn't come because at that moment I wasn't sure what I would say.

"Haarm is mine now, but you could borrow him if you came with me now, Mara. He's a handsome boy, isn't he? And he will be more attractive still when he has met my lord and sworn allegiance. You don't have to live a life of loneliness, Mara. You don't have to pass your days in your sterile abode awaiting the appearance of the boy you can never have. You don't have to serve out the rest of your sentence. You can escape your doom. You can come with us."

"With you?" I said.

"In every way, Mara," she said, and now she was so very near. I heard her voice as a whisper in my ear. I felt, or imagined I felt, her breath on my neck.

Haarm was escaping his fate. Haarm's body would not be slowly, inexorably covered with the tattoos that would forever remind him of a hundred terrible encounters with evil. Haarm wouldn't live years of pain and loneliness and the sadness they brought.

I imagined the months and maybe years ahead of

me. I imagined the distance that must inevitably grow between me and Messenger as he pursued his own obsession for Ariadne.

And, too, I took stock of my doubts. Was this worthwhile, what we did? Did it matter to me if some balance were maintained? It wasn't up to me, it couldn't be. There would be others to take my place.

And what of the day when Messenger deemed me ready to become the Messenger of Fear? What would be left for me when he departed for good and I was fully, absolutely, alone?

I knew I was being tempted. I knew Oriax was manipulating me. I even saw clearly that part of her motivation was mere spite toward Messenger. He had withstood her temptation and she hated him for it.

Haarm was crude and unfeeling, but he was being offered to me and it wasn't like I had better offers lining up. My future was bleak.

But not as bleak as the future I had created for Samantha Early, or as lost as poor, brave Aimal's future. And not as sad as what likely awaited Graciella.

Oriax was evil. She had sung and celebrated as

Derek Grady burned. She had reveled in his destruction. She had wanted Trent for purposes that I could not guess, but I knew that it was his hatred that attracted her attention.

"Come, Mara," Oriax purred. "Let us seal the deal with a kiss."

Did I want to know what her lips felt like? Did I crave the pleasure that I knew would suffuse me?

Desperately.

Desperately.

And her mouth, her now-red and full lips were millimeters from mine.

I closed my eyes and parted my lips.

Yes, I was lonely, and yes in my isolation and sadness I longed for love.

But not hers. The one I longed for was not to be touched.

It was with more than a trace of bitterness that I said those despised words to Oriax: "I am not to be touched."

18

ORIAX AND HAARM AND OLIVER WERE ALL gone. Messenger and I remained, with Nicolet. We stood there in silence, the boy in black, and the girl who loved him.

Instantly I tried to push that thought back into some dark corner of my mind lest Messenger sense it. My cheeks burned and I could not look at him. It wasn't true, I told myself, it was absurd. I barely knew him. I didn't even know his real name. I was just stressed, traumatized, lonely, and afraid, so of course I would be attracted to him.

And yet I knew that in his heart he was compassionate. I knew that he was loyal. I knew that he was strong; no one could long survive as a Messenger of Fear without some source of inner strength. Did it matter that I didn't know his favorite color, or what music he liked, or any of the superficial things I'd known about other boys?

Didn't I know what really mattered?

Yes, but I knew as well that he loved another. Ariadne, whose name was becoming almost a curse to me. Her memory cast its shadow over me, and it would never go away so long as he held on to hope.

The Shoals, I thought. The Shoals. The truth might lie there.

I could go there. I could *know*.

I covered for my blushing and agitated looking away by saying, "Messenger, shall I?"

Had he in fact read my mind and known my deepest thoughts he might well have misinterpreted that. But he was blind, or perhaps *deliberately* blind, to my internal turmoil.

"Do," he said.

So, I did. I wanted the words to sound suitably

solemn, but I cannot deny that there was a quaver in my voice as I intoned, "I summon the Hooded Wraiths to carry out the sentence."

And that's when the last of Nicolet's arrogance abruptly disappeared. She was allowed to speak again, maybe only so that she could scream.

"What the hell?" Nicolet asked, and asked again and again, each repetition louder and higher and faster until the sound of her fear was an almost continuous scream.

Almost a scream. The actual scream came when the Hooded Wraiths stepped from the mist.

They are tall, the wraiths, perhaps a foot taller than the tallest men. They were clothed in black hoods that fell from a point to cover them entirely and sweep the floor. They were a parody of ancient monks, a mockery of druidic fantasies. I saw no face, not even an opening where a face might be, in the darkness of their hoods.

But understand that it is not the size or the robe or the suggestion of physical horrors beneath that robe that is the greatest cause of the fear that flows from them. No, there is something deeper, something visceral, a feeling, a tingling of nerves, a tightening of sphincters, a heaviness in heart and soul that comes not from what is seen or even imagined, but some vastly deeper well of primitive dread.

They carry fear with them like some swift contagion, and it twists your thoughts and crushes your defenses.

They were not here for me, though once they had been. I had nothing to fear from them now, but fear them I did.

The Shoals were their abode. If I meant to visit that dreadful place I would have to conquer that fear.

The wraiths closed on a cursing, screaming Nicolet.

The plane had no identifying logos. There were no flight attendants. I saw no other passenger than Nicolet, belted into seat 12A, a window seat.

I saw bright blue sky through the oval window, and clouds beneath us. The hum of engines was familiar. The fasten seat belts sign was on. And no smoking was allowed.

"Okay, okay, no," Nicolet babbled. "No no nononono!"

The engines began to whine more insistently, as if

they were straining. A sudden sharp bump, and Nicolet was thrown upward against her seat belt, though Messenger and I were not affected.

"You gotta... Okay, I'm sorry. I'm sorry. I'm so sorry! I'll give her credit! I swear to God!"

Sweat poured into her eyes. Every muscle and fiber in her body strained. Blood oozed from her palms as her long nails cut into the flesh.

"Let me out! Let me out!"

The next bump of turbulence was stronger. A voice, professionally controlled but clearly worried, came over the public address system and warned that we were encountering severe turbulence.

"Severe" barely covered the reality I witnessed. The plane was lurching around the sky as if it was a ball being kicked around a playground by a giant child.

Everything shook. Nicolet's body was a blur dominated by a wide, shrieking mouth. The turbulence was so violent that sewage came seeping out beneath the bathroom doors. Some terrible god was raining hammer blows on the fuselage.

Then the floor tilted sharply downward. Nicolet pushed her feet against the legs of the seat in front of her and the shaking was so violent I heard the sickening crack of breaking bone.

We punched through the clouds and out the window I saw the ground, a patchwork quilt of fields crisscrossed by snaking roads and a shimmering river.

Nicolet no longer used words, only grunts and cries and screams came from her. She had in some ways ceased to be human, ceased to be a thinking, reasoning creature. She was nothing but terror. Terror made flesh.

The engines suddenly fell silent.

I heard the harsh atonal song of metal tearing, of rivets popping, and the shaky sound of the pilot yelling, "Brace! Brace! Brace for impact!"

The fields and roads and river were nearer, nearer, leaping up toward us to smash us, to kill us, and the wing that partly obstructed my view began to disintegrate and shed aluminum panels. Hydraulic fluid sprayed. An engine detached and was sucked away in the slipstream.

No hope now. None.

I could see individual cars.

I could see the shadows cast by telephone poles.

I could see the plowed rows of dirt.

And what happened next, though I knew in some part of my mind that it was not real, not really real, would never leave me.

Everything slowed.

The nose of the jet hit the ground and threw shards of metal and glass past the window.

Down the aisle the cockpit door burst outward. The doors of the bathrooms exploded. And inch by inch, foot by foot, the plane plowed into the dirt as it was turned to splinters.

The last seconds, as the destruction reached Nicolet, seemed to drag on for an eternity.

And Nicolet lay on the stage of the Grand Ole Opry.

The sounds that came from her were nothing like her beautiful singing voice.

Daniel was with us.

He nodded at Messenger, and at me. I had no capacity to respond. Had he decided that I myself needed to be taken away to the Shoals, I would scarcely have been able to object. I closed my eyes, unwilling to see them or anything at all.

Perhaps they had seen that I was almost as destroyed

as Nicolet, for when I opened my eyes again, I was in my abode and in my bed.

The book of Isthil lay beside me where I had left it.

With shaking hands I opened it and began to tear out the pages.

19

WHEN I WOKE, AFTER HOW LONG I CANNOT GUESS, the pages of Isthil's book were not crumpled around me. The book, whole and intact, lay beside me.

I walked like a zombie to the bathroom, and then to the kitchen. I stared blankly at the coffee machine.

"I'll make a pot," Messenger said.

"Screw you."

Unperturbed, he began adding spoonfuls of coffee and then water. Neither of us spoke until the blessed juice had drained down and then filled our cups and mouths.

"Sorry," I managed to say.

"I've heard worse," Messenger said. "And said far worse, and far more frequently, to my own master when I was an apprentice."

Okay, that softened my anger just a little.

I made some scrambled eggs and toast for both of us.

"I was tempted," I confessed around a mouthful of food. "By Oriax."

"It's what she does. She's very good at it." Was that the hint of a rueful smile? Maybe a hint of a hint.

"What of Haarm? And Oliver?"

"They are not our concern. Not now. Though they may be in the future."

"And Graciella?"

"I have not been given permission to see her future," he said. "But it is possible that she has learned that the contract she signed is not valid. And from that . . ." He shrugged.

I often talk too much, and I'm sure Messenger thinks I ask too many questions. But for once I had the good sense not to ask.

I did not ask how Graciella could have come to learn

that she might still have a way to find her own path in life. I'd seen what happened to Chandra.

I was not all better. I would never be all better. It would take more than sleep and scrambled eggs to repair me. I had made my choice when I rejected Oriax. I knew she would try again, but for now at least, I had made my choice. But another temptation had taken root in my mind, was growing: I would go to the Shoals. I would search there for Ariadne. I would no longer be haunted by her unknown fate.

Whether Messenger liked it or not, I would discover the truth of his lost love. Because only then would he, or I, have any peace.

"Messenger, I . . . I don't suppose we ever get to call in sick," I asked.

He frowned and looked me up and down, searching for some visible explanation.

"Just cramps," I said.

"Did you eat something bad?"

"No, Messenger. Female cramps. You know . . . I'm fine, but if I could take a day . . ."

Messenger was no more fond of discussing menstruation than any other male, and I almost laughed at the fleeting look of panic that appeared and was quickly concealed. "Of course," he said. "Take a day. Do you have, um . . . whatever you need?"

I resisted the perverse urge to panic him entirely by launching into a discussion of tampons and maxi pads and contented myself with a simple, "Yes."

He left me alone then with a promise of twenty-four hours free. I had the odd thought that I needed to get my mother to call the school attendance line and excuse my absence, but that was another life. That was a life without Messenger, without Daniel or Oriax.

Or the Shoals.

I went first to the book of Isthil, and scanned page after page, looking for any reference to the place that even Messenger referred to only in hushed tones. I quickly became frustrated with the limitations of paper—if only the book was searchable! Can Isthil not release the Kindle version? But at last I found a few couplets on the topic of something called the Temple of Regret.

The brave who pass shall go forth free.
The weak, the fearful, evil, we,

True freedom's comfort never see,
Till gathered up in misery,
And to the dread temple crawl,
The temple built of pain and gall,
There by regret learn, as we all,
That life misled leads us to fall.
And in our silent torment see,
Existence hangs on such as we,
And thus from sin and evil flee,
So man and all his world may be.

It seemed a silly bit of doggerel to describe a place I had been taught to dread. But it was the only reference I could find that even seemed to refer to the Shoals, if indeed this poetic "dread temple" was that selfsame place. Unfortunately Isthil's rhymes did not tell me much, though it implied, as I'd already inferred from Messenger's hints, that it need not be a final destination.

Could I go there? I suspected that I could. Indeed, I believed from things that Messenger and Daniel had said, that such a pilgrimage would be a necessary part of my training as a Messenger of Fear.

So, Mara, I asked myself, if you have to go eventually, why not now?

Because, I answered sensibly, I would be going alone, without Messenger as my guide and protector.

Yet, Messenger dreaded the Shoals for what he might find there. He feared finding Ariadne. I believe he feared he would find her hopelessly, helplessly trapped in whatever purgatory that place presented. The hope of finding his lost love was all that kept Messenger strong. I now knew that it was he who had subjected her to the torments of the Master of the Game. It was he who performed the Piercing that surfaced her darkest fear. And it was he who would have stood by helpless as she endured. It was all his duty as a Messenger, inescapable, but that knowledge would not blunt the jagged edge of his guilt.

The decision was made without me consciously making it. It had been made when I lied to Messenger in order to buy myself time. I'd wasted hours of that time searching the book of Isthil, only to find meaningless gibberish that told me nothing new and did not in any way prepare me. And now, having stalled and gained nothing, I was left still with the same decision: I must go to the Shoals.

I did not need to know its location, I needed only to know that it existed, and then form the clear will to be there. But I was afraid; I have no reluctance to admit that. I was afraid. I searched the room around me for something to carry as a weapon, but what weapon could possibly defend me from what the book called a place of pain and gall? I had seen the Master of the Game. I had seen the Hooded Wraiths. I had felt the malevolent rage of the incubus, and the ever-so-enticing force of Oriax. What weapon could I carry to defend myself from powers such as those?

The Shoals.

I felt myself standing at one of those divergent paths, one coasting along passively with my training. The other path was the one not given but taken as an act of will. In deciding to take that path I was perhaps committing a grave error. I was perhaps altering my own fate in ways that might prove disastrous.

I had played along, gone along, occasionally cried out against unfairness, but mostly I had acquiesced and played the obedient apprentice. Had Haarm's example somehow inspired me to rebel? That didn't feel true, but it might be. I believed he had made a very bad decision, but he had at least made a decision. He had grabbed his fate and given it a good shake.

The Shoals.

Yes. It all led there. I had seen the rest of the process from confronting the accused to the recitation of evils to the summoning of the Master of the Game, and beyond that to the Piercing and the punishment. I had seen some destroyed and some reborn and one escape. But I had not yet seen what happened to those who were crushed by Messengers of Fear.

I would see. I would see whether Messenger's lost love was there.

I would go to the Shoals.

I closed my eyes. And when I opened them again I was enveloped in the vile yellow mist that had from the first been my unwelcome companion. I heard nothing, touched nothing, saw nothing but that swirling, somehow aware mist. I felt its curiosity. I felt its contempt.

"I will see the Shoals," I said in a reedy voice, and with a silent sneer the mist withdrew from me.

I don't know what I expected, perhaps some Dante's pit, perhaps some slasher movie's dungeon, but what I saw as the mist cleared was like nothing I had imagined, at once more terrible by far, and yet, more beautiful.

I stood on a featureless desert plain of cracked, parched mud, like a drought-emptied reservoir. But this plain had no boundaries that I could see, but rather seemed to extend forever in every direction at once, as if it covered the entire earth—if any of this even was the earth that mortals know. My eyes were drawn irresistibly away from that soul-crushing emptiness to a singular feature that rose from the dry mud ocean.

A temple? Perhaps, but unlike anything built by human hands. A mountain rose from the plain, ten thousand feet of basalt so massive it seemed impossible that it did not sink of its own gigantic weight into the plain of cracked mud. The black mountain might almost have been a massive meteorite plopped down from orbit, so unlikely was its location. No rule of earthly geography could account for its overwhelming size in that otherwise featureless emptiness.

Atop this mountain sat a pyramid. It seemed to grow organically from the black rock, without clear boundaries, but as it rose it grew lighter in color, as though altitude had bleached away the black. Black faded to gray, which faded to white, and at the very point glittered like a jewel. The totality of it, the mountain and its pyramid, looked like all the coal ever mined, compressed with increasing heat and pressure until it formed a diamond at the top.

It was impossible for me to judge the distance with no point of reference; it might be a mile away, it might be a hundred, but however far the distance, I felt crushed by the size of that terrible edifice. Gazing at it I found breath a strain to draw, and my heart thudded with ominous heaviness in my chest. My every instinct warned me away from it, and yet, where else was I to go? I could return to my abode, or I could approach.

"I am not condemned to this place," I reminded myself. "I come freely, as a Messenger's apprentice, to see what I must eventually see." I said it aloud, as if whatever malign power that watched over this place would hear and be bound by my logic and good intentions.

I began to walk, but soon intuited that walking at normal speed would take a very long time. I had to reach the place and still search out Ariadne, all before Messenger realized I had gone. I felt like I was skipping school, but skipping school only to take the day off in a place even worse than high school.

I accelerated my pace, something I now do with ease, and soon the parched earth was flying by beneath feet that still seemed to be walking normally, as if each step was a hundred feet long while never requiring a stretch. As fast as I was moving, the basalt mountain and its diamond peak still grew but slowly. And so I hurried still faster, steps that covered hundreds of feet, then thousands of feet, a half mile at a time.

As I approached, the mountain filled more and more of my field of view, spreading left and right, towering ever higher over me, blotting out the cloudless, wanly blue sky, pushing the horizon aside, and still it grew. After what felt like a long time I began to see details of the rock, creases and bulges, boulders that barely resisted gravity's pull and stone pillars like defensive towers placed here and there in a mad and irrational scheme. And then, closer still, I made out a meandering ribbon of red that began in the mud and rose, appearing and disappearing in the texture of the basalt. At first I imagined it to be volcanic, a red stream of molten lava, but no, the red color lacked the light of heat. It was a cold red, a dark red, a red like dried blood.

Someone had come into view, a solitary figure, and I knew who it was. I slowed but did not stop or turn away, and in time came to Daniel. And there, I stopped.

"Mara," Daniel said.

"Daniel."

"You should turn back, apprentice. This is a terrible place."

I nodded. "I know." I noted his choice of verb: *should*, not must. It was my choice.

He looked at me, not unkindly, but perhaps a bit puzzled or maybe merely amused. He had not asked me why I was there.

"Are you not afraid?"

"You know I am."

"Then why?"

I took a while to answer. I thought I knew what I would say, I thought I knew what I felt, but I wanted to choose the words carefully, to eschew anything false or unnecessary. In doing this I forced myself to see clearly my own motivations.

"I love him," I said at last.

"No," Daniel said. "You *wish* to love him, and you

wish him to love you. And there is an *impediment*."

How I longed to sit down, for I was suddenly weary. Hearing the truth spoken so directly had drained the energy from me. I had convinced myself that I was on a mission of mercy, that I was going to learn the truth about Ariadne and with that truth I would stop Messenger from continuing his doomed search for her. This, I had told myself, would free him. Putting his agonies of doubt to rest would be my act of devotion and his liberation and then . . .

And then he would tell me everything about himself. I would learn his true name. I would learn what kind of person he had been and might be again. And then, yes, somehow that would make the beautiful boy in black love me, and I would love him, and Ariadne would be forgotten.

And my own loneliness and emptiness would be gone. I would have my own love to sustain me as Messenger's love for Ariadne sustained him.

"It's not just selfishness," I said to Daniel. "Not every motive is so clear."

"Of course not," he allowed. "Life is complicated, humans are complicated. You do genuinely care for

Messenger, and in time that could even become love. But you are here today to find a way to remove an impediment to your own happiness."

"I just want to understand."

Daniel sighed. "Do as you will. Travel the red path. But I wonder whether what is good and strong in you will outweigh the weakness and selfishness."

"I don't know what—" But he was gone, and my final two words were said to the air. "—you mean."

The red path. I was at once at its base. Above me I could no longer see the diamond-topped temple for the massive bulk of the mountain that stretched from the far left of my view to the far right, so that to see anything else I had to turn my back on the mountain. And yet, when I did, I no longer saw the endless sea of desiccated mud. I saw only the yellow mist, mocking me, denying me even the sense that I had come to this place of my own free will. Had that whole long walk been an illusion? Was this black and sinister mountain the same?

The path was a darker, deeper red upon closer inspection, and made of rectangular flagstones six feet long and half as wide. They were each translucent, with suggestions of shapes and forms I could only glimpse buried down within them, like flies caught forever in amber. I peered closely, but the shapes within only suggested and never revealed. Yet I felt certain that something that had once been human was within each of those terrible stones.

I stepped onto the path, and at once I felt a rush of grief and sadness. There was loss and pain and guilt. And though I saw no face, still less any human action, I felt there was something specific about the stone, something *individual*.

The next stone was similar but not identical. Here the emotion that seemed to rise through my feet and legs to touch my heart was darker, less of grief than of rage.

I knew at a glance that I could not climb this entire path encountering such disorientating feelings with each of the thousands of steps it would require, so I called again on the power that messengers—and their apprentices—can control, and propelled myself more quickly along. Even then I felt a seething sea of emotion vying for the attention of my heart, like a tide dragging at a weary swimmer.

I rushed up that path and passed a woman. She did not see me, moving in a trance like a sleepwalker, crying softly to herself. I passed a man, and later a child, and later still a very old man, and each person looked through me, and each sighed or cried or moaned. I stopped once to look back down the path, and saw that the mist, my faithful if unwelcome companion, was swallowing the path behind me. I seemed now to be on a peak that rose from cloud. Above me I saw the pyramid and indeed it did seem to have been carved or blasted or compressed out of the very mountain itself.

Still I climbed, and passed more hopeless souls, and came finally to what I had expected to find: an arched doorway large enough to allow an elephant to pass through with room to spare.

And above that door were letters. They were in a script I had never seen, but somehow I understood their meaning. Iron letters twenty feet tall spelled SHEOL.

I almost laughed, for of course the pronunciations were so very close. Shoals. Sheol.

Except that one meant a dangerous and concealed peril beneath the surface of water; and the other was an ancient word, a Hebrew word, though I suspected it had

come down to them from more ancient peoples still,
from cursed, forgotten cities at the edge of wastelands.
Sheol.

In English: hell.

20

MESSENGER HAD TOLD ME THAT THOSE WHO WON the game walked away. Those who lost the game endured punishment. Those whose minds survived the punishment were free. And those whose minds did not survive the game descended into madness and were brought to the Shoals.

To Sheol.

He'd also said—or was it Oriax—that there were those who escaped this place. But how? I did not know.

I entered the gate and there, as if the thought had summoned her, stood Oriax. Ah, but not quite the Oriax

I had known. At first glance she might be mistaken for the old Oriax, but as I looked I saw that her beauty, the flawless skin, the Victoria's Secret body, the bewitching eyes all felt thin, like a layer of paint applied over something very different. The image of beauty kept fluctuating, growing lighter and dimmer, clearer and then more fractured, like trying to get a TV signal on an old set with nothing but a wire coat hanger antenna.

"Well, well, if it isn't mini-Messenger. I must confess: I did not expect to see you here so soon."

It was her voice, but not, for the irresistible seduction was absent. That slithering, insinuating, fingers-stroking-bare-flesh voice was ragged now, roughened, coarsened. This was the voice of barely contained rage, not the voice of promised pleasures beyond imagining.

She advanced on me, but stopped quite suddenly. I believe it was because she saw that I was not responding. I believe absent her magic, Oriax knew she had no power over me.

"Why have you come, Mara?"

"To find Ariadne, if she's here."

She laughed, but oh, it was not Oriax's wry

mockery, but a parody of same, a parody performed by a less-than-convincing actor.

"Madness lies within. Do you seek madness, Mara?"

"Your hooves are showing."

They were. The boots flickered in and out, a bit of computer graphics trickery when the software has been hacked. Oriax was the green screen onto which visual lies had been projected, but the special effects no longer quite worked.

"It's this place, isn't it?" I asked, struggling to wring any evidence of fear from my voice, trying to sound strong and unafraid. "You can't maintain the illusion here. The true Oriax is peeking out from behind the curtain."

"The true Oriax." She almost whispered it, and yes there were slithering snakes in that voice, but now they were cobras reared up and ready to strike. "You want to see the true Oriax? Follow me, little fool."

She turned and began walking, supremely confident that I would follow. And what choice did I have? I didn't know this place. I had no map. I had Oriax.

We walked down a cavernous stone hallway that widened and grew as we went, and with each step Oriax herself grew. The seductress's skin was shed in bits and pieces, as if she was disrobing. Or, more aptly perhaps, like a snake molting.

She grew and as she grew, her skin roughened to something more toad-like than human. Her hair fell from her head in locks and then in hunks and finally all at once, revealing a ridged and horned head. From her once-gym-toned behind a tail sprouted, lengthened, and then split in two: whipping, furious serpents, fanged mouths slashing at the air.

The light, too, grew as we advanced, a strange light of a color I had known since first entering the world of the messengers and their foes. It was the yellow of rotting teeth, the yellow of new bruises and dripping pus. It was the yellow of the mist.

Oriax turned to face me and I nearly bolted in panic, but fascination kept me rooted to the spot. Oriax was outlined against the yellow light that pulsed sullenly from some vast open space behind her. She was no longer anything like a human, yet still female, an exaggerated comic book fantasy of femininity.

She was naked, clothed now only in a reptile's skin. Her eyes were blazing red orbs, spheres of blood punctuated with vertical black slits. Her nose was twin gashes that widened and narrowed with each audible breath. Her hands were claws, her feet now unconcealed hooves. Power and malice radiated from her. She stood at least ten feet tall, huge and menacing.

"Do you like me now, mini-Messenger? Do you still fantasize about me sneaking into your bed some night? Will you still shudder ever so coyly at my breath on your neck?"

I should have been terrified. Once upon a time I would have been a puddle of tears and terror on the stone floor. But in revealing herself, Oriax had lost her power over me. This was the Oriax Messenger knew all along, the Oriax he had so effortlessly resisted even as I had practically swooned.

"You know, Oriax," I said, reaching back to my high school mean girls' days, "you used to be hot. But you've really let yourself go."

I had seen Oriax snarky, irritated, frustrated, subtle, and cruel, but I had never seen her lose her temper.

She grew another two feet, a monster of snake skin and ebony hooves. Her tail whipped around her waist, reaching for me, snapping serpent jaws at me.

She roared in a voice that by sheer force of moving air pushed me back. She bared fangs large enough to impale me.

But my fear of her was lessened, rather than heightened. I recognized impotent rage when I saw it. She could not harm me. In fact, I suspected, she could not touch me. Not here, not in her home.

"Take me to Ariadne," I said.

She screamed a foul curse I cannot repeat here.

"In the name of Isthil and her messengers, I command you to take me to Ariadne."

Where did that come from? I had not planned the words; I'd barely thought the thought. I had no notion of being able to command anyone, let alone in the name of the goddess. But the words came from me, and in a strong, clear voice, too.

"You want to meet Messenger's one true love?" she raged. "Then come, and see, and despair!"

She ran down the hall and I ran after her, albeit on shorter legs, but with the power of a messenger that allowed me to keep pace. She came to a stop when the hallway itself came to a stop, at the edge of an open space so enormous I have no ready analogy for it. A stadium could have been tossed into that space and made no more impact than a coin tossed in a lake.

It went up toward light, toward the glittering underside of the diamond. And it went down, down far beyond sight, down into lightless vastness. It stank of raw sewage and salty blood, of fear sweat, and raw meat.

The space itself was overwhelming, and the smell was overpowering, but those were not the sensations that crushed my heart in my chest. There were objects in that hollowed mountain, the objects were human beings, men and women, young and old, all hung in midair, suspended by nothing visible. They rose slowly, or fell slowly, up . . . down . . . They were like scuba divers trying to reach the surface but dragged down each time by too-heavy weights.

They were not alone. Smaller in number but quick as hornets, demons raced from form to form. They hovered close to the humans who rose, and they whispered and laughed and mocked and screamed. The demon cries became a background noise, a soundtrack of rage and hate. I could only clearly hear those closest.

You are filth.

You killed her.

You will never be free.

He cried for mercy and you gave him none!

Sadist!

Pervert!

Murderer!

The humans seemed to be in a trance, jaws hanging open, eyes rolled up in their heads so that the whites were all I saw. They spoke not, nor did they move so much as a muscle. They hung suspended, helpless, tormented by their own evil deeds.

"The unforgiven," Oriax sneered.

"Unforgiven by whom?" I asked.

"By themselves, you stupid ——. They are weighed down by their own guilt. These are but a fraction; many more, millions and billions more, fill the darkness below, and have surrendered to their fates. These few have risen toward the light. And there, mini-Messenger, Mara the backstabber, Mara the one who put the gun in Samantha Early's hand and drove her to blow her brains out, Mara, the murderer who now tortures those no worse than herself on orders from a foul and foolish goddess who struggles to keep all of this—*this!*—in existence."

Oriax's screams had not hurt me, but her words now did. They were the truth, at least part of the truth.

Did I not deserve this same fate? Had I not caused a death?

Did evil not still live within me? Why had I come here? To do good?

Daniel was right: I had come to find a way to erase Ariadne from Messenger's thoughts so that he might be free. Free to love me.

"Here is your moment, Mara, here is your opportunity. You are now not fully human, you are a messenger's apprentice, a creature of the gods. And this is where you choose your path." She no longer raged; her tail no longer whipped at me. She no longer had the Oriax voice that had weakened my resolve at times, but she had the power of truth, however incomplete it might be.

"One path is the messenger's path: horror, the terrible guilt that grows in you with each summoning of the Master of the Game, and above all, Mara, the loneliness. Or . . ."

She let it hang, and I knew I should remain silent, I knew that anything I said would help her to destroy me, but I could not stop myself from asking.

"Or . . . what?"

"Or," she said, "you can become one of us. You can serve Malech. You can work to end this foul system, end this universe, let it start over again and hope the results are less cruel."

I was silent then, and this time the silence worked against me. I had not rejected her offer out of hand. She knew I was listening.

"The beauty and power that I have can be yours. Yes, Mara, you could go back to Messenger no longer the awkward, lovelorn girl, but as you saw me: irresistible, beautiful beyond description. You can go to him then, and he will want you, Mara, and only you. He knows me too well, Messenger, but you? He is already half in love with you, even as unimpressive as you are. Imagine a Mara perfected! Imagine a Mara whose most casual glance can reduce any human to slavering lust."

Did I form the picture in my head? Yes, I confess that I did.

Did I imagine Messenger seeing me exalted, powerful, impossible to resist?

Yes. Yes.

Yes.

But what I said was, "You know, Oriax, it's the twenty-first century, and I don't really think I want to be some comic book fan-boy's notion of a supervixen."

She blinked. Stared, nonplussed.

"Actually," I said, "I was thinking of going to medical school."

Easy to say? No. It sounded easy, I sold it that way—breezy and facile—but no, it was not easy.

Not easy. And yet, I felt my mouth stretch into a smile.

"Maybe pediatrics," I said to Oriax's blank red animal eyes. "Or maybe research, if I have the science chops." I shrugged. "And I think I do."

Then, I took a step toward her. And another.

"Everything you said is true. I am guilty, Oriax. I have done evil. But there's only one path forward after that: to fight evil. That's my only redemption. I didn't know that before, didn't know it when I decided to come here on a selfish and cruel mission to destroy Messenger's love for Ariadne. You've given me a choice, and in that you forced me to think. Your effort to tempt me only reminds me that I'm not that Mara anymore. I am a servant of Isthil, and I work to keep the balance, to resist evil, to protect the good. To keep existence from blinking out."

"You're a fool."

"You made your pitch. I've made my choice. I'm not fool enough to want to be you."

I saw something in her bloodred eyes then. It was not fear, no, I had no real power over Oriax. What I saw in her eyes, on that leathery face, was regret. And suddenly, with chills running down my arms and spine, I understood.

"You," I said. "My God. You were once a messenger! You faced the choice you offered me. You *chose* to become what you are."

"I am the great Oriax!" she bellowed in a voice that made the stone walls vibrate.

"You're a magician with some tricks," I said quietly. "Some very good tricks. But I watched your act closely, and I've seen the sleight of hand. Your magic no longer amazes me. I don't want to be you, Oriax. And I don't want to be the Mara who drove Samantha Early to her grave, not again, not ever."

I laughed in sheer relief. It surprised me and

shocked Oriax. I now knew how to free Ariadne, and, in a way, myself as well.

"I will not be Oriax," I said. "Nor will I be the old Mara. I will be the Messenger of Fear."

She shrank a little then. Still huge and dominating, but somehow reduced. Now it was Oriax who could not speak without revealing her weakness.

"Oriax. Take me to Ariadne."

21

ARIADNE. HOW MANY TIMES HAD I HEARD THAT
name and seethed inwardly?

Ariadne, whose face I knew from the terrifying tattoo over Messenger's heart.

I followed Oriax to her, stepping into the void,
floating through bodies rising and falling, passing
screeching demons that bared their fangs at me but,
like furious zoo animals, never touched me.

Ariadne floated like the others, far from the diamond above, far from the unseen depths of the pit
below. A demon floated beside her whispering, "You

gave him up. You sent him to torture and death, him and his entire family, all save one, and you know *his* fate! You forced him to become your executioner!"

The demon noticed me, his turkey neck whipping his lizard's head around. He hissed like a furious cat.

"Leave," I said to him.

He hissed again, but he left.

I had power. I had authority here. I had the authority of Isthil.

"Shall I tell you how this love of Messenger's life came to be here?" Oriax said.

"No. I don't need you. In fact, Oriax, I think it's time for you to go. Leave me."

My God, she obeyed! The demon who had weakened my knees and crept into dreams I wished I could forget, but never would, roared empty defiance, and then . . . disappeared.

I was alone with Ariadne. Above us, the diamond. Below us, hell itself. She did not see me, her eyes saw nothing. I don't believe she heard me or was aware of my presence. Until I laid my hand against the side of her pretty face. A tremor went through her, and she gasped, but nothing more.

"This is the Piercing," I said, "but you would know that. I will enter your mind, but not to find your fear this time, only to learn the truth."

The pit, the mountain, the floating bodies and flitting demons all faded away, and I was on a narrow cobblestone street. Cars of an earlier vintage rattled by, but so did a horse-drawn cart. It was a shopping district—a display window with three dresses on my left, an enticing cascade of beautiful pastries in the window to my right. The signs read *L'Atelier de Maurice* and *Patisserie*.

My two years of French were up to the task of reading basic signs, though not much more. I was in France, but not today's France, a France gone by. I saw pedestrians, but none with cell phones. I saw cigarettes dangling from lips, men in blue smocks and frayed suits, women in faded dresses and thick-heeled shoes. I heard a grating mechanical sound and looked up to see an airplane with impossible markings: the black cross of wartime Germany.

Down that street came a young couple in their late teens perhaps, arm in arm, laughing, heads tilted together, almost touching.

Ariadne.

And Messenger.

He was a very handsome boy with an easy charm and brown hair cut short. He wore a tan wool suit, no tie, a dark wool overcoat. A plaid scarf wrapped his neck and caught the sudden gust of breeze. He laughed and snatched at the scarf.

He was Messenger, but not. He was at once the same, yet so much younger. This Messenger had seen little of life. He had seen little of pain. He had known little guilt or regret. He was handsome, but he lacked the dangerous beauty and deep sadness that Messenger owned.

But for all their carefree chatter, there was something else going on, something secret. As I watched, Messenger slipped something to Ariadne. No casual observer would have made out the object wrapped as it was in newspaper, but I was no ordinary observer and I saw the revolver clearly. Then he kissed her and quickly walked away down an alley while Ariadne continued on.

I had a choice of whom to follow, but it was impossible still to resist following the young man who would someday become my teacher, my master. It was as he stepped into a small open square with a flower market exploding in brilliant spring color that the two Gestapo agents emerged from a doorway. They fell into step with him and then seized his arms. They searched him, rough hands everywhere, and when they found nothing they slapped him across the face, leaving a red welt.

Even now I had the powers that Messenger had taught me to use and I scrolled quickly ahead, watching them take Messenger, watching him sitting frightened in a small, bare room, shackled to a steel chair, helpless. He had been capable of fear then; he had been only human, just a boy.

When the guards slapped him he cried out. When they punched him and blood sprayed from the ridge of bone above his eye, he sobbed.

And when they slowly, dramatically, opened a canvas sheath and drew out the brutal instruments of torture, he broke.

"Ariadne," he said, weeping. "I gave it to Ariadne to pass on to the Resistance."

I closed my eyes, unable to bear the sight. He had been weak, as I had been weak. He had destroyed Ariadne, as I had destroyed Samantha Early. This was the evil he had done. The weight of it crushed me. How many times over how many years had Messenger told himself he had no choice? How many times had he played that scene again and again in his head? How many times had her name haunted him with a guilt he could not forgive himself for?

I knew what came next and I wished I could look away, but it is a messenger's duty to witness, so I moved through time in that effortless way I had learned, and found I was in the same room. But this time, it was Ariadne shackled. And it was her face that bled from the hail of fists.

She gave them an address.

Her terrified voice said, "If you want the Jew, the one who gave us the gun, he's at Sixty-Eight Rue du Cercle."

They released them both, Messenger and Ariadne, but at different times, and they would not see each other again until much had changed.

I saw Messenger-before-he-was-Messenger standing at the edge of the train tracks, tears streaming down his face, steeling himself to step in front of that onrushing steam locomotive and end his life. I wanted to cry out, "No!" but of course I already knew he was not to die this day.

A mist, a yellow mist, closed around him and he was gone.

I wondered if I had the power to see the moment when he met his own messenger. When he first faced the Master of the Game. And when, shattered as I had been shattered, he refused freedom and chose instead the same terrible penance as I had.

He would not have known that his duties would soon require him to confront Ariadne with the evidence of her own betrayal. He would not have known that she would fail the Master of the Game's test.

Was it not cruel beyond all imagining to make him pierce his true love's mind and find the fear that destroyed her?

I froze the world around me then, closed my eyes, and fought to hold on to the newfound strength I had shown in resisting Oriax. I was not afraid, I was just terribly sad. I was sad for the two young lovers, for the evil that had pushed them to betrayal, at the guilt that had eaten at them both for far longer than I had ever imagined. There had always been something ancient concealed beneath Messenger's boyish looks. He had been frozen in time, not aging in his flesh but aging terribly in his mind, accumulating ever more regrets, ever more suffering.

I did not need to see more. I understood. Messenger had betrayed his love and Ariadne had betrayed a neighbor to his death and the death of all his family.

Ah, but I still did not know the full weight of these events. I thought I had learned all there was to know, but secrets still remained.

Ariadne. I spoke her name in my mind and in hers. I felt her brutalized consciousness turn slowly to me, as slowly as a flower following the sun.

Have you been in this place since then? I asked.

Since then, she answered.

It is time to leave.

I cannot.

You can. If you forgive.

I can forgive all but one.

You must forgive her, too, Ariadne. You must earn that forgiveness and you will be free.

I betrayed him. I betrayed him and his family. All dead because I was weak. All dead because of me. All save one.

The Jew. If you want the Jew . . . His entire family. All but one.

All but one.

That one lives, still, I said. *He suffers, but he lives. And soon he will be free of his long penance, but he searches the world for you, Ariadne. His love has not faded.*

Her emotions were mine, her pain so raw I could not avoid its echoes.

I can never see him, Ariadne said. *His family . . . his mother, his father, his two sisters . . . all dead and him cursed to a life of sorrow and loneliness.*

And guilt, I added. *He suffers the same guilt as you. But he has earned his freedom, and he has earned a right to . . . to love you. Ariadne, decades have passed and still he searches for you, praying that you have escaped this torment and are back in the world of the living.*

There is no freedom from the evil of your own heart.

There is no freedom in helpless self-pity and remorse, I said. *But there is the freedom to fight.*

To fight? The Nazis?

I laughed. *No, we took care of them. The world is different, there are different evils to fight. Will you fight them, Ariadne? Will you spend your life fighting Malech and all his servants?*

We rose, Ariadne and I. When I withdrew from the

intimacy of the Piercing and opened my eyes, I saw that we were rising toward the diamond above us, rising toward the light.

"Forgive," I said. "Forgive him and forgive yourself, Ariadne. And come back to the land of the living."

22

THE NEXT DAY MESSENGER CAME FOR ME.

He was the Messenger I knew, the absurdly beautiful boy in black. But of course I now knew he was far, far older than he seemed. Even his love affair was older than me, older than my mother or father, older than my grandparents. My God, he had loved that girl for seven decades.

And for that time he had carried out the hard justice of Isthil and bore the vivid marks on his body.

"It is time for us to catch up with Trent," Messenger

said, sounding very businesslike. He waited until I nodded.

Needless to say, Messenger being Messenger, he did not whip out an iPad and show me a video of Trent. Instead, I simply went from being where I was, to a cold and slush-lined street.

Trent was in a motorized wheelchair. His carefully nurtured muscles were slack. His limbs were atrophied. He had a mouthpiece that allowed him to control the movements of his wheelchair.

But it was not moving. The battery had died.

He sat helpless, immobile, at a street corner bus stop in Des Moines. His exhalations were steam. His eyes were desperate.

A man walked down the street toward him, spotted him, looked left and right, and grew furtive. Across the street was a Caribou Coffee and past it a small shopping center. On Trent's side of the street was a hospital and the usual cluster of medical buildings.

Trent was on his way to Caribou where his home health aide was to meet him.

The man approaching on foot did not feel himself to be observed except by indifferent motorists, passing on the four-lane road.

Without a word he began to rifle Trent's pockets as Trent sat helpless, shivering, afraid.

The man stole twenty dollars he found in the inner pocket of Trent's coat.

In a voice slurred by paralysis, Trent said, "Please don't. Please don't."

The man pocketed the money, considered the helpless young man before him, and calmly tipped the wheelchair over.

Trent's head lay in the snow. One wheel of the chair spun. And the thief walked away. Trent cried then, cried and his tears ran down to freeze in the snow.

It is terrible to see humiliation and despair, no matter how bad a person Trent was, no matter the damage he had done, or the life he had cost.

But I had more to see. Once again, curiosity was not my friend. And now I saw a shockingly older Trent. He had not aged well. He might perhaps be thirty years old, I supposed, but it was hard to tell. His body was shriveled doll limbs attached to a swollen upper body and a head with long hair.

Trent was marooned on the top floor of a shopping

mall. The elevator before him had a sign that read, *Sorry for the inconvenience: Maintenance.*

He sat there, unable to leave, for two hours as people walked by, incurious, indifferent, or perhaps just mystified as to what they might do.

Messenger released me, and I took a last sip of coffee.

"He's older," I said. "I think he's already lived maybe twenty years like that. Twenty years, Messenger, that's a life sentence." A terribly long time, but not as long as Messenger's own sentence.

"He will awake from this life sentence when we go to him."

I nodded. "All right. I'm ready."

Once again we stood in Trent's basement. He was as we had left him, a strong, healthy young man with a head full of hates.

And suddenly, his eyes opened. Just like that, Trent—the comatose one before me—gasped, sucked in a shaky breath, and woke.

He stared up at me. Stared at me like I was an impossibility. Like I could not be there, probably wasn't there. He turned his head, only his head, to look left and right and his bewilderment edged toward panic.

For the longest time then he looked back at me and at Messenger. That stare seemed to go on and on forever.

His body was trembling, and he noticed it. He frowned in incomprehension. And then, he moved one arm. Just a little. And cried out, "Ahh! Ahh!"

He moved the arm again. And his other arm.

"Ahh!"

Tears formed in his eyes. He was swallowing hard and obviously afraid, but not the fear of growing terror, rather the fear of discovery, of realization and hope. He was crying quite openly, crying without shame or self-consciousness.

Then, sobbing, he moved his legs. When they shifted, he stopped, bit his lip, then moved them again.

We were seeing a boy—no, not a boy anymore, not a boy with sixteen years of experience of life, but a man in a boy's body. An old man, a man with a long life of pain and perhaps much worse than pain.

Slowly, slowly, as if he couldn't believe it yet, Trent rose to his feet.

I had chills. Only a few minutes had passed but I

had dipped into Trent's experience long enough to have some impression of what he had endured subjectively.

To a casual observer he was still the muscular sixteen-year-old boy, but I saw something very different in his eyes now. Not just tears, but something far deeper. Something so very like what I saw in Messenger's own eyes and had not understood until the Shoals.

We watched, Messenger as mesmerized as I was myself.

At last Trent mastered his emotions and I braced for his resentment, his fury. We had subjected him to an entire lifetime of misery and humiliation.

Hadn't we?

Trent whispered something that neither of us could hear. He took a careful, tentative step. He approached, haltingly, as though he could still not believe he was able to walk.

He came within a foot of me and I was still braced for him to lash out.

"Thank you," he said.

I misunderstood his meaning. I said, "You can walk again because you've suffered your punishment and now it's over."

He shook his head slowly. "No. No, I mean, thank you for giving me that life."

"*What?*"

He sighed and passed his hand over his face, wiping away tears, and when he was done he smiled. He smiled, then threw back his head and laughed.

"No," he said, barely able to stop laughing, and now crying very different tears. "No, I mean thank you for what you did. Thank you for giving me that. For all I lived. I . . . I'm not the same person. I'm . . ." He had to pause to catch his breath. "I lived fifty-two years as a quadriplegic. I was angry and bitter, but then . . . then, well, I found love. So much love. I . . ." He shook his head, amazed. But he could not have been more amazed than I.

"And now I come back to this life," Trent said. "My God, it's like . . . I can't even . . ."

Then to my astonishment he said, "Can I hug you?" And he held his arms wide.

Messenger said, "No. We are not to be touched."

Trent nodded, accepting that. "I'm very sorry for you. It must be terribly painful for you."

Messenger flinched and looked away. Then

Messenger said stiffly, "Thank you for your concern. But we have our duty."

"You believed you were punishing me," Trent said kindly. "But you saved me. You saved me from what I would otherwise have become. I'm . . . I'm not that person anymore. I have to . . . to, to, to see my mom, to see my school, to go and change, like . . . everything."

We let him go, Messenger and I, and we ourselves went away. Back to the place that's not my home.

Messenger said nothing and finally I couldn't take it. "Aren't you amazed?" I demanded. "Aren't you thrilled? I want to jump up and down and, I don't know, sing a song or something."

"I am pleased," he allowed. Then, as if he couldn't quite believe it, he added, "Yes, I am pleased."

Then, the miracle. Messenger actually smiled.

It didn't last long, just a second or two, but the boy in black, the Messenger of Fear, produced an actual, human grin. And then it was gone.

And now the time had come, and I was both nervous and excited. I feared that I had set in motion events that would leave me very alone. I was sad, sorry for myself, miserable, and yet, I felt no doubt about my course.

"Messenger," I said, the words heavy on my heart. "Come with me."

I didn't wait for him to argue or forbid. I was suddenly there, and a moment later, so was he.

It was one of the mystical places of the type that Messenger had haunted, knowing that Ariadne had always wanted to visit.

"Stonehenge?" Messenger asked, puzzled. "Why are we at Stonehenge, Mara?"

Everyone has seen the photographs of Stonehenge, the tall, rugged uprights of ancient stone, the few remaining crosspieces that together inscribe a place of such eldritch power that few speak above a whisper there.

But the photos seldom show the surrounding emptiness, a grassy field in every direction. And they never show the quite modern building half a mile away where you can buy a sandwich and a coffee and board an open bus to take you to the henge.

It was a day of mixed sun and cloud, a sky at once promising and threatening, with the wind direction deciding fair or foul.

There were a few Stonehenge Down tourists walking

slowly around the circumference, pointing cameras, striking poses, and sometimes just standing still and silent to feel the power of the place. The tourists were kept at a distance, but we, well, we had come by a different path to this place and so Messenger and I stood at the very center of the circle.

"Have you been here before?" I asked him.

He shook his head, mystified, and it was a small victory leaving him baffled for once. But it was a melancholy accomplishment because I sensed that this would be one of the last times, if not the last time, I saw the beautiful boy in black.

"No. But . . . but I have meant to come," he said.

We were not visible to the tourists; they gazed thoughtfully and saw nothing. Only one person saw us and he stood on a slight rise beyond the parading circle. He had pushed the hood of his sweatshirt back, baring his head to the sun. Daniel watched. Did he know what I was doing? Of course he did—he is Daniel. Did he approve?

Well, he did not stop me.

"Why are we here, Mara?" Messenger asked.

"For a meeting. A reunion."

"If this coyness is revenge for my own taciturnity, I understand but—"

"I went to the Shoals," I said.

He froze. He did not move, speak, or even blink, for an achingly long time. Of course he knew why I had gone to the Shoals. There could only be one reason.

I didn't mean to leave him hanging, but in a moment I knew that I would be forgotten. That knowledge pierced me like a blade. But if pain can ever be good, this pain was.

"You're older than you look," I said, and wiped away a tear.

"Yes," he managed.

"And French."

He nodded so slightly it was barely visible.

"Messenger . . ."

"Yes, Mara."

I could have explained, but it would be superfluous. So I said, "Ariadne."

And she stepped away from the shuffling circle of tourists and walked toward us.

Messenger hid so much from me as he taught me, revealing only the mysteries he felt I needed to know.

He had been gentle with me, spoon-feeding me like a baby. He had protected me from the full strangeness and horror and beauty of his world, his and my world.

He had shielded me, too, from himself, from his pain and his guilt and his terrible sorrow. He had kept his emotions in check. But now I saw not the Messenger of Fear but a boy, his face trembling, emotion tugging at his mouth, his nostrils flared, his eyes filling with and then spilling tears.

I had wanted badly at times for that openness to be something I had earned. I had wanted him to love me, as I had begun to love him. Now I was destroying any chance that we would ever be together.

It hurt.

It felt wonderful.

And it hurt like hell.

He did not move until Ariadne herself, seeing him, broke into a run, a careless, graceless, desperate run and then a sound, a whimper, a sob perhaps, came from him and he ran.

I watched them come within inches before Messenger withdrew and with a desperate edge to his voice said, "Stop! I am not to be touched."

Daniel was beside me. "You surprise me, Mara."

Messenger and Ariadne stood, inches separating them, hands reaching automatically, then stopping, as if both were surrounded by invisible force fields.

"They've been in love for decades, longer than I've been alive, longer than my grandparents have been alive," I said. "That is something too big and too . . ." I sighed. "Too wonderful, for me to intrude in."

"You freed her from the Shoals," Daniel said.

"I freed us both," I said.

"Two happy endings in one day. That's very rare in a messenger's life. And yet, still, it could be happier."

"Yes, Daniel, it could."

"Hah!" He laughed, a genuine laugh, and he nodded. "Well, a young woman who enters the Shoals and emerges with a life saved . . . It would be strange to describe such a creature as a mere apprentice."

Daniel winked and at that instant froze the world around us. Every tourist stood where they were, no eye blinked, no shutter snapped. The clouds in the sky became a still life. The blades of grass no longer revealed the breeze. Only Messenger and Ariadne were still moving, still craving each other's touch, still whispering urgently, still looking into each other's eyes as if nothing else existed.

We walked to them, Daniel and I, and only when we were nearly upon them did Ariadne look at me, and Messenger followed the direction of her gaze.

Messenger made a very unsuccessful effort to compose himself, to retreat within his shell, but tears leave a mark, and the muscles of his face would not obey his stern efforts to assert control.

"I . . . ," he said. "This . . ."

"Shall we let him stammer on for a while?" Daniel asked, mocking gently.

Ariadne gave me a grateful glance. She whispered gratitude in my ear, in French and English, and in the incoherent language of sobs.

"Messenger," Daniel said, sounding suddenly formal. "Your last duty was to prepare your apprentice to take over your role. It is clear that she is well prepared, strong enough and good enough, to do what she must. And thus, my very good friend, in Isthil's name, I free you."

Ariadne reached for Messenger, but instinctively he drew back.

Daniel went to Messenger, stood very close to him, and in a gesture that sent my mind to memories of my own father, put his hand on the back of Messenger's neck and drew his head forward until their heads touched.

They stood like that for a few minutes, Messenger moved beyond any possibility of speech.

Then Daniel pushed him away, and with his left hand took Messenger's left hand. Reverently he slid off the ring of the Shrieking Face. But he did not remove the ring of Isthil.

Then, still holding Messenger's hand in his, he took Ariadne's hand and said, "Messenger, you have faithfully fulfilled your duty to Isthil and to the Heptarchy, and to the balance. Well done, my friend. Well done."

Daniel clapped his hands briskly, looked a bit askance at me, and said, "This part may be a bit embarrassing."

Suddenly Messenger's long black coat with its skull buttons was gone. And then the gray shirt. And then Messenger stood naked in the English sun, his body a nightmare in ink.

Then, one by one, the tattoos disappeared. There were dozens. Hundreds. An account book of pain and misery, the scars of a long battle with evil. They faded . . . faded . . . and were gone. Until only the tattoo over Messenger's heart remained to fade slowly away.

Now Messenger stood clothed in stylish but somewhat dated garb, a wool suit and a narrow tie, the outfit I'd seen him wear so long ago in chronological years but so recent to me. He was handsome, that boy, very good-looking, but now it was a merely human beauty. Maybe that took some of the sting out of it for me. I don't think Ariadne saw any change at all. After all, she had known him first as a boy, and only briefly as a boy transformed by service to Isthil.

And then, grinning a huge sunny smile, Daniel brought Ariadne's hand together with Messenger's and said, "My friend and faithful servant: you are to be touched."

Tentatively, disbelieving, ready to pull back, Messenger's hand and Ariadne's touched.

How am I to explain that moment? I felt so terribly bereft. I felt the weight of decades of loneliness to come. I felt a loss that nearly equaled what I had felt on losing my father. And yet my heart was so full of joy for him, for them. For life itself. I had been weeping, and now I wept some more, but at the same time I completely forgot myself and grabbed Daniel's hand.

Oh, and was that ever a moment. The time I had accidentally touched Messenger had been a torrent of pain that still haunted my mind with images I must someday find a way to exorcise. But Daniel's touch was like opening a door on paradise.

I stared at him in astonishment and saw a creature like yet very unlike the low-key Daniel. He was light itself, gold and silver, sunlight and moonlight, and I saw within him multitudes, multitudes of those who, like Trent, and now, like Ariadne, had come through evil, through regret, through guilt and pain, to redemption, and acceptance, and joy.

Daniel held my hand for a while, letting me bask in that light, then with a wry smile he disengaged and was once more a young man in a hoodie, young and as old as time.

He looked at me very seriously and said, "We do terrible things to preserve the balance. We do it not just to ensure existence, but because existence can be very . . . nice."

I laughed. "That was way past *nice*."

He nodded. "Yes. Can be," he said, nodding and smiling rather smugly. "Let us leave them. They have decisions to make. And I believe they want to kiss."

"But I—"

"You will see him again. One more time." Then, catching my eye, he said, "One more time."

23

I WAS WRUNG OUT. I WAS EXHAUSTED. I HAD DONE and seen and felt too much.

I fell facedown on my bed and slept before dreams could catch up to me. I don't know how long I slept, but when I awoke it was with clear eyes and a sad heart.

He was in the kitchen. He had made coffee. And as I emerged I heard the sound of the toaster lever being pressed down. He was making me a toaster strudel.

A good-looking boy dressed in jeans and a white shirt and a leather jacket. He looked almost shy as he said, "Hello, Mara."

"Messenger."

He shook his head ruefully. "No longer."

I noticed then that he had an accent. He'd never had one before, but now the r's were down in his throat.

"You look good."

"I look like myself."

"What happened to the suit?"

He shrugged. "We decided . . . I mean that, I was given a choice and we . . . We could be slipped back into our own time, or stay in this one. We chose to live in this time, to see the future together."

"I'm happy for you," I said, and I was, though my heart ached.

"I'm happy . . . we are happy . . . because of you." The word "happy" came out as "appee." "That was a very brave thing. It was an act of courage and . . ."

"And love," I whispered.

"Yes," he said.

It should have been awkward, but somehow it wasn't. We stood silently together, and for once my silence was not impatience waiting for him to speak. When there is too much for words, silence says all. I was content for the moment just to share that silence with him.

At last he said, "If my heart had not already belonged to Ariadne . . ."

"Thank you."

"You know what is to come next?"

I nodded. "I think so."

"We travel this time not with my powers or yours: Daniel summons us."

I suppose I should have gotten used to sudden transitions, but I was still amazed, and I guessed that I might never entirely lose that wonder. We were gone from my abode and stood now in the Shamanvold, that hidden cavern decorated with soaring bas-reliefs of the Heptarchy. The golden tablets bearing the many strange names of messengers down through the ages towered above us.

The bas-relief stirred, and the image of Isthil, great and terrible Isthil, stepped from the stone and stood before us in what I can only call glory. We bowed our heads, not because we must but because no mortal can look upon her and not be moved.

"You have done well, Messenger," She said.

Messenger seemed to shake, a tremor, quickly mastered.

"Your name I now inscribe upon the tablets that mark the service of each faithful messenger."

Like some movie special effect, I saw letters traced by fire on the gold. But I had no time to peer more closely, for Isthil beckoned me and I went to her, moving like a sleepwalker.

"I give you this gift," She said. She opened one hand and there lay the ring of the Shrieking Face. I shuddered seeing it, but I reached nevertheless and slipped it onto my finger.

"I give you this as well," She said, and nodded at Messenger who, reluctantly I thought, slipped the ring of Isthil from his hand. He held it for a moment, looking at it resting in his palm, and then with two fingers slid it onto my finger. He did not touch me in doing so. I understood.

"In my service you will suffer," Isthil said. "In my service you will labor ceaselessly to preserve the balance so that this time, existence shall not fail. Do you accept this burden, Mara?"

Yes, it would have been funny if I'd said, *Hell no*. Part of me wanted to. But a deeper part of me understood that I had done a terrible wrong, a wrong that would only be righted by my willing service.

"I do," I said.

"Serve me well," the goddess said. "And in time, you will be free in body and in soul."

Was I crying or was I laughing? Sadness and joy were each too real and too powerful for me to hope to control myself. I was destroyed. I was reborn. I saw a long and awful path of pain and utter loneliness ahead. But I knew now that at the end, I would live in the freedom of the forgiven.

I dashed away tears, and when I looked again the goddess was gone, but Daniel was with us.

"You must say your farewells," he said gently.

Messenger came to me and opened his arms. I wanted so very much to go to him, to be wrapped in his embrace for the first and last time. But I said, "I am not to be touched."

Messenger shook his head. "I know the images that will fill my mind. I know the pain it will cause, but the greater pain would be in not saying farewell."

He took me in his arms, and I felt him stiffen as each of the horrors we had witnessed together once more flooded his mind. But he did not pull away, and I held him for a while. How often had I dreamed of that moment? But now it was different than the emotions I had imagined. I was not holding the Messenger of Fear. I was not holding the boy I had longed for. I was saying good-bye to a friend.

We separated at last.

"Go to her," I said, making no attempt to conceal my tears.

"As you wish, Messenger," he said.

"But hey . . ."

"Yes?" he asked.

"I suppose you won't be able to see me. I'll be . . ." I sighed. "And you'll be . . . But I wonder if you'd mind if from time to time, when it's all too much, you know, I wonder if you'd mind if I sometimes looked in on you."

"I will see you here," he said, and touched his heart.

Then, he was gone.

I was alone with Daniel.

And I realized that I was dressed differently. I wore a dark coat that fell to my knees. There were boots on my feet. Rings on my fingers. And to any mortal eye I allowed to see me, I would appear as a girl of uncommon beauty.

I used the sleeve of my new coat to dry my eyes. I took my time because if there's one thing Daniel did not lack, it was time.

I looked up at last. "I have things to do, don't I?"

"You do indeed," Daniel said.

"I still don't know his name."

Daniel nodded toward the golden tablet where the letters were cooling but still glowed.

"Michel?" I read. I don't know what I expected; it was a good French name. And I could see him as a "Michel." Now. But in the end it was just a name, and not very important.

Just as my name was no longer important.

For I was no longer Mara.

And I was no longer an apprentice.

I would bring terror to the wicked, and to teach me humility, I would be marked with the memories of that terror. I would be alone for a terribly long time. I would feel pain and sorrow. But I would feel joy as well. I would serve Isthil and the balance She maintains.

I would fight to preserve existence itself.

For I am the Messenger of Fear.

ACKNOWLEDGMENTS

It may surprise some readers to learn that I don't make books all by myself. I just write the words. But I don't design either the exterior or the interior of the book, because the results would be sad looking. I don't arrange for the book to get to bookstores or libraries—who would I even call to arrange that? I don't know. I don't really even tell people about the book unless it's on Twitter, so there are professionals who take care of that for me, too. And, the truth is, although I write every word, I do it with the benefit of insight and experience from great editors, and a great publisher. So, I want to thank at least some of the people who make all that stuff happen: Barb Fitzsimmons, Joel Tippie and Amy Ryan from design; Kathryn Silsand from managing editorial; Lauren Flower and Alana Whitman from marketing; Rosanne Romanello from publicity; Kelsey Horton from editorial; and of course, the boss and my pal, Katherine Tegen.

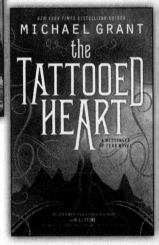

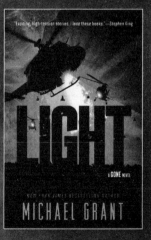

JOIN THE
Epic Reads
COMMUNITY

THE ULTIMATE YA DESTINATION

◀ DISCOVER ▶
your next favorite read

◀ MEET ▶
new authors to love

◀ WIN ▶
free books

◀ SHARE ▶
infographics, playlists, quizzes, and more

◀ WATCH ▶
the latest videos

◀ TUNE IN ▶
to Tea Time with Team Epic Reads